DRUID APPRENTICE

A NEW ADULT URBAN FANTASY NOVEL

M.D. MASSEY

MODERN DIGITAL PUBLISHING

PREFACE

This novel deals with the very delicate subject matter of psychological abuse and rape.

While teaching women's self-defense courses for more than two decades, I've spoken with dozens of survivors. Thus, I know how triggering this subject matter can be to survivors of sexual and emotional abuse.

These topics are *not* dealt with in a graphic manner within the pages of this novel. However, I feel it is my responsibility to make the reader aware of the subject matter before they delve into this ninth volume in the Colin McCool urban fantasy series.

And on a related note, if you are in an abusive relationship, please call the National Domestic Violence Hotline at 1–800–799–7233 or TTY 1–800–787–3224.

Your conversation will be held in the strictest confidence, and their trained staff will help you get the support you deserve.

1

I fucking hate fighting giants.

And yet there I was, soaked to the bone and ankle-deep in mud, psyching myself up to face a particularly nasty *jötunn*. Of course, I had my reasons for being on this God-forsaken piece of property in the middle of nowhere, Texas. Likewise, I had my reasons for avoiding giantkind, including some awful memories of my best friend dying, and the fact that they reminded me way too much of the darkest parts of who I was now.

Then, of course, there were the apparent drawbacks inherent in picking a fight with a fifteen-foot-tall, cannibalistic humanoid. Getting chewed on like a Snickers bar wasn't exactly my idea of a peaceful ending.

Standing in front of the cabin as it pissed down rain, knowing full well that I was about to tussle with one of their kind, well—to say I was in a bad mood would have been an understatement. And on top of that, my druid mentor Finnegas had forbidden me from shifting into my full Fomorian form. The idea was for me to start relying more on magic and less on hulking out when things went sideways. While I'd partially shifted to ensure I didn't get smooshed before I could get a spell off, I was still giving up the size advantage to the giant.

I may as well get this over with. Here goes nothing.

"Norris! Norris Belsterson! This is Druid Justiciar McCool, representing the faery court of Queen Maeve of Austin. By order of the Queen, you are under arrest. Please come out with your hands up, and be advised that if you resist arrest, I am authorized to use lethal force."

A deep voice replied in an odd accent that was half Texas redneck and half Scandinavian pig farmer. Although muffled by thick log walls, and despite the pounding rain and distant thunder, the giant's words carried clearly to where I stood, some twenty feet from his front door.

"Snorri Býleistr's son did nothin' to your queen, drood. Go away and leave me in peace, 'afore I wallop you somthin' awful."

I wiped the rain from my face with a sigh. "Just for once, it'd be nice for a creature to give up without a fight," I muttered. "Would that be too much to ask?"

"Not the way you look," a disembodied voice replied from somewhere to my right. "Hate to break it to you, but you're about as scary as a young Rick Astley in drag."

"That's pretty scary if you think about it, Larry. Now, shut up and stop interrupting me while I'm working."

"Fine, fine," the chupacabra said in his thick Brooklyn accent. "But when this giant stomps your pale ginger ass into mincemeat, don't expect me to dial 911."

I sagely decided to ignore the chupacabra, turning my attention to the task at hand once more. Going inside that cabin wasn't an option. The place was warded up like nobody's business with dangerous, near-god-level magic. It'd take months to unravel those spells, so I needed to convince the giant to step into the open where I could take him down.

"Work with me here, Belsterson. You broke the rules, and

now I have to take you in. Why don't you make this easy on everyone by coming peacefully?"

"I didn't do nothing!" he bellowed back.

"Seriously? Norris, c'mon—every giant, ogre, troll, and buggane in the demesne knows Maeve doesn't put up with that shit. You can't just go around eating cattle and horses like Pez and expect to get away with it."

"I was hungry, druid!" the giant roared. "I ain't supposed to starve, am I?"

"No, but there are ways to go about these things that you chose to ignore. You left footprints, Belsterson—actual, giant-sized footprints. Now, the locals are up in arms about Bigfoot eating their cows, the story is all over the news, and social media has been lit up with armchair cryptozoologists blaming everything from aliens to skunk apes for the missing livestock."

"Weren't no harm in it!" the *jötunn* replied. "The mundane folk are always on about that stuff."

"No harm? Maybe if you'd just kept it to farm animals, sure. But you also ate a couple of gnomes, Norris—walking, talking, law-abiding members of fae society. Did you think Maeve would let that stand?"

"They's just tiny folk, drood, worse'n rats. Ain't nobody gonna miss any of the *tomtenisse* when they's gone."

"Maeve misses them, Norris, because they're her subjects, and thus pay tribute. She's funny like that."

"I only 'et three of them! Ain't no crime to eat three little gnomes. Practically did her a favor, I did."

"Hard to argue with that logic," I muttered as I pushed the sleeves up on my trench coat. The rain was coming down harder and I was losing my patience, so I took a deep breath before shouting my ultimatum. "Norris, I can see that this conversation is going nowhere. I'm going to count to five, and if you're not out here by the time I hit four, I'm going to level that cabin."

I DOUBTED I could level the cabin, protected as it was—but Norris didn't know that. Despite the wards and pouring rain, I was fairly certain that I could light the *jötunn's* house on fire. He was a frost giant, after all, so the mere threat of fire would likely be enough to get him to come out.

Thankfully, Finnegas had been teaching me the rudiments of druid battle magic, which started with the refinement of the primary offensive spells that most druids knew. Almost all druids could cast fireballs and lightning bolts, because manipulating nature's energies was pretty standard stuff. But a battle druid learned to cast spells that were many degrees deadlier, mostly by combining different kinds of energy or by focusing large amounts of energy into a much smaller area.

I suppose this is as good a time as any to test out that ball lightning spell.

Ball lightning was a combination of electricity and extreme heat, and according to Finnegas, it was the first spell battle druids learned. Out of all the paltry number of offensive spells I had at my disposal, it was the most likely to bust through Belsterson's wards and start a fire. Besides, it looked a hell of a lot like one of the special attacks from *Streetfighter*, and any chance to cast a badass spell like that was hard for me to pass up.

After giving him a few more seconds to mull my threat over, I addressed the front door of the cabin a final time. "You had your chance, Norris. Don't say I didn't warn you."

"Ain't skeered o' the likes o' you, drood!" the giant shouted back.

"We'll see about that," I mumbled, rubbing my hands together and mentally gathering energy from the air around me as I spun up my spell. Drawing more heat and static electricity from the sky and atmosphere above, I continued to complain under my breath. "Make me get out in the pouring rain, eh? Now it's Hadouken time, you gnome-gobbling shit-stain of a pituitary defect."

"One..."

Silence.

"Two..."

Nothing.

"Three..."

I raised my hands in front of my chest, palms facing each other, focusing the energy of the spell between them as I pulled silicon oxide and carbon from the soil beneath my feet. Electricity crackled between my fingers, and rain sizzled as it hit the sphere of silver-white fire that rapidly grew while hovering in the air between my palms.

"Four..."

This asshole is really going to make me do it. I hope you have decent home insurance, buddy.

"Last chance, Belsterson!" I shouted as the glow around my hands intensified.

After a moment of silence, the giant replied from within his cabin. "Keep yer panties on. I'm coming out!"

"Panties? He's sure got your number," Larry said.

"This is already a hostile work environment. Frankly, I can do without hearing your smart-ass remarks on top of it," I hissed out of the corner of my mouth. "So, zip it."

"Don't blame me for your exotic tastes in undergarments," the chupacabra sulked.

"Larry, I swear by all that's sacred, I *will* feed you to this giant."

The cabin's front door opened, and a hunched over, hulking figure squeezed through. The doorframe was man-sized, so the giant had to turn his shoulders sideways to fit. It took him a moment to emerge onto the front porch, so I held the spell at the ready in case he decided to charge.

"He doesn't look so big," Larry remarked. "Heck, I could take him."

Larry was right—Belsterson wasn't so big after all. At most, he was eight feet tall, which would be large for a human, but almost runt-like for a giant. Rather than appearing out of the ordinary, he looked almost normal in his huge work boots, blue jeans, and an enormous green rain slicker over a plaid flannel shirt.

From the shadows of his hood, beady blue eyes glowered at me over a nose that had been smashed flat by being broken one too many times, partially hidden by pale blond hair that fell into his face. A full but neatly-kept blond beard and mustache covered the rest of his punched-in face and prominent under-bite, giving him the appearance of an oversized, pissed off Shih Tzu. If I had to describe him in one sentence, he looked like a pro wrestler turned lumberjack hipster who'd just learned that his favorite coffee pub got shut down due to health code violations.

Belsterson's eyes fixed on me for a moment before darting to my right. "Snorri sees you, rat dog. Watch yourself, or you may end up in Snorri's pot."

"That's it, I'm outta here," Larry proclaimed as he splashed off in the direction of my car.

The giant chuckled, a deep rumbling sound that I felt as much as heard. "Looks like your ugly cop dog is a coward."

I cocked my head. "What, him? He's not my backup. Larry's just a groupie—one I can't seem to shake."

Belsterson nodded and stuck his lower lip out, which took little effort considering it was halfway there already. He glanced at the ball of fire and electricity between my hands.

"Thought you was gonna let me come peaceful-like," he remarked.

"Are you?" I asked.

"S'long as you don't zap me with that spell." I shrugged and let the spell fizzle out. The giant stepped off his porch, arms extended and palms up, just like criminals do in cop shows on TV. "Guess you'd better cuff me then, eh, drood?"

He continued to approach me as I replied. "Actually, Maeve's people are gonna pick you up. I simply need to give her the sig—"

Before I could finish that sentence, Snorri Býleistr's son closed the distance between us with two quick strides, clobbering me with a powerful punch that sent me tumbling ass over teakettle across the clearing.

WHAT DO you want to do with your life?

That thought ran through my addled brain when I came to, some thirty feet from where I'd been standing when the giant had struck me. It wasn't something I'd spent a great deal of time pondering, not recently and not ever. What I wanted had never been in question; I'd been reacting to circumstances and events and just trying to survive ever since I'd discovered the World Beneath in my teens.

I sat up, wiping the rain from my eyes and shaking my head in an attempt to clear the cobwebs. I'd only briefly lost consciousness, and now quick, thundering footsteps warned me of the giant's approach. I rolled out of the way just in time to avoid becoming human toe jam, a millisecond after Snorri's massive right boot left a print in the mud six inches deep and three feet long.

Ah, that's how he closed the distance between us so quickly—his size is an illusion.

With my magical sight, I was able to see Snorri's true form, and it was impressive. Some supernatural creatures possessed strange magic, the kind that could warp reality and bend the laws of physics. An excellent example of that was Maeve's home, a sprawling hive of ever-shifting halls and rooms, all hidden inside a 4,000-square-foot Victorian manor. In this case, Snorri's magic allowed him to alter his size, or his cabin was much more than it appeared, or both.

Regardless, facing a fifteen-foot-tall behemoth instead of an eight-foot-tall pseudo-giant changed the equation considerably. The fact that he meant to kill me didn't make matters any less difficult. Snorri had hit me with all the power and might a giant of his size possessed. Had I not stealth-shifted before confronting him, I'd have been a goner. In his current form, he towered over me, and I was about to have a hell of a time bringing him down to my level.

I scrambled backward, desperately trying to get out of the giant's reach. Unfortunately, a five-yard-tall giant has arms that are longer than the average human male is tall. His hubcap-sized hand reached down for me, hairy fingers spread wide to grasp me around my body, likely in an attempt to crush the life from me. I couldn't crab-walk fast enough, so I reacted from instinct, blurting out a trigger-word and releasing a spell directly into the giant's palm.

"*Tintreach!*" I shouted, extending my hand until it almost touched Snorri's. Electricity arced from my palm to his, exploding as the energy from my lightning spell entered his flesh at full force. I'd already covered my eyes before the branching tendrils of magic reached him, as I knew the flash of light could easily blind me, even though I'd cast the spell.

Kaboom!

I was fully shielded from the more damaging effects of the spell, so every last volt and amp of that lightning strike struck Snorri's hand. When the flash subsided, I quickly uncovered my face and opened my eyes to see the damage. As it happened, fear and desperation had caused me to release quite a bit more power than I'd intended, a fact revealed by the resulting damage.

Blackened and charred flesh surrounded the spot on the giant's hand where my spell had landed—or, at least, the half that was left. Snorri had reached for me with that hand because he was left-handed, as many supernatural creatures were. Fun fact, that was the reason why some cultures once thought it was evil to be a southpaw. But now, the giant's thumb, index, and middle fingers were missing, as well as a good portion of his palm.

Snorri's eyes grew wide, and his face was writ in horror as he realized what had happened. Then, the pain must've hit, because he opened his mouth wide enough to show every last one of his double-row of teeth. He let out a roar so loud it vibrated in my chest and shook the ground beneath me.

The giant stared at his now mangled left hand, still bellowing in agony as he grasped his wrist to staunch the bleeding. He tore a strip of cloth from his ten-XL shirt, wrapping it around the wound even as his eyes bored into me with hate so noxious I could feel it on my skin. I took that opportunity to scuttle backward as if my life depended on it.

As Snorri quickly dressed his wound, I observed that, like most giants, he had twelve fingers and twelve toes. So, he'd probably still have some use of that hand. Being no dummy, I wasn't sticking around to point that out. I jumped to my feet and rabbited off into the woods, with the giant's thundering steps not far behind.

Damn it! Should've fired off another spell while he was stunned.

That was one of the many issues I'd faced in learning to rely less on my Fomorian side and more on druid magic. For too long, I'd turned to physical violence as my first line of defense in virtually every encounter. So, I thought like a swordsman and a brawler, and not like a druid. Chaining spells together might've been second nature to your average battle druid or war mage, but I'd yet to develop those instincts.

Thus, I'd squandered the brief window of opportunity that my initial counterattack had provided, and now I was on the defensive again. And Snorri would not make the mistake of letting me snap a spell off at him twice. From the sound of his footsteps and the vibrations I felt through my shoe soles every time they hit the ground, I knew he was right on my tail.

If I turned and faced him, I'd barely have time to draw a weapon before being trampled, never mind having the time to fire up a spell. Running away was only a temporary solution, since his legs were easily twice as long as mine. While I had to run around trees and large bushes as I went along, Snorri could walk over or crash right through them. And every time I tried to change course, the giant cut me off, almost as if he wanted me to maintain my current heading.

If he's herding me, I'd damned sure bet it's toward somewhere I don't want to go.

And backup? Besides Larry, I had none to speak of. The factions only brought me in on jobs they didn't care to mess with, and that meant I almost always worked alone.

In short, I was royally, hopelessly fucked. What was supposed to have been a relatively routine apprehension—and a convenient opportunity to test out a new spell or two—had now turned into a life or death struggle, with my own life hanging in the balance.

Think, Colin. Think!

Soon, the woods thinned, and I exited the trees into a relatively clear area that headed up a short rise. At first, I thought I might be able to gain some ground there, but no such luck. As I crested the rise, I saw that what lay before me was no hill, but instead a seventy-five-foot cliff that overlooked the scenic Pedernales River below.

2

A tree fell with a tremendous crash behind me, startling me out of the *oh shit* moment I had when I first saw the cliff ahead. A quick glance over my shoulder informed me that Snorri was about three steps away from smashing me into Colin jelly. With nowhere left to run, I ran full tilt at the cliff. Then, I leapt over.

Now, a savvy magic user would have some slick-ass spell handy for times like this—say a feather spell to slow your fall, or a limited levitation charm that would allow said magic-user to glide gently over to the opposite cliff. But me? I had no such clever back-up plan, since I wasn't exactly the savviest of druids.

Once my feet left solid earth, things happened in slow motion for the span of several seconds. First, I heard Snorri's gasp of surprise behind me, stretched out like a dying man's final breath. Then, I noticed my legs pumping at the empty space beneath me, as if trying to gain purchase on molecules of air in a vain attempt to prevent the inevitable. A bright ray of sunlight shone through the clouds in the distance, and a passing bird gave me a somewhat sympathetic look that said, "Man, it must be a bitch to not have wings."

Then, everything sped up all at once, and I was falling.

As the ground hurtled up at me—or rather, as I hurtled down at it—two thoughts crossed my mind.

First thought?

This is going to suck balls.

Second thought?

If this works, I'm going to fuck this giant up.

Now, a sane person would never think to jump off a cliff to avoid getting smashed and eaten by a giant. That'd never happen, because the human self-preservation drive is too strong. No, anyone who wasn't batshit crazy would have stood and fought, knowing that at least they'd have a small chance of escape.

Some might even rationalize the situation in an attempt to convince themselves that it wasn't all that dire. Thoughts would cross their mind, like, *What if the giant just wants to rough me up a bit before letting me go?* and *Geez, I wonder if I can reason with the fifteen-foot-tall cannibal with extra teeth and fingers expressly made for the purpose of rending human flesh?*

That wasn't me, though, because I'd been down this road before. Not the part about being on the giant's lunch menu, although I knew it'd be a done deal if he caught me. But the part about jumping off a cliff was old hat—so I knew what came after terminal velocity and rapid deceleration, and it was not my imminent demise.

See, there was a time when my insides had been so knotted up with self-hate and guilt that I'd tried to kill myself numerous times—"try" being the operative word. And man, did I try everything. Guns, blades, large vehicles moving at fast speeds, poison, fire—and yes, long falls from high places that ended abruptly on hard, flat surfaces.

In each instance, Death refused to take me. Or rather, my

Hyde-side refused to let me die. Instead, it simply took over and patched me up, good as new.

Yep, every time I attempted to take my own life, my *ríastrad*, or "warp-spasm," kicked in. That other side of me emerged to prevent my demise. Stopped heart? Started again. Shattered bones? Mended. Spine severed? Merely a flesh wound. Pulverized flesh? Knitted whole once more.

I'd once hated my alter-ego for that. But not anymore.

Back then, I'd thought of my Fomorian side as a separate entity—that was my way of denying any guilt for the things my Hyde-side had done before I gained control of it. Now, however, I knew it was as much a part of me as my DNA—because in essence, that's what it was.

Normally, that part of me remained hidden until I called on it or until it decided to come out and save me from a hideous, excruciating death. Of course, it still hurt like hell, that was a given. The nearly dying part was always agony, and the rapid shifting and healing that came after sucked giant, boulder-sized donkey balls.

And falling from great heights was no exception. Being smashed into a vaguely human-looking sack of gelatinous human goo, and then having all that goo almost instantly rearranged into a nine-foot-tall cross between the Hulk and Quasimodo, well...

Let's just say it wasn't my idea of a good time.

So, when the ground finally came rushing up to greet me at fifty miles an hour, I was thinking that things would get really, really bad for a second or two, and then they'd get really, really good again. A few seconds of agony in exchange for teaching Snorri not to fuck with a descendent of Fionn MacCumhaill, the guy who'd also inherited the *ríastrad* from Cú Chulainn, son of Lugh? Oh yeah, I'd take that deal, any day of the week.

But the luck of the Irish is never a cure for poor planning, and there was one crucial detail I'd forgotten when I launched myself off the cliff. Dummy that I was, I totally forgot that I'd stealth-shifted earlier to increase my odds of survival against Norris the Cannibalistic Giant. So, when my body connected with the rugged, rocky terrain at the bottom of that cliff, it was agony alright.

Unfortunately, because I was already partially shifted into my Fomorian form, I didn't even come close to dying. Nope. And that meant my *ríastrad* was not fully triggered, and good old Mr. Hyde-side definitely was not coming out to play.

Fuck. Me.

SNORRI WAS HALFWAY down the cliff when the excruciating pain of multiple broken bones brought me back to consciousness. Apparently, that cliff was even too high by the giant's standards, and I guess that was saying something. My only comfort was that he was having a hard time of it, mostly because the hand-holds were too small for giant-sized hands, so he was forced to take his time coming down.

Knowing I had only seconds before the *jötunn* arrived to finish the job, I did a quick mental inventory of my injuries.

Broken wrist and fingers, check. Shattered ankles, check. Flail chest, check. Busted pelvis, double-check. Dislocated shoulder and knee, check, check.

Obviously, I wasn't going to fight or spell my way out of this situation, not in my current state. And I certainly wasn't in any shape to flee. So, that left me with just one alternative—the one I wasn't supposed to resort to today.

"Ah, fuck it," I said, although it came out sort of garbled, more like, "Uhfuzzit," presumably because my jaw was broken. Then, I prepared to shift.

On a good day, I could manage the full transformation from human to Fomorian in as little as twenty seconds, if I was in top form and uninjured. Serious injuries slowed the process considerably, because intense pain affected my focus and made it difficult to complete the change. But desperation is a phenomenal motivator, so I held my breath and triggered the process.

It was much worse than I'd expected.

In the past, when my Hyde-side had taken over and initiated the shift autonomously, it had happened almost instantly. That was the deal when my alter-ego took over—it was in complete control, and it had much better control over the transformation than me, even after many months of practice. But since I was now in control of my Fomorian half, the shifting, rearranging, and healing of my injuries happened at what seemed like a snail's pace. That resulted in a prolonged process that I could only liken to being put through a wood chipper and glued back together again with iodine and salt.

Did I scream? You bet your granny's fanny, I screamed.

And, of course, that attracted Snorri's attention. When he figured out what I was doing, he dropped the last forty feet or so to the bottom of the cliff. As luck would have it, I was still only halfway through the change when his feet hit bottom.

I'd never been attacked while injured and in the middle of the change, so I had no idea what would happen. The *jötunn* was likely to simply rip my head from my shoulders while I remained incapacitated, and I doubted that even my Hyde-side could heal from that. I needed to do something to save myself, and fast.

With no better alternative, I focused on healing my jaw and right arm, which I hid beneath me while covering my face with my other arm. This was absolutely the last thing I wanted to do, since my left humerus was sticking through the skin in two places. I sweated bullets and blood while focusing on controlling my breathing, urging the change to speed up while prepping the simplest spell possible.

"Heard 'bout yer other side," Snorri said as he strolled toward me. "Nasty, that one. Can't be havin' that, so's I think I'll jes' squish ya' good now. Say yer prayers, drood."

I turned my head ever so slightly, just enough to glance out of the corner of my eye as Snorri lifted his massive leg to stomp me. Immediately, I rolled onto my back and thrust my right hand out, pointing my open palm at the exposed flesh on the underside of his foot.

"Bladhaire!" I hissed, still in agony as my bones and flesh healed and rearranged at a funeral pace.

Flames shot out of my hand, blazing forth in a brief gout of fire and heat that completely enveloped the underside of the giant's foot. I watched with satisfaction as his skin blackened and blistered. While the spell was among the simplest I knew, fire was a frost giant's weakness, and even a simple flame spell was sure to do some damage.

Snorri howled in rage and pain, grabbing his foot as he hopped around the clearing. The river was nearby and he headed for it immediately, eager to stop the pain and prevent further injury from occurring. Tall as he was, the giant made it into the river in two hops, immersing his foot in the cool waters with a sizzling hiss. Meanwhile, I put every last bit of energy and effort I could muster into completing my change while the seconds ticked by.

By the time Snorri turned toward me again I'd completely healed, and my body was in the final stages of the change. His lip curled in a snarl that revealed his double-row of teeth, reminding me that I'd very nearly ended up in his belly. The giant locked eyes with me, and if I saw a momentary flicker of fear there, it was for good reason—even though I was still only half his size. It wasn't for nothing that the Tuatha Dé Danann had once feared the Fomori above all other races.

My bones were now longer and thicker, stretching my frame to roughly nine feet—ten, if it weren't for the huge hump in my broad upper back that caused me to hunch something terrible. The entire musculature of my body had thickened as well, increasing my mass to roughly four times that of my normal weight and bulk. My left arm remained thinner than my right, and it ended in a claw-like hand that seemed purpose-made for ripping things asunder. Conversely, my right arm was swollen with bulging muscles and sinews, and it ended in a massive wrecking ball of a fist. Thick, almost calloused skin covered my body from head to toe, and my eyes were deep-set beneath a Cro-Magnon brow that jutted out over a crooked, smashed-up face and a too-large mouth full of jagged, yellow teeth.

"Now, giant," I rumbled in a deep, menacing voice as I pushed myself to my feet. "Let us see if the fierce reputation of the *jötnar* is as well-deserved as the sagas claim."

THE WEIRD THING about going full-on Hyde-side was that my personality changed as well as my appearance. When I let my Fomorian DNA have its way, I generally became much more ruthless, cold, and calculating—all traits the war-like Fomori were said to possess in spades. That sometimes evidenced itself in my speech patterns, as I tended toward slightly more archaic and flowery turns of phrase when I was in full-shift mode.

"Big words, for such a little giant." Snorri smirked as he replied. "Les' see if you can back 'em."

The giant grabbed a nearby boulder that sat in the shallows near the shore and hurled it at me with speed that belied his size. I was prepared for such an attack, however, as I'd seen how giants fought before and knew they loved to toss large objects. Ducking under the boulder as it sailed past, I was already sprinting to meet Snorri at the shoreline as he stepped out of the river.

Since the giant still towered over me even in my fully-shifted form, I decided to take him off his feet in order to negate his size advantage. When I was close enough and running at considerable speed, I dove at his knees while attempting to tackle him. Unfortunately, the giant had expected my attack, and he kneed me straight in the face as I was diving in.

Normally, that sort of blow would've stunned your average giant or ogre. However, my Hyde-side was all about the pain, and instead of allowing myself to be deflected, I took the brunt of the blow and hung onto Snorri's leg. Holding his leg up with one arm, I stepped behind his other leg, tripping him while I shoved him hard with my free hand.

The giant fell backward into the river with a splash. I crawled on top of him, kicking him in the nuts along the way. However, Snorri was no slouch when it came to wrestling, and he was able to buck me off him and make it to his knees. I rolled and came up to my feet, then jumped and drop-kicked him in the chest. Snorri partially avoided the kick by turning his shoulders, deflecting much of the force and causing me to land awkwardly on my back.

The giant fell atop me, pinning me beneath the water with one of his hubcap-sized hands. I struggled to free myself, but before I could squirm out of his grasp, he straddled me in order to use all his weight to hold me down. I sat up, hoping to get a breath of air, but Snorri used that opportunity to begin choking me with both his hands. He leaned forward, using the bulk of his upper body to force my head back beneath the river's surface.

This was a simple but effective tactic, since it kept me from using magic by preventing me from saying the trigger words to my spells. And fool that I was, I'd given Snorri just what he wanted by choosing to fight him in the river. In my rush to engage him, I'd completely overlooked the fact that the water would negate my most effective spells.

And then there was the fact that I couldn't breathe water.

Sure, I could hold my breath for some time in my Fomorian form, much longer than I was able to normally. But even in this form, my body needed oxygen to function, and I was burning through my reserves fast by struggling against the giant's weight. Snorri was also cutting off the blood flow to my brain, compounding the effects of my current inability to breathe.

My first response was to bridge my hips in an effort to roll him off me, but each time I tried, my feet simply sank into the muck beneath us. I tried to peel his hands off my throat, but his grip was strong as a vice and his hands were slick with mud from forcing my head into the river bottom. When that tactic failed, I yanked at his wrists in an attempt to pull his hands apart, but it was like pulling at two iron beams. I even attempted to push him off me, but my arms weren't long enough. The more I struggled, the more things got fuzzy around the edges, and I knew I was in danger of blacking out.

So, I decided to change tactics. I began to flail around as if I were on the verge of drowning. Truthfully, the human part of my brain was close to panic, but the Fomorian side of me was in charge and it wasn't about to go down like that. Faking that I was losing consciousness, my movements slowed and weakened, then I exhaled every last bit of air from my lungs in a stream of bubbles before relaxing completely.

Snorri held me under a moment longer, then released his grip on my throat. I was close to blacking out, and my lungs burned as if I'd inhaled one of my own fireball spells. Still, I knew I had to wait for the precise moment, else I'd end up in the same situation—and this time, Snorri wouldn't let up until he knew I was dead.

I felt the giant shift his weight back, and then his hips lifted off me as he rocked back onto his feet. That was all the space I needed, and I immediately sat up and latched onto the giant's inner thigh with my teeth, grasping both arms around his leg to prevent him from dislodging me as I gnawed and chewed my way down to the bone. Giant skin was thick and tough, but in this bestial form, my teeth and jaw muscles were up to the task.

Snorri's fists beat at me around my head and shoulders all the while, but I remained undeterred, determined to defeat this bastard before I blacked out. Fighting the urge to lift my head up and draw a breath, I continued to rip through the muscle and flesh of his leg like a dog until I felt the hot, salty rush of blood in my mouth that told me I'd hit an artery. I bit down hard, and then I yanked my head away, ripping a huge chunk of Snorri's thigh out in a gush of blood that covered me completely as the giant's life bled out into the river.

The giant's blows subsided, allowing me to push away from him and stand as he fell to his knees, pale and weakened by the rapid, massive blood loss he'd suffered. I wiped blood from my eyes and spat a gob of flesh in his face as I rose, then took a first desperate gasp of air, choking on some blood in the process.

"Treachery—that's how ya' bested me, drood," the giant protested as he swayed drunkenly in the water. "T'weren't fair at all."

Weakened from the prolonged battle, I'd already begun to shift back into my human form. Fearing I might be swept away by the river, I lurched back to shore before I replied.

"I won, you lost, and that's all that matters," I rasped, staggering as I heaved air in and out of my lungs. "You fought well, Snorri, and I'll say the same to anyone who asks."

Snorri's eyelids drooped, and his eyes were nearly vacant. "And you, drood?" he whispered. "What will you do, now that you've slain Snorri Býleistr's son?"

"Me?" I said, wiping my mouth as I slung giant blood and spittle into the water. "I'm going to get paid."

3

"You did what? The *jötunn* was supposed to stand trial, druid. The queen will not be pleased."

Rolling my eyes, I held the phone at arm's length as one of my least favorite people in the world continued to bitch. Eliandres was one of Maeve's pet assassins, part of a matching set that included his partner, Lucindra. The prick had been the one to call me in on the job, a task that he'd likely been assigned because Maeve knew how much I hated him. She liked getting under my skin like that.

Setting the phone down on my dusty bookshelves, I peeled my rank, wet t-shirt off and threw it in the corner of my room. Then, I took a whiff of my pits, wincing at the smell. Damn, but I needed a bath. No cold outdoor shower for me, though—I very much preferred the idea of taking a long swim in the clean, cool waters of the pond in the Druid Grove.

"Druid? Druid! Are you still there?"

Reluctantly, I grabbed the phone off the shelf.

"Yes, I hear you. Bitch all you want, Ellie, but the job's done. I even dragged Snorri's body into the brush and cast a 'look away' spell on it—so, you're welcome. Although it won't stay hidden for long. I suggest you send someone to dispose of it before it starts to smell and draw attention."

Eliandres released an exasperated sigh. "You won't always be protected by your position and influence, druid. Your master grows old and weakens by the day. When he's gone—"

I growled and cut him off before he signed his own death warrant. "Trust me, buddy—you do not want to finish that sentence. If Maeve doesn't like how I handled this job, then the next time a giant starts eating her subjects, she can deal with it herself."

"The Queen had good reason—" Eliandres stopped mid-sentence. "Never mind, McCool. You'll find out in due time. Expect payment in the usual manner."

The phone went dead with nary a "have a good day" on Eliandres' part, which was par for the course whenever I dealt with the fae these days. Ever since I'd cut them off from that great big extra-dimensional magic battery they called Underhill, they all hated my guts. Although taking the fae down a notch or two had been one of the highlights of my life, I'd be dealing with the consequences of my actions for decades to come.

Not like I cared or anything. Fucking fae could ingesteth a satchel of Richards. I had bigger problems than my popularity among the city's supernatural denizens. Heck, the only reason I was still pulling Justiciar jobs was to pay the overhead on the junkyard. If it wasn't for the mortgage and payroll, I'd already have bailed on the gig.

As for Larry, the chupacabra was nowhere to be found after I finished Snorri off—and that was just as well. The one place he wasn't welcome was inside the Grove, partially because Roscoe and Rufus hated his guts. But mostly, it was because the Druid Oak wouldn't take him there—apparently, the Grove was allergic to him, and it'd broke out in weeds the first and last time he'd visited.

When left to his own designs, Larry was prone to leaving for hours or days at a time. Personally, I'd come to enjoy the brief moments of respite I got when he wasn't around. The test tube experiment was handy for doing recon work, but he continually failed to respect personal boundaries and he never stopped talking. So, for now, I'd treat his absence as good riddance.

Now for some rest and relaxation.

Since I was planning to see Fallyn later, I grabbed some clean clothes from my room Earthside. Then, I headed for the Druid Oak, which served as the magical gateway to the pocket dimension that was my Druid Grove.

Time flowed much differently in the Grove, which was one of the reasons why it had become my new favorite retreat. While it might seem as though I'd spent weeks inside the place, only a few hours would have passed when I stepped out again. Much of the "time" I spent there was dedicated to studying magic and druidry with Finnegas, although I often retreated to the Grove when I needed rest and a place to think.

I'd been doing a lot of that lately, working out my emotions in the wake of Jesse's second, untimely demise.

Even though we'd been at odds during much of her brief resurrection, I'd taken her second death hard. I couldn't help but feel it was my fault that she'd come back, and my fault that she'd gotten killed again. I also wondered if I'd squandered an opportunity to reconcile with her when she'd become human after I'd inadvertently bonded with the Grove. I kept second-guessing the choices I'd made, wondering if I could've done things differently to achieve a better outcome for Jesse.

Finnegas told me once that sometimes to save the thing you love, you have to let it go. The only problem was that I *hadn't* saved Jesse, and because of that I was having a hell of a hard time letting her go.

The old man also said that time wouldn't erase my regrets,

but it would give me perspective on them. Based on that advice, I'd been spending more and more time in the Grove. Certainly, this made it much easier for me to squeeze my studies in between Justiciar work and preparing for the next catastrophe— because there would always be another crisis. But it also made for some awkward conversation when I ran into my friends. To them, it might have only been a day or two since we last spoke, but to me it often seemed an eternity.

"Hey, really good to see you, man—it's been ages!"

"Um, dude—we just hung out together last night."

or...

"Hey, did you see the season finale last night? It was crazy!"

"Nope, missed it. I was in another dimension, and we don't get Wi-Fi there."

Yeah, the whole time differential could be a real pain in the ass. Despite that, I kept reminding myself that things could be worse.

How? I had no idea, and I didn't care to speculate. But I was certain that life would reveal another fucked up situation to me soon. Until then, I intended to enjoy the relative quiet I'd had since I'd kicked the Dark Druid's ass. Relative being the key word, of course, as far as the Justiciar stuff went.

And, of course, there was Cerberus.

After we'd set up Agent Mendoza and his goons at Big Bend, we thought for sure that he'd run back to Washington with his tail between his legs. But no such luck. While I hadn't had any direct confrontations with Cerberus since I'd gotten back to town, black vans and SUVs had been following me everywhere. I'd taken to traveling using the Druid Oak for a time, then realized I was simply arousing their suspicion further. So, between all the other shit I had to do, I'd also been driving around every day doing mundane shit, just to give the feds the impression I was "normal."

And did it work? Hell no. As far as Cerberus was concerned, I was public enemy number one. And as soon as they could prove it, they'd probably try to snatch me off the street and take me to a lab somewhere. What it all boiled down to was that Mendoza refused to let it go. That fucker was like a dog on a bone where I was concerned.

And the really fucked up thing? It made it extremely difficult to see Fallyn. After Big Bend, Samson wanted nothing to do with the government heat I'd drawn, and he let me know in no uncertain terms that I was not to bring that shit down on the Austin Pack. That pretty much put the kibosh on noshing with his daughter, and it didn't get lost on me that it was probably exactly what the Pack Alpha wanted.

Samson could be such a dick at times.

There was an upside, though. Over the last several weeks, I'd spent many an hour doing "normal" stuff like working on cars at the junkyard, drinking coffee at Luther's, and training Muay Thai and jiu-jitsu with Hemi. Heck, I'd even started taking courses again online through the local community college. It wasn't the same as going to class every day, but I didn't care because it was all a welcome distraction from my druid studies.

And if I didn't think about things too hard, some days it almost felt like I hadn't gained the unwanted attention of the federal government—and the Celtic gods to boot.

So, there was that.

As I walked out of the junkyard warehouse with my bundle of clothes under my arm, I noticed someone sitting on the loading dock. Finnegas was waiting for me, smoking a roll-your-own cancer stick with his elbow propped up on an old Igloo cooler. Out of respect, I cleared my throat, even though it was a given he knew I was there. You didn't live for two millennia without developing a nearly infallible sense of tactical awareness, after all.

"So, no comment on how the giant gig went down?" I asked as I plopped down next to him on the bare concrete of the dock.

The cold seeped through my damp jeans almost immediately, but I ignored it. Truth was, I missed the junkyard smells of engine grease, moldy upholstery, and rust. Suffering the chilly autumn air was a small price to pay for enjoying it all a bit longer, before we had to retreat to the Grove once more. Despite that, my body gave an involuntary shiver as the cold ran through me.

Finnegas flicked ash from his cigarette and pointed at me with it. "If you were smart, you'd have dried your clothes with magic."

I tsked and smiled wryly. "My control isn't that good yet, and you know it. I'd rather not singe my pubes off, so I'll deal with wet pants for now, thank you very much."

The old man snickered. "I keep telling you that you need to practice the small, inconsequential skills just as much as the big, flashy spells."

"I know, I know. 'The mastery of druidry hinges on controlling the most minute weaves of power and magic.' If you've said it once, you've said it a million times since we started training again."

My mentor scratched his nose absently with a knotty, liver-spotted knuckle. "That's because I want you to get it through your thick noggin, you numbskull. The more time you spend with the Oak and Grove, the more your power will grow. If you don't learn precise control now, mark my words—you'll regret it later."

"Later? Hell, I'm regretting it now, Drill Sergeant Finnegas.

The way you've been pushing me lately, it feels like I'm going through druid hunter training all over again."

Finnegas hissed as he exhaled smoke through his teeth. "When the Tuath Dé finally decide to deal with you, druid hunter training isn't going to save you. Despite what you might think, your *ríastrad* won't either. When that time comes, you'll be thanking me for running your skinny ginger ass ragged now."

"Ewww. Not sure I'm comfortable with my two-thousand-year-old druid mentor talking about my ass."

The old druid blew smoke out of his nostrils. "Just for that, I'm doubling our study time this week."

"Meh, I'll just sleep it off in the Grove."

He raised an eyebrow at me. "That Grove is becoming as much of a crutch to you as your Fomorian DNA. It was hard enough to teach you druidry before you learned to control your *ríastrad* and bonded with the Druid Oak. If the Grove wasn't helping us accelerate your studies, I'd ground you from using them both."

"You have to admit, it is kind of nice to have nearly unlimited time—"

The old druid's expression soured as he cut me off. "That's just it—we don't have unlimited time! Soon, the gods will come calling, and I'll be gone. And if you're not ready—let's just say it's best if that didn't happen."

It sucked hearing him talk like that. My greatest fear at this juncture was being left alone without Finnegas to help me navigate the coming shit-storm. I'd already lost my dad and Jesse, and I'd nearly lost the old man once to addiction and despair. Since he'd cleaned himself up, I'd come to depend on the old coot, and I simply didn't know what I'd do when he was gone. So, most days, I pretended like he wasn't on his last legs.

I shrugged, a futile gesture of rebellion and denial. "C'mon,

Finn—you've been around for two millennia. It's not like you're going anywhere anytime soon."

"'Soon' is a relative term, son." He glanced at me with a frown. "Don't look at me like that—makes me feel old."

I was about to voice a smart-assed reply, but the lines in the old man's face, the slight tremor in his hands, and his stooped, tired posture stopped me. Clearly, his time really was growing short. And of all people, he'd chosen to invest what little time he had left in me. He'd taken to spending long stretches in the Grove with me, teaching me and pushing me to absorb as much of his vast knowledge of druidry as possible. For that reason alone, the old man deserved more than a smart-assed retort.

"I, um..." The words got stuck in my throat.

Finnegas held a hand up. "I know—you don't have to say it. Listen, this old dog still has a few tricks left in him. Let's head back so you can wash that stink off you, and I'll nap while you practice controlling minor weaves of heat and cold energy to effect atmospheric changes in isolated micro-environments."

"In other words, while I practice drying my clothes with magic?"

"Yup. Now, grab that beer cooler for me—my back's not what it used to be."

———

FOLLOWING a long swim in the pond and a few hours of alternately singeing and freezing my jeans, I'd worked up an appetite and needed a break. Using my psychic connection to the Grove, I checked in on the old man. The sentient pocket dimension answered me with a series of mental images—the sun setting over a peaceful glade, a cat napping in soft sunlight, and the low drone of crickets in the forest at night—meaning, Finnegas was out cold. Not wanting to disturb him, I decided to quietly step out and grab us some food, knowing the time differential was such that I'd be back long before he woke up from his nap.

After throwing on some clean jeans, a t-shirt, boots, and my leather biker jacket, I instructed the Oak to take us to a thickly-wooded stretch of Bouldin Creek near South Congress. Assuming we'd arrived—the Oak could travel wherever it wanted, nearly instantaneously—I slung my Craneskin Bag over my shoulder and tucked my holstered Glock in my belt before heading out. But before I told the Oak to warp me back into my own dimension, I asked the massive, magical tree to see if the coast was clear.

Answering back in the affirmative, the Oak ensured me that there was no danger to be found in the immediate vicinity Earthside. Out of habit more than necessity, I touched the warm, rough bark of the druid tree. The sensation was both comforting and overwhelming, because for an instant I felt and saw everything the Oak and Grove felt—every plant, animal, and insect within its boundaries. Beyond that and on a deeper level, I sensed the low, vibrant hum of magic residing deep within its heartwood,

Taking a moment to enjoy the experience of communing with the Oak and Grove, I then asked it to send me home. One moment I was standing in the Grove, and the next second I was Earthside in SoCo. Double-checking what the Oak had told me, I extended my druid senses outward, briefly connecting my mind with each of the small animals and birds that currently resided within a one-block radius.

No SUVs with blacked out windows, no black helicopters circling overhead, no snipers on rooftops nearby. Looks like the coast really is clear.

It wasn't that I didn't trust the Oak to give me good intel—far from it. It simply wasn't in its nature to lie, especially not to me, the Master of the Grove. However, the Oak had a tendency to focus on supernatural rather than mundane threats. Anything that it deemed beneath me in skill and power would likely go unnoticed as it ran its sweep of the area, and that included human federal agents who possessed little or no magical talent.

While it was nice to know that the Oak thought so much of my abilities, it still wouldn't do to be jumped by a bunch of agents with tasers, then kidnapped and renditioned to a magic-proof detention center in a foreign country. Finnegas had assured me such facilities existed, so I'd gotten extra careful when making forays into the city.

Obviously, I didn't have to worry about such things when I was at the junkyard. My wards were more than enough to keep Mendoza's technomagic and hedge witches out, and they'd warn me if there was a breach. But in the city, if I wasn't in a public place with plenty of witnesses, there was always the chance they'd try to snatch me. For those reasons, I took precautions while doing my best to avoid Cerberus whenever possible.

On those odd times when they did find me, shaking a federal law enforcement surveillance team was always good for practicing my counter-surveillance skills. Not to mention, it was deeply satisfying as well. Finnegas had told me numerous times to stop doing it, because apparently, shaking a government tail only made them that much more determined to watch your every move. Whatever. It was in my nature to give authority a huge "fuck you" whenever possible. Thus, I saw no harm in having a little fun at the feds' expense.

I was about two blocks from Luther's, and three from the sandwich shop where I intended to grab my dinner. Fallyn loved their pastrami sandwiches, and that gave me an idea. I pulled my phone from my Craneskin Bag and quickly sent her a text.

MEt me 4 sammiches?

The reply came nearly instantly.

Sur. I can slip away. 15 min?

I'll b ther.

Smiling broadly, I tucked my phone back inside my Bag. No cell signals could escape the pocket dimension within, and that kept the feds from tracking me by GPS. I whistled a tune as I slipped from the woods onto the sidewalk, heading north on Congress toward Luther's cafe and the sandwich shop.

As I walked on, nothing seemed amiss. The usual amount of traffic whizzed by, a few tourists passed me on bikes and electric scooters, and there was no shortage of pedestrians out either. I was absolutely certain there was no way that Cerberus would pull anything here, in broad daylight and in front of all these people.

Hence, when the manhole cover I stepped on disappeared into a dark hole of nothing, it completely took me by surprise. And when I kept falling instead of landing in a drainage tunnel beneath the city sidewalk, that's when I knew I was truly fucked.

4

It felt like I was falling, but I immediately recognized I was caught in a transporter spell. Transporter spells were similar to portal spells, but more crude in the casting. A portal spell was a direct gate from one dimension or place to another, made by magically punching a hole through perfectly-folded time and space. Long known as the favored way for gods and extremely powerful magic users to get around, they were relatively safe. That is, so long as you didn't get caught in a portal while it was closing.

On the other hand, transporter spells used naturally-occurring wormholes to move people and things from one place to another. This was infinitely more dangerous, because you might not come out where you planned. Plus, you never knew what might be passing by in the Between Spaces as you went from Point A to Point B.

Oh, I know—it sounds hella cool to travel through a wormhole. But if there was a one-in-five chance of someone dying every time they took the bus, would anyone use city transit? Of course not.

On top of the safety issues, transporter spells took just as much energy to cast as magic portals, and that was basically a metric shit-ton of mystical horsepower. For these reasons, the spells were used about as often as a spade-less shovel—and most magicians considered them just as worthless.

However, they did have an upside—namely that it took less skill to cast a transporter spell than it did to create a magic portal. Thus, a less-skilled magician with access to a lot of power might spark one up in a pinch, especially if they were transporting something or someone that was expendable.

In other words, it was exactly the sort of thing a group like Cerberus might do to capture a person of interest.

Since Mendoza saw me as a threat, I figured it'd be no skin off his nose if I got eaten by Void spawn while being renditioned to Guantanamo. Which, I'd recently learned, was still very much open for business—and Cerberus' favorite place to question and experiment on supernatural creatures. Samson's military contacts had also mentioned that Cerberus was rumored to have a lab near San Antonio, underneath a secret CIA installation—but those were just rumors.

I wonder... would I be able to mentally connect with the Druid Oak from Cuba?

That thought was interrupted when I abruptly landed on a cold concrete floor in a dark, dingy room that smelled like bleach, dried blood, piss, and shit. Due to the effects of gravity, I'd managed to build some momentum when I fell in the manhole, which meant that I hit the floor with enough force to cause me to stumble. I was still in my human form—a gamble, I knew—but I didn't want to give Mendoza any reason to keep me in captivity, so I'd decided to maintain the ruse.

Of course, it might not have been Mendoza who'd just kidnapped me. I had a lot of enemies, and that was a fact. Over the last couple of years, I'd pissed off the fae, the Cold Iron Circle, certain members of New Orleans' vampire population, the Tuatha Dé Danann, and various gods from other assorted pantheons. The truth was, it could've been anyone who snatched me... but I was betting on Cerberus.

As my eyes adjusted to the gloom, I made out my surroundings. I was in a cylindrical concrete room roughly twenty feet in diameter and thirty feet tall. The walls were etched in glyphs to ward against the use of magic—but not against shifting. I checked my cell phone to see if I had any reception, knowing instinctively that I wouldn't.

No magic, and we're far enough below ground to block cellphone signals... or they're using a signal jammer. Interesting.

Besides the wards etched into the walls and a few old blood stains on the floor, there wasn't much else of note. The only other distinctive feature of the space was a single, curved observation window roughly twenty feet above. I had a feeling it was made of thick bulletproof glass, or perhaps some super-strong polycarbonate composite that would be resistant to my supernatural strength. I was no expert about such things, but it made sense.

Well, this isn't cliché at all.

The room beyond the window was dark, but I had the feeling I was being watched. I called out to no one in particular, maintaining my "I'm completely human" act.

"Hey, is anyone there? I think I fell into a manhole or something. Hello, can anyone hear me?"

I kept screaming and yelling for help for the next hour or so while searching the space using the flashlight app on my phone. After a sufficiently reasonable amount of time had passed, I sat in the middle of the room hugging my knees. From that point on, it was a waiting game, so I decided to learn as much as I could about my surroundings—without the use of magic.

The first thing I noticed was an almost imperceptible draft coming from above, which told me the space was ventilated, probably via small holes or slots at the top of the shaft. Straining the limits of my natural and somewhat enhanced hearing, I heard just the barest of noises coming from above. It wasn't much, just the sounds of someone shifting in their seat, and the soft scuff of a shoe sole on carpet. But it told me someone was watching me.

Finally, I took a few minutes to identify and determine the origin of every single smell in the room. From the walls and floor, I got the aforementioned stench of bleach, blood, and waste. But beneath that, I detected an array of pheromonal odors spanning a range of emotions, including anger, fear, and despair. And then, layered beneath all of that, were the scents I was looking for—smells that were unique to the supernatural denizens of our modern world.

And what a collection it was: vampires, 'thropes, fae, yōkai, trolls, zombies, and a few things I couldn't identify. Whoever had built this room had used it to contain all manner of creatures that fell under the heading of "other than human." From what I could tell by the depth and quality of their scents, some of those beings had been here a while—perhaps weeks or even months.

I was fairly certain I could escape from the room any time I wanted, either by calling to the Oak to get me out or by shifting and busting out that observation window to see who or what was on the other side. But I didn't want to tip my hand. Whoever had decided to abduct me had piqued my interest, and if it was Mendoza and company, I wanted to see how this played out.

If they really were abducting supernatural creatures and holding them in captivity for scientific study, that was something I simply could not abide. Granted, I hated some of the supernatural races with a passion, and for good reason. Still, it might be one of my friends who ended up in this cell one day, and that pissed me off something fierce.

I gave a few more half-hearted calls for help, along with a couple of "let me outs"—then I stretched out on the floor and pretended to go to sleep.

And now, I wait.

ONLY A FEW MINUTES had passed before my captors decided to change the game. Directly beneath the observation window at floor level, a section of the concrete wall silently slid away, revealing a dimly-lit hallway beyond. The walls and ceiling of the passageway matched the concrete gray walls of the observation cell, and those walls were likewise etched in anti-magic runes.

Can't say much for their decorator, but I'll give them points for carrying the theme throughout the facility.

A cool draft blew in through the open door. Rather than freshening the air in the cell, the breeze stank of rot and death. It was a scent I was familiar with, because I'd spent six hellish months in a world where that rank odor always meant danger was imminent. Soon I heard shuffling footsteps, coming down the hallway in a broken rhythm that sent a chill down my spine.

Ghoul.

I backed away from the hallway, hugging the opposite end of the cell. Since the room was circular, there wasn't much chance I could hide by the door and ambush the creature, so that left me with three options. First, I could use magic, the main problem with that approach being that it would divulge a lot more about my skills and talents than I cared to reveal.

Second, I could pull Dyrnwyn from my Craneskin Bag and make short work of the ghoul. But again, that would mean showing more of my hand than I'd like. And if I was right about the identity of my abductors, I would very much prefer to keep my Bag a secret.

That left me with my third option—stealth-shifting and taking the thing out in hand-to-hand combat. Timed properly, I was certain I could make it look like I'd simply overpowered the thing. All I'd have to do is snap its neck, and then play it off like I got lucky.

No way is Mendoza falling for that. Still, it's better than the alternative.

I crouched down, curling up into a ball to make myself less noticeable. If I was lucky, the damned thing wouldn't detect my scent before I changed. Considering all the conflicting odors that permeated the walls and floors in the space, it was even odds that I'd get a few extra seconds if it didn't notice me.

With no better option, I initiated the change and watched the door. Seconds ticked by as the thing's shadow darkened the hall beyond, stretching toward the entrance as it unwittingly closed the distance between us. I was halfway through the transition when it reached the door, snuffling and grunting like a wild hog rooting for food.

It was hideous, as all the lower undead were, but I could tell that it'd been dead for a while. The ghoul had been a large white man before he died, maybe six-foot-four, with broad shoulders, thick forearms, a balding pate, and a potbelly that said he'd enjoyed one too many double cheeseburgers and pints of IPA before he passed on. However, after taking in his blood- and gore-stained Farmer John overalls and wife beater, I decided the culprit must've been too much Pearl beer and chicken fried steak.

Half the thing's upper lip was missing, revealing an ashen, receding gum line over crooked, yellowed teeth with rotting flesh stuck in the gaps between. His eyes were so bloodshot as to make the sclera pink, with pupils that were dilated wide enough to make the irises completely black. That, along with the large swaths of skin missing along his exposed arms, face, and neck and the maggots that squirmed in the exposed flesh, all served to give the ghoul an unearthly, almost demonic appearance.

Demonic? May as well be. Closest thing to it, outside of hell itself.

I finished shifting just as the ghoul caught my scent. The creature reared its head back, letting out a terrifying, screeching wail that was intended to call all the surrounding undead to join in his feeding. Thankfully, this one was alone.

Time to go to work. Better make this look good.

I stood, arms extended and palms out in the universal sign of peace and surrender. "Hey, man, just chill. I don't want any trouble, alright? I just want—"

That's all I got out before the ghoul charged me, resulting in a real-life version of the famous Tueller drill—sans knife and firearm of course, but no less deadly. Back in 1983, a police sergeant named Dennis Tueller had wanted to see how quickly a knife-wielding attacker could close the gap and stab a cop with a holstered weapon. He determined that about twenty feet and under was too damned close, because at that range, the cop got stabbed before they could draw and fire their weapon nine times in ten. Interestingly, most of the attackers in his experiments crossed that twenty-foot distance in under two seconds.

The ghoul did it in half that time, and honestly I'd have been in a world of hurt if I hadn't stealth-shifted. My reflexes were good in my fully-human form, the result of my heritage as a natural-born champion of humanity. About one in a thousand humans were born champions, blessed with peak human speed, strength, reflexes, and senses. Finnegas said the effect was nature's way of balancing the scales for us against monsters and the supernatural races, but in this case, those abilities would not have made a difference.

Fortunately for me, my Fomorian DNA did. Just as the

monster reached me, I stepped offline and to my left, pivoting as I redirected the ghoul's lunging grab. Forcing his arms down so they wouldn't get in the way, I simultaneously grabbed the back of his overalls and shoved him with just a touch of superhuman strength, adding to his momentum as I sent him head-first into the concrete wall.

On impact, the creature's skull collapsed with a satisfying crunch, and I was pretty sure the loud *crack!* I heard was its neck snapping at the base of the skull. I watched it drop to the cement, now truly lifeless as nature had intended, and stepped back feigning horror and disgust for whoever might be watching. And, of course, I kept my eyes on the hallway in case they sent anything else to eat me.

Instead of another attack, I heard a loud electronic buzz, then the click-hiss of a sealed door opening at the end of the hallway. A voice I recognized came over a hidden PA system, echoing in the silence of the observation cell.

"Mr. McCool, if you would meet me in the hall, I would very much appreciate it."

Mendoza.

"Fine," I said, aiming my words at the observation window. "But if you send anything else at me, we're going to have words —angry, hurtful words."

SURPRISINGLY, when I exited the hallway leading out of the observation cell, Agent Mendoza waited for me alone. He was dressed as I'd seen him last—in a dark suit, black dress shoes, white button down, and power tie. Unlike our last meeting, his tie had been loosened, his shirt unbuttoned at the collar, and he sported a three-day beard. The agent's clothes were rumpled, and he had dark circles under his eyes.

In short, he looked like shit. And the knowing look in his eyes told me he wasn't buying my confused college kid bit.

Let's poke this dog and see if it bites.

"You look like shit," I remarked.

Mendoza pursed his lips and nodded. "I haven't had much sleep lately. I suppose I have you to thank for that, although I'm not blaming you for my recent misfortune."

"Misfortune? Do tell."

Mendoza gave a sour smile, then shrugged. "Come with me, and I'll explain everything."

Without looking back, he headed down the hallway. At that moment, I could've had the Oak zap me out of there, but I honestly wanted to see what the agent was up to. With nothing better to do, I trailed him down seemingly endless industrial corridors, all painted that ugly gloss gray you only ever see in Navy ships and military installations. I strained to hear anything that would indicate where we were, but all I heard was the distant hum of a large diesel generator, and a lot of silence.

Secret base? Check.

"You know you made me stand up my date," I said.

Mendoza looked back at me as he stopped at a door marked, "Conference." "What? Oh, sorry about that. We picked up your cell location via StingRay—that's a cell phone reception device —so we had to move fast."

"Hmpf," was my only reply, mostly because I felt stupid for not expecting them to intercept my cell calls and texts.

Mendoza punched a code into the electronic keypad next to the door, and it opened with a click. "It was just luck that we had a surveillance van in the area when you made that text. Still haven't figured out how you're getting around, you know. You've posed one mystery after another since you popped up on our radar, McCool."

"I do card and coin tricks, as well," I quipped.

Mendoza chuckled as he held the door open. "After you."

I entered the room with a shrug, finding it was nothing out of the ordinary. Off-white walls, industrial carpet, roughly fifteen by twenty-five feet, with an oblong conference table in the middle and a projector screen on one wall. The place smelled like plastic, stale farts, and spilled coffee. A laptop was set up at one end of the table, along with a pitcher of water, carafe of coffee, and small stack of Styrofoam cups.

"Sorry," Mendoza apologized, "I couldn't find any cream or sugar. Place has been shuttered since Big Bend, and most of our support staff have been reassigned. You played us good there, by the way."

"No idea what you're talking about," I lied.

He chuckled. "Have a seat, McCool."

Without waiting for me, he sat in front of the laptop and poured himself a cup of coffee. After he'd taken a sip, I did the same. The coffee sucked, but it was black, hot, and strong, and it'd been a long night.

"Alright, tell me why I'm here."

"Fair enough." He tapped a few keys, and the screen lit up with an old, faded photo of a dead 'thrope inside what appeared to be a prison cell. "Sarajevo, 1994. An American soldier on a peacekeeping mission is attacked by what was first reported to be a wild animal in some back alley of the inner city. He almost died. Three days later, his wounds had completely healed. Twenty-seven days after that, he transformed into that thing in the photo and killed his entire squad."

I sipped my coffee, poker-faced. "Sounds pretty outlandish to me."

"Does it?" Mendoza's lower lip jutted out as he nodded. "I suppose it would, to the average person. But then again, you're not average—are you, Mr. McCool?"

"Again, I have no idea what you're talking about."

"You took out a Level Two SNE like taking a walk in the park."

I scratched my nose. "SNE? You lost me there."

"'Supernatural Entity.' That one was of the undead variety, while the stiff in the photo is some sort of shapechanger, a were-wolf. We've studied others as well—vampires, witches, and the like. Despite capturing the odd monster, we know precious little about that world. Your world."

Hmm... he's compartmentalizing his intel—hiding what he really knows to see how I react.

I laughed and rubbed my forehead with the palm of my hand. A headache was coming on, and it was all due to dealing with the jackass in front of me.

Fuck, I hate these government types.

We suspect you're controlling it, via telepathy, or magic, but we haven't yet determined which."

I sighed. "I'm just a normal human being, Mendoza. I don't have psychic powers, I'm not a—what'd you say? A witch? And I'm not part of some secret conspiracy to summon demons from hell," I said, holding up my right hand. "Honest."

"Right. That thing you so easily handled downstairs? Two weeks ago in Baton Rouge, it took out a team of tier-one operators like they were Boy Scouts. My group was sent in to capture it—despite being on the Homeland Director's shit-list—and it took four tac operatives and two PNEOs to bring it down."

"Again, language. PNEOs?"

"Damn, you're stubborn," he said with a shake of his head. "'Paranormal-Enhanced Operatives.' You'd probably call them hedge witches. And although we've managed to augment their abilities with technology, hell if we've been able to recruit anyone with any real magical talent. Fact is, we're mostly flying blind where magic is concerned."

"Do tell," I said, with no small amount of sarcasm in my voice. Even though I was determined to maintain my act, I wanted to hear what he had to say.

"Oh, so you've decided to play along? Since the event in Sarajevo, the DoD has been investigating paranormal events involving cryptids and unknown humanoid species. Sadly, we've had damned little luck in penetrating that world. Oh, we know there are powerful magic users, and probably a bunch of supernatural races we don't know about. But getting anyone to tell us anything about it all has been like pulling teeth from a dragon." I snorted, and he arched an eyebrow. "Yeah, I'm pretty sure those exist too."

"Huh." I leaned back in my chair, lacing my fingers behind my head as I crossed an ankle over my knee. "You mean to say these PNEOs—hedge witches—haven't clued you in?"

"Nope. Early on, we recruited a couple of people who were in the know—after offering them huge amounts of money, of course. And when those informants died horrible, inexplicable deaths, we got stonewalled from there on out. The PNEOs we have now were recruited and trained from scratch, by identifying personnel from within federal law enforcement agencies and branches of the military that had untapped magical talents."

"Why do I get the feeling you've had less than satisfying results with that program?"

He shrugged. "It's hit or miss. We have access to some rather rare documents, magical tomes and such. But without skilled guidance, even the most talented operatives can only cast the most rudimentary spells. Hell, even that cost us lives. Ever seen someone self-combust? It's not pretty."

"I can only imagine," I replied.

"I bet. Word on the street is, you immolate people on a regular basis."

"Thought you said you got stonewalled." I replied, genuinely curious.

Mendoza steepled his fingers. "Confidential informant. And no, I'm not divulging any names. It took us forever to find someone who had half a clue about—what do you people call it? The 'world beneath our own'? Last thing I need is for our informant to get fried in a freak lightning storm, or die in an inexplicable gas explosion, or have a mysteriously violent allergic reaction to MSG."

"You say that as if it's actually happened before."

He rolled his eyes, tilting his head back with a chuckle. "Oh, it's happened, and then some. You fucking people are brutal, and ruthlessly efficient. Hell, I wouldn't even be talking to you if we didn't need help. These events have been happening more and more frequently lately—that's how you ended up in our sights, by the way—and we desperately need someone to help us prepare."

I rubbed half my face as I squinted at him with one eye. "Prepare? Prepare for what?"

Mendoza pounded on the conference table with a balled fist. "The invasion, of course. We have it on good authority that someone is planning a mass incursion of SNEs from another dimension. And we need your help to stop it."

I locked eyes with him for a moment, and that moment stretched on for several more. Then, I busted out in full-on, ball-straining laughter. I mean, complete donkey braying, tears-streaming-down-my-face cackling. It took me a while to settle down, and to his credit, Mendoza sat calmly until I'd finished.

"Whoa, that's rich," I said, wiping my eyes as a few more giggles bubbled up. I took a few deep breaths to calm myself, then my face grew serious—as serious as I could make it, anyway. "Alright, Agent Mendoza. Listen closely, because I'm not going to say this again."

He crossed his arms over his chest. "I'm listening."

"For starters, there's not going to be an incursion, or invasion, or whatever the hell you want to call it."

"And you know this how?"

"Theoretically, let's just say I have firsthand knowledge—very firsthand—that it has been stopped. Nipped in the bud. Squashed, like a bug on a windshield."

The agent took a deep breath, exhaling slowly. "Ooh-kay. Theoretically, let's say that's the case. We still need people on the inside who know the score, who can guide us as we prepare for future disasters."

I raised a finger. "Ah, but that leads me to my second point. That is, if all this stuff you allude to actually exists, then it has existed for centuries. Hell, for fucking millennia. Right under the noses of emperors, presidents, and kings. And if that's the case—if these 'others' kept it under wraps all this time—it stands to reason they have a vested interest in keeping it that way."

"Stands to reason," he replied.

"Taking that all into consideration, if I was someone who had been clued in on that imaginary mystical world you've so vividly described, well... I'd say you're in way over your fucking heads. And if I was that person, I'd inform you that you have no idea what you're dealing with—none."

"If that were true, then what would you suggest?"

"In that case, my advice would be to leave it the fuck alone." I stood and looked around. "Now, I think I'll be leaving. So, could you please tell me where the hell I am, and who the fuck is driving me home?"

TWO OF MENDOZA'S people tossed me in the back seat of a nondescript passenger van, cuffed and hooded, of course. They were both large Anglo men with buzzcuts, and each sported an earbud radio and off-the-rack suit. They lacked that certain military bearing most soldiers had, so my guess was they were federal agents who had been recruited into Cerberus, likely from the Secret Service or Air Marshals.

Their boss leaned in and lifted the bag off my head. "Sorry again for the restraints and hood, but this facility is above top secret. We can't let anyone know our location. I'm sure you understand."

I'd already sent instructions to the Oak via our mental link, asking it to mark my current whereabouts. The Druid Oak sent back an image of Devil's Tower in Wyoming, of all things. I had no idea if that was the location of Mendoza's secret base, or just an indication that the spot had been noted. Since they were driving me back home, I was going with the latter... but I damned sure hoped they weren't sending me through another wormhole along the way.

"I hope this is the last time we meet, Agent Mendoza."

"Doubtful, and you know it," he replied. "I really wish you'd consider working with us, McCool. Based on what our C.I. says, I think you're fighting them, and I also suspect you're doing it on behalf of the human race. An alliance with Cerberus would be useful in that regard. We could provide you with financial backing, weaponry, tech, personnel—heck, I could put you in charge of your own tac team."

"I'm just a college student who likes to wrench on old cars," I said. "And I prefer to keep it that way."

He sighed in frustration, scratching his forehead. "Have it your way. But I have a feeling that someday, you're going to come to us for help. When that day comes, you'd better hope I'm still in charge—because I can't guarantee that a successor would be so favorably inclined toward you."

When I failed to answer, he dropped the hood back over my head.

"I'll be seeing you, McCool."

"Not if I see you first."

The drive back was uneventful, but long. Based on the number of turns they took, the agents had chosen to do a thorough cleaning run to make sure they weren't being followed. They also drove around in circles so I wouldn't be able to guess how far their secret hideout was from Austin.

It made no difference, since my very rudimentary training in chronomancy and chronourgy had given me an uncanny perception of time. By my estimation, they drove for almost six hours before we arrived at our final destination. With all the extra driving they did, I figured their base was within four hours of South Austin.

As the van came to a stop, one of the agents removed my cuffs and pulled my hood off. "Don't try to follow us," he growled.

"Hey, you're the ones stalking me," I said as he glowered at me.

The other agent walked around the van, opening the side doors from the outside since the inside handles had been removed. Based on the ambient traffic noises I detected above us, it looked like we were in an underground parking lot—most likely at one of the hotels downtown.

As I stepped out of the van, I wondered how many people they'd abducted using that particular vehicle. For all I knew, they had an entire fleet of abducti-mobiles, all unmarked on the outside, with dark tint and the interior handles removed from the passenger doors.

"You know, you guys should start a side hustle. 'Renditions-R-Us,'" I said, spreading my hands apart as if revealing the letters in midair. "You know, like Uber, but for secret government organizations. I bet it'd be a big hit on the east coast."

The agents ignored my jibe, refusing to be roused. Without another word, they got into the van and drove off, leaving me to wonder where I was. Just for grins, I took the elevator to ground level and walked outside.

Damn it.

I was at the university, on campus. It'd be a long walk back to the junkyard if I didn't ask the Oak to retrieve me. I decided to check my messages instead. Sure enough, Fallyn had been texting me like crazy.

I sent her a message back.

Sry 4 stnding U up. Pik mE up @ Brazos n MLK?

She answered almost immediately.

B thr in 5. Xpect trouble?

I typed a quick reply.

No. Expln wn u get hEre.

K.

That was the cool thing about Fallyn. She understood that my life was crazy as fuck. When the unexpected happened, she wasn't prone to freaking out, and she never blamed me for stuff that was beyond my control. After months of dating Bells, always feeling like I was in the doghouse for something or other, Fallyn's even temperament was a welcome change.

Minutes later, the she-wolf pulled up on a chopped-out Harley with fat, white-wall tires, wire-spoke rims, ape-hanger bars, and a short front rake. She pulled off her helmet and shook out her flowing chestnut hair. She wore tight jeans over biker boots and a fitted leather jacket that accentuated her lithe, muscular frame. I couldn't help but admire the girl with those high cheekbones, pert yet regal nose, and Goldilocks lips that always teased at a smile, like Fallyn was enjoying some private joke that only she was in on.

"So, you wanna tell me about it?" she asked, frowning sympathetically.

"Over food, if you don't mind. I was starving six hours ago, before I was abducted. Right now, I could eat a horse."

"Hop on, then," she said, nodding at the seat behind her.

"Aw, man, you're going to make me ride bitch?" I asked.

Fallyn gave a low growl. "Watch it, buddy. You might have a cute ass, but that doesn't give you carte blanche to say whatever the hell you like."

"Hey, blame your dad for that. He's the one who taught me how to speak one-percenter."

Fallyn rolled her eyes at me, then put her helmet back on. "Just get on the damned bike, McCool, before I leave you behind."

I chuckled as I swung a leg over the seat, wrapping my arms

around her lean, slender waist. Snuggling close, I breathed in her perfume and musky, canine scent.

"Alright, hard-belly—but you're buying."

TWENTY MINUTES LATER, we were at Thundercloud wolfing down subs—no pun intended. Fallyn could put the food away, being a werewolf and all, but I was giving her a run for her money. She paused between bites to wink at a couple of frat boys who'd watched wide-eyed as she destroyed two foot-long subs in under five minutes.

Suddenly, her cocky grin turned into a frown. I swung my head around, looking for the cause of her distress.

"Frat boys giving you grief?"

"Naw, I'm pretty sure they're gay and checking you out. It's that creepy guy back there, the blond—he's the one that's got my hackles up."

I turned to look again, but the place was empty except for the frat guys. "I don't see him. And those guys definitely aren't setting off my gaydar." One of them winked at me. "Oops, never mind."

"You see him?"

"No, but you were right about at least one of the frat boys."

Fallyn's head swiveled as she scanned the place. "Damn, he must've taken off. I think I saw him yesterday too, just staring at me while I was at Luther's."

"Hmm... want me to find him and rough him up?" I asked with a teasing smile. Fallyn could take care of herself, of course, but I still liked to act like the protective boyfriend every once in a while.

She tossed a tomato slice at me. "I think I got it, tough guy. But if I need you to bust anyone up, you'll be the first to know."

"Deal," I said, inhaling the rest of my sub.

She slung a stray piece of sandwich shrapnel off her hand, pausing to take a sip of her soda. "So, Mendoza wants to be all buddy-buddy now? That's quite the one-eighty he's pulled. Weird."

I chewed a mouthful of meatball sub and washed it down with a pull off my extra-large sweet tea. "Meh, it makes sense when you think about it. I mean, had you heard of them before they showed up at the junkyard?"

"Nope, but that doesn't mean they haven't been around a while. Samson says he's known about them for decades."

"Finnegas pretty much said the same thing. But think about it—do you know anyone who's clued in that would risk their life by sharing info with the feds? I don't. Heck, it'd be a race to see who got to them first—the fae, the vamps, or the Circle."

She took a long pull from her soda. "My money would be on Luther. He seems nice, but he'll do just about anything to protect his coven."

"Don't I know it. I've seen him in action a few times, and the dude is scary as fuck. When he decides to throw down, he legit makes you want to shit your pants."

She screwed her mouth up sideways, squinting at me with her light hazel, almost yellow eyes. "Ya' think Samson could take him?"

I pushed myself back from the table, taking a few seconds to ponder her question. "Damn, I never thought about it. It'd be a hell of a fight, that's for sure. Why? Is there friction between the Pack and Coven?"

Fallyn waved my question off, giggling. "What? No, no way. Dad and Luther are thick as thieves. Two wily old bastards who know the treaty with Maeve only stands if they stick together. Naw, they're good."

I sighed with relief. "Shit, you had me worried for a minute."

I grabbed my bag of chips, pouring the last few crumbs in my mouth. "What do you think I should do about Cerberus? Do I leave it alone, or what?"

"You definitely need to tell Samson and Finnegas what's going on. But to me, it seems like Mendoza just left the ball in your court. I have a hunch he's decided you're on the side of angels. I wouldn't be surprised if he goes all out to recruit you."

"Hah! Fat chance I sign on with Cerberus," I said, reaching for a potato chip on her side of the table. She slapped my hand hard enough to leave a bruise. I shook it out as I feigned indignation. "Ow! Sheesh, nothing gets you riled like someone trying to steal a bite from your plate."

"Food guarding is a normal behavior for canines. Look it up," she replied with a smile. Her voice turned syrupy-sweet as she continued. "Now, after that gross infraction of Pack etiquette, would you please grab me another sandwich?"

I leaned across the table, narrowing my eyes as a smile played at the corners of my mouth. "And what will I get if I do?"

She leaned in, lips brushing my ear as she whispered her reply. "You'll never find out if you don't."

Laughing silently, I stood. "Then I suppose I'd better refill your drink as well?"

"See? That's the kind of strategic thinking that attracted me to you in the first place." She winked at me playfully. "Well, that and the fact that you have no qualms about chewing a mother-fucker's throat out."

The next morning, after spending several hours in the Grove with Fallyn—and after she left, the equivalent of a few weeks there training with Finnegas—the old man and I stopped by the junkyard to help Maureen with some admin work. It was still early, but we wanted to catch her before the morning crew arrived at nine. As we approached the office, the half-kelpie's voice reverberated through the walls of the metal building that served as the junkyard's HQ.

"I know we've maxed out our feckin' credit—that's why I'm callin' ta' ask ye fer an increase, ya' idjit!"

We both pulled up just short of the front door, not wanting to walk in the office while Maureen was in full ass-chewing mode. Being fae, her tantrums were often epic, albeit short-lived. When she was in a mood, it was best to let her settle down before entering her domain... and the office had become that and then some, of late.

I winced, leaning against the building. "Didn't that job I pulled for Maeve cover our expenses for the month?"

Finnegas rolled a cigarette, licking the paper to seal it before lighting up. "Eh, probably. But this place wasn't exactly pumping out cash when your uncle was alive. Bless the man, but Ed was too kindhearted to make a business like this profitable."

The old man was right about Ed—he'd been too nice for his own good. My uncle had loved taking strays in, which was why he'd always had more people on staff than he needed. Besides that, he was always helping people out by giving them credit on parts, free repairs, and the like. And because of that, a lot of the equipment around the yard that should've been replaced, wasn't.

"Did the crane break down again? Or the crusher?"

Finnegas puffed on his cigarette and shrugged. "Ask Maureen. She's the one keeping this place afloat." He glanced sideways at the office wall as the half-kelpie's kvetching reached a fever pitch. "Might be best if we come back later—after she's had a chance to cool down."

"Good idea. We could help the morning crew get a head start on pulling parts."

He shook his head. "Actually, this might be the perfect opportunity to work on some magnetism spells. I—" Finn's left eyebrow shot up as his eyes darted around the junkyard. "Something's coming!"

I reached in my Bag, grasping Dyrnwyn's smooth, worn hilt. The sword warmed at my touch, which told me it sensed the presence of evil. Before I could pull the sword free, Finnegas laid a hand on my arm to keep me from drawing it, pointing at the front parking lot. The first of our employees had just pulled up to start their shift, and the last thing we needed was for the morning crew to see me swinging a flaming sword around.

"There's no time anyway," the old druid said. "Head for the Oak, then get as far away from here as you can—it'll follow you, believe me. Once you're clear, have the Oak bring me to your location as soon as you're able."

"But Finn, the wards—"

"It's the Dullahan, Colin, and no gate, ward, lock, or barrier will keep him out. Do as you're told, and hurry!"

"And if he doesn't follow?" I asked.

"Oh, believe me—he'll follow. If he's been freed from where I sent him the last time, it can only mean one thing—the gods are coming for you. Now, go!" he said, pointing a long, bony finger toward the junkyard proper.

Torn between staying with the old man and luring the Dullahan away from the junkyard, I hesitated a split-second before sprinting for the Druid Oak. I needed to be near the tree when the fae's grim reaper arrived. If he really had come for me, I wanted him to have line of sight when the Oak sent me away.

As a psychopomp, the Dullahan possessed powerful magic, the sort that allowed him to circumvent magical locks and wards, and to cross time and space to pursue his prey. When I traveled from place to place via the Druid Oak, the Grove's magic left a trail that could be followed, for a brief time. I wanted the Dullahan to see that trail so he'd follow me and pose no danger to Finnegas, Maureen, and the junkyard staff.

Could I have retreated inside the Druid Grove? Yes, of course. However, the Dullahan was known for his ability to traverse dimensions. Although I could access a lot more magic inside the Grove, something told me I did not want the headless horseman following me inside that sacred space.

Seconds later, I was standing next to the Oak, poised for action and senses on high alert. The tree must have picked up my distress, or perhaps it sensed the Dullahan's approach. It sent me images of a mountain lion creeping through the forest undergrowth at night, followed by an image of a deer fleeing away at speed. Obviously, it held the opinion that discretion would be the better part of valor in this instance. I touched the tree's trunk to reassure it, feeling the rough bark under my fingertips and sensing the massive magical power that slowly pulsed within like a giant, mystical heartbeat.

I agree, but we can't run yet. I need to draw it away from the junkyard, so wait for my signal.

The tree sent an image of an eagle, poised on a high ledge with wings spread as it prepared to take flight. At that moment, the sky grew dark, and ghostly hoofbeats began echoing across the yard. I plugged my brain into the Oak's senses, closing my eyes as I used the tree's magic to enhance my ability to "see" in the magical spectrum.

At first there was nothing except for the glow of energy coming off the tree itself, and the glimmer of my wards surrounding the perimeter of the junkyard. Then, in my mind's eye, a dark, shimmering oval appeared twenty yards away, in the direction of the front gates. Six feet wide and twice as tall, the portal was easily large enough for a horse and rider to leap through. I opened my eyes, keeping one hand on the Oak's trunk as I waited for the portal to appear in this reality.

Soon the air split, just at the spot where I'd sensed the portal forming moments before. Through the rift in time and space I saw what existed on the other side, wherever the Dullahan had come from. It was a hellish landscape—dark, misty, and void of any living thing.

Tech Duinn—the land of the dead. I bet that's where he takes his victims.

Hoofbeats echoed from the mists beyond, growing louder as the rider approached. The dense fog parted and the Dullahan emerged through the portal, riding a huge steed with glowing red eyes and flesh that appeared to have been flayed skinless from nose to tail. Blood dripped from the creature's raw, rippling body, trickling down its legs and splashing from its hooves in splatters and droplets with every step.

The beast saw me and bared a mouthful of teeth—not the

typical herbivore dentition that normal horses had, but a mouthful of sharpened canines and incisors meant for ripping and tearing flesh. It snorted and stamped its forehooves, pawing violently at the ground. When its poison breath touched the undergrowth beneath those hooves, the plant life wilted immediately.

A nuckelavee. Looks like old headless got an upgrade.

A giant of a man sat astride the horse, dressed in a long frock coat made of human skin worn over a dirty white shirt and black pants tucked into riding boots. I could tell the coat was made of human skin because the Dullahan had used not just the hide of his victims to fashion his overcoat, but their faces as well. Each of those faces appeared to be locked in an eternal scream, silently protesting the agony and humiliation they'd suffered at the hands of the fae reaper.

The Headless Horseman held the horse's reins in one large, gloved hand, and under his other arm rested his disembodied head, the face split in a permanent rictus of a smile. The Dullahan's dead eyes locked in on me, leering hungrily at the seemingly helpless human prey before him. He ran a bloated, rotting tongue across his mold-green lips, as if anticipating the taste of my blood—or perhaps my soul.

The specter calmly sat his head in his lap. There it seemed intent to stay, despite the way the horse stamped and pawed at the ground. He wrapped the reins around the saddle's pommel, once, twice, before drawing them tight. Reaching into his overcoat, he pulled out what at first looked like a length of chain, but then I realized it was a human spine—several, actually, held together by some force of magic beyond my understanding.

At the end of the spinal cord whip was a dark, slightly curved blade, shaped like a short scimitar or perhaps a harvest sickle. Soundlessly, the Dullahan charged, swinging that long, wicked blade in looping circles overhead.

"Look, Mendoza, I don't know what the hell you spooks are up to with all your *X-Files* bullshit, and I don't care. You expect me to believe there are werewolves and vampires, and that the thing that came at me in that cell was a zombie?"

"You said it, not me," he interjected, tapping a few more keys on his laptop.

"Yeah, because I watch TV just like everyone else these days! I got no idea what kind of sick game you're playing here, and I don't care. All I want is for you and your goons to leave me alone, and for you to take me back to my place so I can get a decent coffee and a good night's sleep."

The agent nodded, as if deciding something to himself. Then, he turned the laptop screen around to face me. The image on the screen was grainy and in black and white, but it was me. Not human me, but the Hyde-side version of me—in all my raging glory.

"Recognize him?" Mendoza asked.

"What, is that a leaked photo from the next MCU movie?"

"You can drop the act, McCool. We know you're connected to the creature in some way, although we don't precisely know how.

That's our cue—get us out of here, now!

I DUCKED THE TWO-FOOT-LONG, razor-sharp elven blade, rolling to my right as the edge bit deep into the bark and cambium of the cottonwood tree I'd been leaning against. All I'd needed was a moment to catch my breath, just a few second's reprieve, but my assailant was having none of that. Chest heaving and muscles burning, I sprang to my feet and sprinted through the thick eldritch fog in an attempt to lose the Dullahan in the forest once more.

Nothing like being chased by the supernatural version of The Terminator. I suppose I should thank my lucky stars—at least this guy doesn't spout dopey lines in a thick Austrian accent.

The horseman momentarily struggled to free his weapon from the tree, providing me with a few precious seconds to gain ground. I'd stretched that lead to a good fifty yards before hoof-beats indicated the chase was on yet again. Not wanting to make things easy on him, I chose a path that took me through the densest part of the woods. It ran along the south bank of the Pedernales River, in the northernmost section of the eponymously-named state park. Thankfully it was still early in the day, so there was no one to witness this spectacle but the forest animals who hid and scattered as we passed by them.

I'd asked the Druid Oak to take us here, well away from the junkyard—and Maureen and Finnegas. Despite the old man's request to be brought along for the fight, I decided to handle this one on my own. While there may have been a time when Finn could've taken the Dullahan with one hand tied behind his back, the old druid's glory days were over. He was still powerful in knowledge and magical skill, but not in body, and a weak body could only channel so much magic before it failed.

Apprentice or no, I wasn't going to allow my mentor to sacrifice himself for my sake.

The hoofbeats grew louder as my pursuer closed the distance between us, muffled as they were by unnatural mists that blocked my connection to the Grove. If not for the interference, I would've already called the Oak to me so I could have it transport us both out of here. But despite my best efforts, I'd been unable to communicate with the Oak and Grove since the fog had risen from the ground around me.

Upon finding our connection severed, my plan had been to circle back to the Oak. But after thirty minutes of stumbling around the woods while evading the Dullahan's relentless pursuit and avoiding his attacks, I'd yet to come across the clearing where I'd left it. More than once during that time, the bastard had nearly taken my head off, and I was currently at the limits of my human, albeit enhanced, physical stamina.

Fuck this, I'm tired of running. Time to make a stand.

Even in my human form I was a match for most run-of-the-mill creatures, having been blessed from birth with the peak physical attributes of a natural-born human champion. Yet my fully-human form was no match for the Dullahan, a fact I'd discovered during our last meeting. On that occasion, the fae psychopomp had knocked my demigod buddy Hemi out cold without breaking a sweat.

And if it hadn't been for Finnegas stepping in, I'd have been dead. The old man had used druidic magic to send the damned thing to the Underrealms—saving my ass in the process. After my first go-round with the Dullahan, I knew that the human me stood no chance against him.

Back then, I'd had zero control over my *ríastrad*, the so-called "warp-spasm" I'd inherited from the Fomorians via Lugh by way of Cú Chulainn's bloodline. When my warp-spasm triggered, to say I became a highly formidable hand-to-hand combatant would be an understatement. Based on past experience, I was certain I'd be more than a match for the Dullahan if I let my Hyde-side come out.

But it occurred to me that I might not want to reveal my new-found shifting abilities to the Dullahan. As far as I knew, my foe had no idea that I'd learn to control my Formorian powers. Presumably he'd just returned from wherever Finnegas had sent him a little more than a year prior, pissed off and out for blood. And if that was the case, I'd gain an advantage by not letting him know that I was on his level. With the element of surprise on my side, I might be able to take him out before he sank that huge chain-sickle into my neck.

Wait a minute—can psychopomps die? Guess there's only one way to find out.

I reached into my Craneskin Bag and pulled out Dyrnwyn, the famed flaming sword from Welsh legend. Once I had the sword firmly in my grasp, I began to stealth shift, accessing my Fomorian genes to magically increase my strength, speed, reflexes, and durability to preternatural levels, all while maintaining my human appearance. After my inner transformation was complete, I adjusted my grip on Dyrnwyn's hilt and shifted my weight to the balls of my feet, facing the direction of the staccato hoofbeats that heralded the Dullahan's approach.

———

ONE THING no one ever tells you about a life-or-death battle is how you'll react. And it's always the same, regardless of how many times you've previously faced death. The metallic acidity of fear and bile in your mouth, the urgency in your bladder, bowels, and gut, and the way your brain selectively sharpens and mutes your senses. Your heartbeat pounds in your ears and you smell the iron tang of blood in the air, all while your vision narrows so you can only focus on one thing—the enemy who wants to take your life.

Currently, the threat garnering one hundred percent of my attention was the seven-foot-tall headless horseman on the 2,000-pound skinless steed bearing down on me like a runaway train. Needless to say, it was terrifying. When you're facing the fae equivalent of the grim reaper as he charges you riding a nuckelavee, swinging a two-foot-long scythe blade on a chain made from human bones, well—it'll definitely make you wish you wore your brown underwear.

Thankfully, my Fomorian DNA acted as a sort of buffer against my instinctive human fear. Had I completely changed and gone full-on Fomori, that fear would've been a distant memory. As it stood, I felt a bit nauseous and my hands were shaking, but it wasn't nearly as bad as it might have been. Moreover, I'd been in similar situations many times before, and I knew that stillness was death in battle.

Time to move, or die.

I sprang into action, willing Dyrnwyn to conceal its nature as I ran full tilt at the Dullahan, screaming bloody murder. The battle cry was more to help with my nerves than to put fear into my enemies, but it seemed fitting since I was playing chicken with 2,400 pounds of hell-spawned death. The gap between us narrowed with my every step, and two seconds later, I was within range of the horseman's scythe.

The soul-taker's decapitated head cackled silently as he whipped the blade at my neck in a movement that was so quick, I almost didn't react in time. Thankfully, I'd anticipated that move, and gravity was on my side as I made my play. The heads-man's blade flew close enough to nick my ear as I dodged left and dropped beneath it, sliding like a runner into home plate as I willed Dyrnwyn to ignite.

The nuckelavee was fast and powerful, but it was also a large animal and cumbersome due to its bulk. I might not have been its match pound for pound in my current form, but I was that much nimbler. Savoring the fear I saw in the fae horse's glowing red eyes as it realized its fate, I slid past the creature with the flaming sword extended to my right.

The blade blazed like a star gone nova as it sliced clean through the nuckelavee's right foreleg and hind-leg. The beast screeched in pain and rage as horse and rider both went tumbling into the trees behind me, while I skidded and rolled to a standing position. As I turned to face them, I casually checked to see if my ear was still intact. It was bleeding like mad, but my Fomorian DNA would heal it shortly.

Could've easily been my neck. He's quick with that thing. I'll need to do something about that.

The Dullahan disentangled himself from beneath his steed, all while the nuckelavee made vain attempts to get back to its feet. Since two of its legs were missing just below the knee, all it could do was roll back and forth and screech in pain, hate, and rage. For a moment I felt a twinge of sympathy for the creature, then I remembered that nuckelavees were known for drowning people and eating them.

In spite of the steed's evil nature, the noise it made was reason enough to put it out of its misery myself. Thankfully, there was no need. The Dullahan spun his chain blade in a tight arc, ending the motion by swiping the blade through the horse's neck so hard the scythe buried itself in the ground. He freed his weapon in a spray of black dirt and even blacker blood as his head floated out of the bushes, settling under his right arm where it scowled at me.

I backed away with Dyrnwyn held before me in a vertical guard. Hopefully I could deflect the scythe before it separated my head from my shoulders. The Dullahan advanced on me, step by determined step, covering more ground than I would've thought possible in just a few long strides. He was nearly close enough to strike when I stumbled over a tree root, and his disembodied head leered in triumph as he launched his weapon at me.

I rolled left, a line of searing pain crossing my back as the scythe scored my skin in passing. I heard a satisfying *thunk* as the blade sunk cleanly into the root I'd tripped over moments before. Instinctively, I reached out with my druid senses, willing the tree's roots to envelope the scythe completely in order to trap it. Sensing rather than seeing the tree's roots wrap around the blade, I knew by the clanking of the chain as the headsman yanked on it that it was firmly stuck.

I rolled back to my left, chopping down with all my might. The flaming blade sliced through the bone chain connecting the weapon to its wielder. Now, all the Dullahan had was a bone whip—intimidating, but not nearly as deadly as a blade on a chain.

Springing to my feet with Dyrnwyn blazing bright, I ran toward him at full tilt, intending to finish the fight while I had him at a disadvantage. But before I could reach the fae headsman, the air behind him split into a dark oval window that revealed the black mists of Tech Duinn beyond. With his ghoulish mouth set in a hard line, my enemy stepped away from me in retreat. Before I could reach it, the portal closed, taking the Dullahan back to the Celtic Underworld—for now.

7

Once the Dullahan had vanished, the fog receded and I was able to communicate with the Oak once more. I instructed it to take us back to the junkyard, where Finnegas waited for me. The old man was practically blowing smoke out of his ears as he paced a line in the dirt and weeds of the yard.

"Damn it, boy—what'd I tell you to do? I said lure it away and then bring me to help you get rid of it, not fight it all on your own."

I rubbed a hand across my face, checking my ear in the same motion. Of course, it had already healed.

"Well, I took care of it. I beat him and the Dullahan went back to Tech Duinn. Or, at least, I think that's where he ran off to."

Finnegas tugged at his beard as he glowered at me. "You think you're so smart, using your *ríastrad* to solve every problem that comes your way. If you'd have called me to help, I could have easily banished that thing again—"

I bit my tongue, not wanting to say that I didn't think he was up to it. Instead I stared at the ground as he continued his royal ass-chewing.

"—but now, the Headless One knows you have control of your Fomorian side—and whatever god or gods who sent him will know you've finally mastered those powers. Now, they'll come at you in force. Believe me when I say they won't trifle with you next time, and neither will the Dullahan."

I threw my hands in the air with a growl. "Honestly, Finnegas—what's new? The Tuath Dé and their offspring have been fucking with me since I was a kid. So what if they decide to send their first string after me? It's not like I haven't fought gods before."

My druid mentor snapped his fingers, and a lit cigarette appeared in his mouth. The old man rarely used magic to accomplish mundane tasks, and I knew the display was a sure sign he was well and truly pissed. He took a long drag off the coffin nail before pulling it from his mouth, stabbing the air with it as he spoke.

"How many times do I have to tell you that you aren't strong enough to fight the gods? You've yet to scratch the surface of the powers the Oak and Grove provide, you've not even passed your druid apprenticeship—despite having been under my tutelage for years—and you rely way too much on that damned Fomorian blood to get you out of every tight spot and scrape you find yourself in."

I knuckled my forehead. A headache was coming on. "Look, I get why you're concerned. But don't you think they sent the Dullahan after me because they're scared of me? Now that I've beaten him, maybe they'll back off for a while."

Finnegas stared at me, slack-mouthed, with his cancer stick hanging off his lip. Then he busted out laughing, snagging the cigarette with one hand in time to prevent it from flying across the yard. Knowing there was nothing to do but wait for him to settle down, I looked on with my arms crossed as I let the scene play out.

The old druid wiped his eyes, stamping out his cigarette butt as he started to roll another. "Oh, you kids," he snickered. "Sometimes I forget how young you really are, and how much naivety comes with that lack of experience. Of course they're afraid of you. But by besting the Dullahan in one-on-one combat, you've dialed their fear up to eleven. The Headless Horseman was a test, Colin—one that you passed, and brilliantly. Now, they're going to be aiming for you with both barrels."

"Um... huh. I never considered that they might be testing me."

"Of course you didn't, because you don't think like an immortal being. Well, semi-immortal, anyway. Gods *can* die, after all." He sat on a stack of tires, puffing away as he looked off into the distance. "You sure have a knack for stepping in it, I'll give you that. What was it that girl called you? A first-rate shit magnet?"

"If memory serves, I believe the modifier she used was 'world-class.'"

"Pfft... she got that right." He took a long drag and blew smoke out his nostrils. "When you piss off the gods, you put everyone around you in danger. Are you sure you're willing to risk placing your friends in their crosshairs?"

"If it comes to that, I'll draw them off like I did today," I replied with a lot less certainty in my voice than I would have liked.

"Uh-huh. That's if they don't go after your friends first. The gods are fickle, Colin, and spiteful. They enjoy crushing the human spirit, and it's not unlike them to make sport of it. Any advantage they can gain, they'll use. And they'll happily draw your suffering out until you've nothing left to lose."

I clenched my fists, angry about being an unwilling chess

piece in the games of the Tuath Dé. "I won't let that happen, Finn."

He barked a short laugh. "Good luck with that. They can play a long game, and that usually means the gods get what they want—in the end."

"So, why hasn't anyone ever stopped them? You know, put them in their place?"

His eyes locked on mine. "Don't even think about it. Despite the 'god-killer' moniker, you're nowhere near powerful enough to take on the gods. Best thing you can do is keep your head down and hope they take their time planning their next move. Maybe that'll give us the opportunity to get some more training in, and give you a slight edge."

"So, there is hope after all."

"Hah! Shit in one hand and hope in the other, and tell me which one fills first." He licked a fleck of tobacco from his lip, chewing on it absently. "One thing's for sure, though—you can't trust the Grove to keep you safe from the Dullahan. There's not a lock, ward, or wall strong enough to keep him from his prey. We'll have to instruct the Grove to move around a lot, and in unpredictable patterns, to keep him off your trail. But eventually he will catch up to you, either in this world or while you're in the Grove."

I kicked an empty soda can across the yard. "Seems like I'd want him to attack me inside the Grove. I killed plenty of nasties in there while we were stuck in the Void. I'd bet on having that advantage, any day of the week."

Finnegas shook his head. "They'll know that, and they'll plan to remove you from the Grove somehow. That's how I'd do it, and I'd divorce you from your Fomorian powers as well."

"It's been tried before, by the Dark Druid," I replied. "And he failed."

"They'll come after Fallyn, you know. And I don't need to tell you what'll happen if Samson thinks you're responsible for something happening to his daughter."

"I'm aware," I said.

Finnegas stood, pointing his cigarette at me as he stared with authority. "Then you'd damned sure better go warn him before it comes to that. But I'll leave that to you. I'm not your gods-damned nanny, you know."

———

I WASN'T EXACTLY LOOKING FORWARD to having this conversation with Samson. Long before Fallyn and I had gotten involved, he'd made it pretty damned clear that he didn't want me dating his daughter. Much to his displeasure and despite his best efforts, his daughter would not be deterred. As for me, I'd resisted as long as I could—but once Fallyn had me in her sights, it was pretty much a done deal.

Samson's wishes hadn't stood a chance.

Of course, that was the problem. Alphas were used to getting what they wanted, especially when it came to telling their pack members what to do. And when it came to their offspring, well —let's just say an alpha could take parental protectiveness to a whole new level.

It was a wonder that Samson hadn't ripped my head off when he'd found out about Fallyn and me. However, she was pretty much the only Pack member who stood up to him, and also the only one who could get away with it. I was pretty sure Samson's daughter had read him the riot act about interfering in her love life well before he could track me down and kick my ass.

Which was just as well, considering that I wasn't about to take an ass-kicking from him just because his daughter had a thing for me. He might have been my Pack Alpha, but I showed him deference out of respect, not fear. Samson couldn't exert his will on me through the Pack bonds, because my Fomorian side wouldn't allow it. He knew that, and I think it rankled him, making our relationship even more tense than it was already.

So, a confrontation between us would only end in a fight, and that was something neither of us wanted. As I pulled into the clubhouse parking lot, I hoped he'd remain calm and civil while I explained the situation—and my plans for making it right.

Sledge and Guerra were on door duty at the clubhouse entrance. Sledge didn't have to do it, as he had plenty of 'thropes to pull the weight. But I was pretty sure the huge werewolf liked being the first thing visitors saw when they arrived at the clubhouse. Both wolves stared at me as I walked up, and Guerra gave me a grudging nod.

I stopped before I hit the concrete steps at the entry, giving them the advantage of higher ground. The last thing you ever wanted to do was get in a 'thrope's personal space. Power moves like that might work among humans, but when you were dealing with Pack, even minor challenges were best avoided.

"Sledge, Guerra. Anything I should be aware of before I go in?"

The Pack's sergeant-at-arms raised his chin at me. "Been a while, Colin." He extended his hand and I took it. The big 'thrope pulled me into a bro hug, nearly knocking the wind out of me when he slapped me on the back. "Everything's copacetic tonight. Got a few probies pulling bar duty, and the regulars are all here. Other than that, it's a slow night."

"Good to hear," I said. "Samson around?"

Guerra stood stock still as he answered. "In the back, as usual." The dour-faced Mexicano was a dead ringer for Danny Trejo, down to the actor's stoic screen persona and craggy, pockmarked face. "And he's got a case of the ass 'bout something tonight, druid. Fair warning."

I nodded. "Thanks for the heads up, fellas."

Sledge snickered as he shot Guerra a look. "Been with us almost a year, and he still talks like a fucking choir boy."

"Fuckin' ay right I do," I said with a straight face as I walked into the bar, with Sledge and Guerra's raucous laughter trailing after me.

THERE WAS a hush over the clubhouse when I walked in, the sort of pseudo-silence created when everyone was talking, but no one wanted to be heard. Here and there, eyes darted toward me and away again, as if the mere act of looking at the wrong person might draw their alpha's ire. It was the wrong time to be disturbing Samson. Of that, I had no doubt.

While I was scoping the place out, the bartender beckoned me over with a tilt of her head. She was tall and pretty, and an old hand at handling the very rowdy 'thropes who made up the Austin Pack.

"Heya, Mitzy. What's up?" I said as I sidled up to the bar.

She busied herself with cleaning pint glasses, even though they were rarely used here. Pack members tended to drink out of bottles and cans, except when drinking hard liquor. Werewolves had a hard time getting drunk, as did other therianthrope species. So, drinking games were popular in the clubhouse, and one of their favorites was seeing who could do the most shots before passing out. They went through a lot of alcohol.

"You goin' back to see Samson?" she asked as she poured a shot of bourbon for me. Mitzy had grown fond of me when I was just a probie, and I of her. I'd pulled barback duty for her a lot back then, and she'd always shared her tips with me because I showed up early and stayed late. She was good people.

"Why else would I be here? I'm not exactly popular around the clubhouse, you know."

Mitzy gave a quick shake of her head. "I wouldn't, if I were you. He's a special kind of pissed off tonight, and I think it has something to do with you and Fallyn. Might be best to give him some time to chill out. Maybe come back when he's not..."

"Pissed off?" I said, giving her my best devil-may-care grin.

She nodded curtly, looking me in the eye. "Old 'thropes can be dangerous when they're riled, Colin. I know you're tough and all, but still—it's not a good time to bother our alpha."

"Huh. Guerra told me the same thing when I came in." I scratched my head absently. "Normally I'd take the advice to heart, but this just can't wait."

She polished the glass she held ever more furiously. "Your funeral, then. Good luck."

"Mmhm. Yeah, that's something I've never had." I raised the shot glass to Mitzy and slammed it. "See you at my wake."

She gave me a look that said men were idiots to ignore the advice of women. I mostly agreed with the sentiment, but still headed back to Samson's office. Everyone in the clubhouse grew silent as I approached the door, each holding their breath in unison as they watched me meet my doom.

Whelp, time to rip this bandage off.

I made a fist, holding it up to the door, but pausing just before I knocked.

"I know it's you, McCool," a gruff male voice said from the other side. He wasn't yelling, but his voice carried regardless. "Get your ass in here and close the door behind you."

Out of the corner of my eye, I saw a biker draw a finger across his throat. His buddies chuckled silently. I looked their way momentarily, staring them down. None met my challenge.

It was a dumbshit move, and it could've ended in a brawl, but I was kind of tired of taking shit from half the Pack.

With one last wink at Mitzy, I headed into the office. Samson was the only person within, but he was more than enough to frighten the hell out of anyone. He looked like a bald, bearded, tattooed Chuck Norris, with the slight stature to match, and he shared the actor's steely-eyed stare and intimidating presence. Add to that his status as a very old werewolf and alpha, and... well... he was not someone you casually fucked with.

The Alpha sat concealed in shadow on the far side of the room behind his desk. He had his feet propped up, with a cigar in one hand and a glass of whiskey in the other. Besides the tobacco smoke, the place smelled like stale beer, male hormones, sex...

And anger. Lots and lots of anger.

"Have a seat."

It was a command, not a request. I crossed the room and sat. The tension in the air was palpable.

"Samson, I—"

"I know why you're here, dumbass. Son of a bitch, but I'll never figure out what my daughter sees in you. Hell, even she says you're the world's biggest shit magnet—"

"World-class," I interjected, immediately regretting it.

"Do not fucking interrupt me!" he shouted, lowering his feet from the desk so he could slam his fist down on the scarred, stained surface.

Cigar ash flew everywhere as he crunched his stogie between his fingers. He leaned into the light, revealing the veins popping out on his forehead. The Alpha glared at me for several seconds as if daring me to speak again, but I kept my eyes down and had the good sense to remain silent. An instant later, the tension in his face and neck disappeared, and he sank back in his chair, deflated.

"That was my last Cuban."

"Sorry," I replied, meaning it.

He exhaled heavily. "I should kill you for putting her on their radar. Do you know what it'll mean for the Pack if we end up in a war with the Tuath Dé? It'll shatter the peace between the fae and the Pack, and we'll end up fighting a war on two fronts."

"Maeve would never allow it," I proffered hopefully. "She wants to keep the peace as much as you do."

———

THE ALPHA TOOK a sip of whiskey, swishing it around as he considered my words. "Sometimes I forget how young you are, and that you've never lived through a faction war. Others will come, Colin, if the gods tell them to come. They'll overrun Maeve and those loyal to her—those who don't defect—and then they'll take over her demesne."

"Samson—"

He cut me off with a chop of his hand. "Just sit there and listen, damn it. You're a danger to them, Colin—a serious threat. And while you might have a couple of the Celtic gods on your side, the rest'll fear you. To them, you represent the ugly side of a race who once beat the Tuatha, combined with the race who forced them into hiding. Add in the fact that you're a druid, and you're their worst nightmare—a human-Fomori hybrid who could someday match them in magic and power."

He downed the rest of his drink, setting the glass down on the desk with care. Clearly, he wasn't finished speaking. I sat silently, wishing I'd had a few more in me before I'd entered the Alpha's den. After he'd gathered his thoughts, Samson continued.

"Every immortal spends at least some of their time thinking

of worst-case scenarios. They might spend centuries busting their noggins over who or what could hurt them. Then, they make plans to survive those scenarios if they ever happen.

"Well, guess what? You're the extinction-level event they've been dreading for ages, the one person who might end their reign for good. And when it comes to gods, boy, they will not allow a threat like you to exist. To do so is simply not in their nature.

"They'll come after you relentlessly, first by probing your defenses, learning your strengths so they know where you're weakest. Then, they'll test your resolve. Everyone and everything you care about will be fair game. They will give no quarter —none at all—and they'll dismantle you piece by piece, until nothing remains of you or the people you loved but ash. When it's done, they'll salt the Earth behind them, and you and yours will be nothing more than a cautionary tale about what happens when a mortal challenges the gods."

With that, Samson leaned back and stilled himself, like a sphinx who'd delivered his final riddle. I got up and grabbed a fifth of bourbon and a rocks glass from the shelf full of liquor he kept in his office. After I'd topped his off and poured one for myself, I sat back down.

"It sounds to me like you speak from experience," I said. "Am I right?"

He clapped silently before grabbing his drink from the desk. "Give the kid a cookie. Sure, I've tangled with the sons of bitches before. Not these gods, mind you, but others. And I still have the scars to prove it."

"But you lived."

He snorted softly, scratching his nose with a knuckle. "Yeah, I did. But others didn't. What I lost in the process, well —there's no replacing it." The grizzled old wolf set his drink down, leaning in with his elbows on the desk. "I'll not have the price you pay be my daughter's life, McCool. You have to let her go."

I took a drink, hoping it might numb me to what I was about to say. "That's what I came here to tell you, Samson. I need you to keep her away from me, so she doesn't get mixed up in the mess I'm about to face."

"And how the fuck do I do that?" he asked archly. "She has a mind of her own, kid. You know that as well as me. Even if I did come up with a way to keep you two apart, the fucking gods would find her, regardless."

I nodded. "I know. So, I figure we have only three choices."

He rubbed his hands together slowly, as if to warm them against a chill only he felt. "I'm listening."

I raised a finger in the air. "Option one—I give myself up."

The old wolf chuckled. "If it came down to it, I'd choose Fallyn over you in a heartbeat. But, much as I hate to say it, the world needs you. Why? Because it needs druids. You'll be the last of your kind once Finnegas takes his final rest, so let's do our best to avoid that scenario. 'Sides, the old man would never allow it."

"I'm not too keen on that option either," I said sarcastically. "By the way, glad to know you care."

"Pfft. I care for you as much as any poor bastard who decides to date my daughter. Consider yourself lucky that I haven't killed you—yet. Now, what's your next option?"

"The second option is to send her somewhere far away from here, someplace where the Celtic gods can't find her or reach her."

"I know a place, but she'd never go. Not willingly, anyway."

"I agree. So that leaves option number three."

His eyes narrowed. "Which is?"

I cleared my throat involuntarily before mumbling incoherently.

"What?" the Alpha demanded. "Speak up, damn it."

"I said, 'I break her heart.'"

Samson gave me a predator's glare that sent a chill down my spine. I knew better than to startle an apex predator in a situation like this, so I froze, keeping my eyes on his chest. After a few tense moments he sniffed the air, once, then again. Suddenly, his shoulders relaxed and he slumped back in his chair.

"Shit, kid, you practically reek of heartache and regret. You really do care for her."

"I do. Which is why this has to be done the right way, for good. It has to be convincing, Samson. And you need to be there for her when all is said and done."

"She might try to kill you, you know." He said it matter-of-factly, without a hint of irony in his voice.

"I... thought of that. If she becomes violent, I have a contingency plan in place."

"There's nowhere you can hide from them." Samson took a slug of whiskey, gulping it down like he was taking a bitter pill. "They'll find you wherever you go, unless you cut a deal somehow."

"Is that how you did it?"

He nodded. "I did. It cost me a lot—more than I thought I'd be willing to give."

"What's worse, though?" I asked. "Losing what you love, or letting it go?"

He stared at the bottom of his glass, deep in thought. "That's what's fucked up, kid. Years later, I honestly still don't know."

8

Samson and I agreed to maintain our lines of communication while keeping Fallyn out of the know as much as possible. I didn't like the idea of hiding things from her, nor did I enjoy the prospect of breaking things off with her in the worst way possible. However, I liked the possibility of her being killed by a vengeful Celtic god a lot less.

It sucked, but it was what it was.

My first stop after leaving the clubhouse was checking in with Maureen and Finnegas. Maureen had texted me to let me know they were shoring up the wards on the junkyard, just to be safe. I knew they were both worried, so I figured it was best to keep them in the loop about everything—except what I planned to do about Fallyn and me.

I arrived back at the junkyard well after dark and found the two of them walking the fence line as they fiddled with my wards. Normally, I'd be pissed if someone messed with my spell work. But in Finn's case I'd make an exception, considering he was the one who'd taught me how to cast magical wards and traps in the first place. The old man could run circles around me when it came to warding up a place, so I merely stood by and watched while they did what they could to make the junkyard safer.

When they had finished, Finnegas sat down heavily on the tailgate of the yard truck. Meanwhile, Maureen pretended she didn't notice how much a small bit of spell work had worn the old druid out. And for my part, I acted like I didn't see the concerned looks Maureen gave Finnegas when he wasn't paying attention.

Well, this is awkward.

I grabbed a couple of beers from a nearby cooler, popping the caps and handing a bottle to each of them. "Looks like you two have been busy."

Finnegas wiped the bottle across his brow, in spite of the cool evening air. "Your wards were in good shape, and I know you maintain them like I taught you. I just made a couple of improvements that'll make it harder for the Dullahan to pierce the perimeter, next time around."

"That's if there *is* a next time fer that one," Maureen said, slurping on her beer before continuing. "Those bastards are likely on ta' the next step in their plan, now that they've seen ya' give their best boy a knuckle supper. Naw, ya' can expect an even worse foe ta' come at ya' next—someone stronger and more cunning."

I glanced at Finnegas, seeking confirmation for Maureen's assessment. His face was drawn and he looked paler than usual. It definitely had me worried.

"Stop looking at me like that," he snapped. "I'm not dead yet, and I won't be for a while. Couldn't leave anyway, even if I wanted to. Too much left to be done."

Maureen laid a hand on his arm, as if to stop him from saying too much. "What the Seer means ta' say issat he's too damned stubborn ta' lay down for those Tuatha bastards."

"I'm aware of that," I said, nodding. "But—and don't get mad at me for saying so—maybe you should leave the spell-casting to me from here on out, and save your strength for when we really need it."

I figured Finnegas would argue the point with me. Instead he grew pensive and quiet, merely nodding in response.

That's definitely not like him. Not at all.

Now it was Maureen's turn to pretend she didn't see the concern on my face. I stared intently at the half-fae woman until she returned the favor, then flicked my eyes back to Finnegas as if to say, "Are you seeing this?" She looked sad for a moment, then slapped her hands on her thighs, smiling for all the world like nothing was amiss.

"So, boyo—why don'tcha tell us what you've been up ta' lately?"

Her abrupt change in demeanor caught me off guard, but I saw what she was doing so I played along. "Well, um—yesterday I did a little counter-surveillance on Mendoza and his goons. And tonight, I dropped by the clubhouse to warn Samson about our unwanted visitor."

Finnegas smirked at me, perking up a bit. "He already knew, I bet. That old wolf is as wily as he is short. Did he threaten your life if something happens to Fallyn?"

"Does the pope wear funny hats?" I said. "We worked it out, but I promised to keep it between me and him."

"That's good, lad," Maureen said. "Ya' don't wanna' be pissin' that old trope off. He's a good one ta' have on yer side in a tight spot."

I gave them a quizzical look, raising my hands in the air. "So, what's next?"

"Maureen and I will try to determine which of the Celtic gods are behind the Dullahan's attack. And as for you"—the old man pointed a long, bony finger at me—"you need to shake some trees around town, and find out if anyone knows anything in the fae community. Word travels fast amongst the Fair Folk, and one of them is bound to have heard something."

I sighed. "Can I least get some sleep first?"

Finnegas crossed his arms and nodded. "Inside the Grove? Sure, but not before you practice the battle magic spells you've learned so far. Focus on the offensive magic we've been working on—you're going to need it."

Groaning inwardly, I downed my beer and tossed the empty into a nearby metal barrel that served as a waste receptacle. "If I'd have known druidry would be this much work, I'd have let that stupid vampire dwarf kill me."

WHENEVER I NEEDED info on what was going down with the fae, my first stop was usually Rocko's place. But since I'd screwed up the fae's connection to Underhill—cutting them off from much of their magic in the process—Rocko had asked me to stay away from his club. He said it was nothing personal, but my presence was bad for his business.

Still, the Red Caps and I were on friendly terms, mostly because they'd made a ton of profit since I'd closed the gateways to Underhill. Many members of fae society led dual lives, with one foot in our world and the other in their own. But not all fae could easily pass for human. Without access to Underhill's magic, those fae who magically concealed their identities had been at a loss in the events that followed my trip to their home world.

That's where the Red Caps came in, providing illusory charms and trinkets to those fae who lacked innate glamours of their own. Of course, they charged a hefty fee for renting those magical items to their brethren. Those who couldn't pay were turned away, and if you defaulted on your payments, well—you might find yourself sleeping with the fishes, so to speak.

Where they got the charms, I had no idea. But it was a good racket as far as Rocko was concerned. While the rest of the fae might hate me for what I did to them, the *fear dearg* felt almost indebted to me because of it. Almost.

I held no love for the Red Caps—bloodthirsty, thieving little bastards that they were—but I didn't want to screw up relations with them either. So, I hit the other fae hangouts around town. These mostly consisted of dive bars and juke joints where the *aes sídhe* could mingle unnoticed by mundanes, and also prey on the odd, unwitting human who might wander into their midst.

I dropped by a couple of places on the south and east sides of town, sleazy little rat holes that purposely looked like shit to keep the tourists at bay. But either no one knew anything, or no one was talking.

So, I decided to head out to Luckenbach.

Luckenbach, Texas was a little nine-acre plot of land that represented an unincorporated town in Gillespie County about fifty miles north of San Antonio, and seventy miles west of Austin. Made famous by the eponymous Waylon and Willie song, it was home to the Luckenbach Dance Hall, Luckenbach General Store—more of a souvenir shop, really—a food stand, and a few outdoor stages and seating areas.

The place was renowned as a country music venue, a pleasant if clichéd tourist trap right in the heart of the Texas Hill Country. Plenty of well-known music acts had played there, and the "town" often hosted festivals and concerts ranging from chili cook-offs to makeshift county fairs. For Texans and country music fans, no trip to the Hill Country would be complete without making a stop in Luckenbach.

But what most people didn't know was, if you travelled a short way down the road past the tourist trap, you'd come across an old, decrepit, whitewashed clapboard building. The tin roof was rusted but solid, although you wouldn't know it by looking at it. White paint had peeled away from the siding in various places, and the windows appeared to be original, circa mid-1800s. A long, weathered covered porch ran the length of building's front, complete with hand-hewn hitching posts made from juniper cedar logs that might have been older than the building itself.

It was the sort of structure that you'd pass and say, "Oh, look at that old, forlorn building. Someone should fix that up before it falls down completely." But once you drove by, the fact that it even existed would slip from your memory immediately.

That was because Rube's Icehouse was never meant for human eyes at all.

The joint's proximity to Luckenbach was part of the reason why the location had become such a well-known hangout. Old fae magic called to humans, although most were not aware of it, and they were drawn to Rube's. But since the Icehouse had a powerful obfuscation spell on it to keep mundanes from coming around, they ended up at the dance hall down the road instead.

Funny how those things work out.

Over the years, the place had become instead a hangout for various country fae, the type who didn't care for the city nor for mixing with city folk. Most were Germanic fae who'd settled in the area with immigrants traveling to Central Texas from the Rhineland in the 1840s. Many of those families had brought along with them household spirits like *heinzelmännchen* and kobolds, as well as nature fae who'd been worshipped as minor deities by those people.

Hidden within the immigrant groups who'd crossed the ocean to settle here were other supernatural races as well. They included *lutzelfrau*, the odd *doppelgänger*, *weisse frauen*, *schrate*, and more. To escape notice, those creatures posed as the people they'd come along with, following them to the New World to prey upon them or protect them as was their nature.

And here they remained. Some had adopted mortal identities, living among the local populace as farmers, ranchers, or merchants. Others remained in their capacity as guardian or helper spirits, watching over the same families they'd always served. But when they wanted to gather with their own kind, they almost always gathered at Rube's.

It was supposed to be a great place to get info if you were one of the in-crowd. Many of the fae who frequented the place were older than the city fae—thus, they were connected to their forebears in ways the modern fae had long forgotten. If anyone in Maeve's demesne were to know which Celtic god was behind the Dullahan's most recent attack, they'd likely be found at Rube's Icehouse.

There was only one problem with walking into that joint, and it was why hunters and other clued-in humans stayed far away from the place. Getting in wasn't a problem, so long as you knew it was there and had the juice to overcome a powerful look-away, go-away spell. No, it was getting back out again that was the real challenge.

That's because no mortal who'd entered the place had ever come out of there again.

IT HIT me as soon as I saw the place, a half-mile distant on that lonesome country road. Just the barest whispering in the back of my mind. Nothing overt, mind you—more like a stray spider's thread brushing my cheek.

Looks deserted, a nowhere nothing place. Old, abandoned, disused, neglected, beneath notice. Not worth a second glance.

Fully expecting the effects of the spell, I maintained a line of sight with the building as I drew nearer. That's when the magic really started kicking in. It began with a tickle near the base of my spine, like a chill waiting to happen on a cold winter day. Then it sank into my gut, a deep foreboding that told me something awful had happened in that building, and whatever did it might still be around.

With some effort, I kept my eyes locked on the place, but my hands kept turning the steering wheel the opposite direction. I was going to wreck if I didn't do something, so I reached into my Bag and grabbed Dyrnwyn. Immediately, the feelings subsided, at least enough for me to pull into the dusty gravel parking lot in front of the structure. As soon as I pulled my car near the building, the compulsion faded completely. Apparently if you made it this far, it was assumed you belonged.

There were cars parked there, as well as a few motorcycles, a tractor, two 70s-era bicycles, and a horse and buggy. I'd failed to notice any of them before pulling into the lot, although the spaces around the roadhouse were almost completely filled by the odd menagerie. I chose an empty spot around back between a newish, chromed-out Harley Davidson trike and a sleek black '48 Dodge Town Sedan that looked like it had just been driven off the lot.

I couldn't help but feel that eyes were on me as I de-assed from the Gremlin. When my gaze flicked to the windows, all I saw were shadows and dust within the walls of the place. This stood in stark contrast to the music that came from within— Blind Lemon Jefferson's "See That My Grave Is Kept Clean." I didn't know if it was a coincidence, a warning, or a joke. I decided it was probably a combination of the latter two options, so I pulled my Craneskin Bag close and made sure I had my weapons within easy reach.

When I walked around front, the porch was empty and void of anything that might mark the place as occupied, save an old, rickety wooden rocking chair with cracked and fading baby blue paint. I stepped onto the porch and reached for the door handle when a deep, gruff voice startled me into stillness.

"Son, you sure you're in the right place? Don't get many visitors 'round here, these days."

The accent was German, but only vaguely so, as it held more Texas twang than Old World inflection. I turned toward the speaker, who rocked slowly in the same chair that'd been empty just seconds before. The man was draped across the rocker bonelessly, as if he and the chair had agreed to commit a mutual, perfect act of repose.

He looked old, around seventy I'd say, with a craggy, bearded face dominated by a prominent, bulbous nose. His weathered features had seen many a summer in the sun, and many times that in miles. He wore faded jeans, Western work boots that were decades past being broken in, and a tan cowboy-style shirt with the sleeves rolled up to his elbows. His pale blue eyes regarded me, not unkindly, beneath a sweat-stained straw hat with a rattlesnake band, complete with the head frozen mid-strike in front and the rattle hanging loose in back. It looked like something Jerry Reed would've worn in a trucker movie from the 70s.

"Is this Rube's Icehouse?" I asked, knowing the answer.

The old cowboy turned his head, spitting tobacco juice in a straight line that struck a fly on the porch some ten feet away. "It might've been called that, once. Most folks don't recall such things. But then, you ain't most folks."

"Appears to be going around," I said, knowing that the old man was not what he seemed.

"Oh, I've not been most folks for quite some time," he said, reaching behind the chair to grab a worn, scratched acoustic guitar that I hadn't noticed earlier. "An' from what I understand, the fella who owns this place don't like it when folks use that name."

Suddenly, I realized who he was. "You're the Mountain King."

"Speakin' of things that ain't been called such in years." He strummed the guitar, working through a D-C-G chord progression that was typical of many country ballads. "You can call me John, if that's alright. Sit."

He motioned to his left, and a weathered, straight-backed kitchen chair appeared. Its woven rush seat was so frayed, I feared it wouldn't take my weight. I sat down anyway, waiting patiently until the old gnome spoke again.

"There's a price for entry," he said. "Always is, for mortals. Everybody agrees to the price, but none are ever willin' to pay it in the end. S'why none of them ever leave."

"What's the price?" I asked, truly curious.

He strummed a few more chords, this time playing a blues riff reminiscent of B.B. King. "Can't say beforehand. Spoils the surprise. Part of the deal is that you can't know before you go inside. Rules are rules, after all."

"Huh. So, what if I'm not really mortal?"

"You're a 'thrope, then?" he asked, more a statement than a question.

"Of a sort, yes," I replied.

He glanced at me sideways from beneath the brim of his hat. "Then, we fight for right of entry. But you ain't gonna' like how that turns out. Best you pay the other price."

In no rush to fight an ancient being like *Herr Rübezahl*, I considered my options. A battle with a creature of his type could very well be to the death, and I had neither the desire to die nor any wish to kill him. But I also knew that making a blind deal with the fae was equivalent to signing your own death warrant. Undoubtedly, the price would be disproportionate to the favor received, and likely something so horrible as to make death preferable to rendering payment.

On the other hand, my goal wasn't to gain entry to the road-house—it was to acquire information about my enemies. It occurred to me that the person I was speaking with was as likely to have useful intel as any fae I might meet inside. So, why not make a deal with him for information instead of passage?

"I'd rather not fight you, and there's no way I'd enter into an open-ended pact with any member of the fae races."

He plucked a few strings on his guitar, tuning it until each string hit just the right pitch. "Wise. But that means you came here for nothing."

I nodded sagely. "Hmm... perhaps." For show, I rubbed my chin and sighed like a man perplexed. "So the trip isn't a complete loss, what say you and I engage in a contest?"

The Mountain King perked up at that. "A contest, eh? Of what kind?"

I continued to rub my chin. "Well, it's obvious I can't match your musical talent. And, with the wisdom and knowledge you've gained over the centuries, it's doubtful I could beat you in a game of wits."

"True, true," he agreed.

I snapped my fingers, feigning enthusiasm. "I've got it! How about a test of strength?"

A smile flickered at the corners of the gnome's lips, so quick it almost wasn't there. "A contest of brawn, you say? With such a strapping young man? Hardly seems fair."

"Tell you what—we can arm wrestle so no one gets hurt. And I'll even use my weak hand."

He frowned, but from the gleam in his eye I knew he was

hooked. "You don't say? And what'll be the prize for the winner?"

"If I win, you'll answer five of my questions."

Rübezahl squinted at me. "Three. And if you lose?"

"I'll let you pick a single item to take from my Bag."

After eyeing my Craneskin Bag for a few moments, a grin split the old gnome's face.

"Deal!" he exclaimed.

Rübezahl leaned in over his guitar, extending an open hand to me. I took it and we shook hands, sealing the pact. Now, all I had to do was beat the guy at arm wrestling.

It was a gamble for sure, because based on the legends I'd read, *Herr Rübezahl* had the magical ability to grow many times his size. But I was also banking on the fact that he'd underestimate my strength, and would fail to grow to his full height. Plus, I had another trick up my sleeve.

"Where are we doing this?" I asked.

The gnome pointed to a tree stump, near a field on the far side of the parking lot. The Mountain King sauntered across the lot and I followed, watching him in the magical spectrum. By all appearances he was still a normal-sized person, and that's what anyone with mundane eyesight would've seen.

But I wasn't any mundane human.

As we walked, my druid senses pierced through his glamour and I saw the real Mountain King instead of the grizzled old cowboy I'd spoken with earlier. He looked much the same really, right down to his clothes, but the earth trembled beneath his feet as he walked, and he grew in size and stature with every single step.

By the time we reached the stump, *Rübezahl* had grown to about eight-and-a-half feet tall. Not large enough to reveal that he'd grown once we grasped hands, but enough to give him a distinct size, weight, and strength advantage at arm-wrestling.

Of course, I'd been busy with a transformation of my own during the short walk, but I doubted my stealth-shifted strength would be enough to seal the deal.

We paused in front of the tree, and I pulled two objects from my Bag. Knowing that *Rübezahl* was already keen to the nature of my very unique sartorial accessory, I waited to see how he'd react.

"Ho now, what's this?" said the gnome. "No one said anything about allowing magical items."

I held up one of the objects I'd pulled from the Bag. It was a leather gauntlet, the kind we'd used for sparring with wasters back when I'd first started training under Finnegas. While it had no inherent magic of its own, it was an instrumental part of my plan to defeat the gnome.

"Nothing magical about it—see for yourself." I tossed him the glove while palming the other object to conceal it. *Rübezahl* caught it, examining it suspiciously. "It's harmless and completely devoid of magic. But my hands sweat, you see. The glove is just to help my grip."

The gnome's brow furrowed deeply, and his bulbous nose twitched furiously. "I suppose it's alright. Now, let's get this show on the road."

Rübezahl leaned over the stump, placing his left elbow on the flat, roughly-hewn surface that would be our field of battle. I slipped the glove on my left hand, surreptitiously sliding the other object inside the glove so the gnome couldn't see it. Once hidden, it took only a minor exertion of my will to make the small disk of oak split into five rings that slid into place over my fingers and thumb.

Sidling up to the stump, I locked grips with the gnome and dropped my elbow to the stump's surface. I felt *Rübezahl's* huge mitt envelope mine, despite the fact that his hand looked much smaller. A wicked smile split his face as he tightened his grip.

"Ready?" he asked with a twinkle in his eye.

"On three," I said.

"One..." *Rübezahl* replied.

"Two..." I countered.

"Three!" we shouted in unison.

Instantly, I willed the oak rings on my hand to seek the rough wooden surface of the stump opposite my grip. The Mountain King, while powerful in his giant-sized form, stood no chance. When it came to trees and plant-life, and making things of nature do my bidding, I was king—or, at least, Master of the Grove.

And in this case, that was enough.

9

With the help of the druidic skills I'd gained since bonding with the Oak and Grove, I slammed *Rübezahl's* hand down on the stump before he realized he might lose. I exerted my will for a few seconds more, holding his hand in place while he struggled to free himself from my grip. The ground shook around us, visibly this time, as the gnome's expression darkened.

"You cheated!" he shouted, his voice echoing off the rolling hills in the distance.

I released his hand and backed up, giving myself enough space to react in case he resorted to violence.

"I merely followed your lead," I said, looking him in the eyes. His real eyes, that is, which were about three feet over his illusory head.

He slammed his massive fist down on the tree trunk, splintering the surface and sending shards of woods and bark everywhere. None touched me, of course. I made certain of that.

The gnome glowered at me. "A druid. I should have known."

"You should have asked," I replied.

"Did you lie about being a 'thrope?"

"Nope. I am a shifter, of sorts. The only one of my kind, but a shifter nonetheless. The Alpha of the Austin Pack will vouch for that."

A look of realization dawned across his face. "It appears I've been well and properly fooled, although I should've seen what was right in front of my face. Ah—what's done is done. You've three questions, so don't waste 'em."

"If it's alright with you, I'll save two of them for later."

His expression soured slightly. "I suppose. Wasn't in the agreement as to when you could ask them. Go on, then, ask your first question."

"Which Celtic god wants me dead?"

Rübezahl's eyes got a faraway look as he stared at me, then through me. I could've sworn I saw something *other* in his gaze, as if a gateway to another world had opened inside his head. But then it was gone, and I was left wondering whether I had witnessed something mystical and unknown through the gnome's eyes, or only imagined that I did.

"Hmm... Plenty of 'em, druid. The Crow, the Fisherman, the Warrior, the Lover, the Mare—should I go on?"

I opened my mouth to ask why so many gods wanted me dead, but caught myself before I spoke. No sense wasting a question on something I already knew. Instead, I needed to focus on getting a solution instead of another riddle.

"I need to know which one commanded the Dullahan to attack me recently."

"That's not a question," *Rübezahl* responded. "And I don't know, anyways. I'm not all-knowing, damn it."

I considered my next question carefully. I only had two left, and I wanted to leave one in reserve. It wasn't often that I had the opportunity to have one of the fae beholden to me, and that was something I wanted to relish. Besides, I might need that third question to get me out of a tight spot one day. The Mountain King was a powerful being, after all.

"Who should I speak with to find out which Celtic god commanded the Dullahan to attack me yesterday?"

The gnome who was also a giant chuckled and tugged on his beard. "Now you've put your thinking cap on. Good for you! The fella' you want to chat with is Brother Carroll, who lives at the hermitage in Christoval."

"Christoval, Brother Carroll. That's weird, but okay."

The gnome smiled at me like the cat who ate the canary. If my previous dealings with the fae were any indication, he was probably dicking me over somehow. Unfortunately, I had little choice but to follow up on the lead he'd provided. Although I didn't know how I was being jacked with, I narrowed my eyes at the Mountain King, just to let him know I was on to him.

He spat tobacco juice at a grasshopper, pinning it to the ground. "Unless you intend to ask that last question... will there be anything else?"

"Meh, I'll save it. Could come in handy down the road."

Rübezahl remained blank-faced. He stared at me for a while, waiting for me to screw up and say "thanks" or ask some innocuous question. Finally, he sighed and slowly vanished from sight.

I leaned against the stump and pulled out my phone. There was surprisingly good cell reception here, which actually wasn't surprising at all considering how many German fae frequented the roadhouse. It was a sure bet that one of them had futzed with the local cell tower, or somehow influenced humans to place a tower or repeater nearby.

I tapped a name on my speed dial list, and moments later, I had Maureen on the line. "Yes, lad, what d'ya need?"

"Maureen, do you know anything about a Brother Carroll who's a hermit or something at a monastery in Christoval?"

The phone was silent for a time, then Maureen finally answered. "Aye, the man is known ta' me."

"Oooh-kay. Well, I just had a chat with *Rübezahl*, and he says that this Brother Carroll guy knows who sent the Dullahan." Silence again. "Hello, Earth to Maureen. Are you there?"

Her voice was serious as she replied. "Yes, ya' idjit, I'm still here. Fecking hell, can't a lass think 'afore she opens her pie hole?"

"It's just that—"

"Just that what?" Maureen asked with a dangerous edge to her voice.

"Oh, nothing—it's not important. You were saying?"

"I was about ta' say, ya' need ta' be very careful around that one. He's not what he seems, and ya' can't go trusting them folk anyway."

"Which folk, Maureen?"

"Those Christians, who else? Ever since St. Patrick, they've been mucking up things fer the Irish. The land was better off before he arrived."

"Um, Maureen—"

"I know you go ta' that Eastern church, but it's not the same. Meanin', yer' not the same. You don't jest do whatever some priest tells ya' ta' do."

"I'm hanging up now, Maureen," I said with just a touch of sarcasm in my voice. "Warning heard and heeded. I'll definitely be on my guard around those evil monks."

"Smart ass," she replied. "Jes' be certain ta' watch yer back when ya' visit him. Them monks cannot be trusted!"

She ended the call abruptly, leaving me curious regarding what was so special about a Catholic monk that the very mention of his name gave Maureen pause.

EXCEPT FOR THE large SUVs with blacked-out windows tailing

me in the distance, the drive out to the hermitage was long and boring. Every so often the vehicles would change, but it was obvious I was being followed. Apparently, Mendoza wasn't going to take no for an answer. I didn't like being tailed, but at least it was better than being attacked and abducted.

Besides, I had enough to worry about without being at odds with Cerberus. Hell, I was already working for the Fae, the Pack, and the Coven, so why the hell couldn't the druid justiciar also do gigs for the Hoomans? Of course, the Druid faction was supposed to be representative of all humans, but since there were only two of us, I hardly felt like we were a fair representation of our species.

Celtic gods hunting me, Samson on my ass, and Mendoza tracking me to boot. Nothing like having a full plate.

Of all the aforementioned problems, Mendoza's interest in me was farthest down my list of priorities. Sure, he was becoming a pain in my ass, but clueless as their outfit was, I figured I could handle them. It was a problem I'd have to deal with another time, because right now I had an angry Celtic god —or gods—to deal with.

Back on task, McCool... getting close to the monastery.

The hermitage was south of San Angelo, which was halfway between Fort Worth and El Paso, way out in the middle of nowhere. I'd heard it was a nice city, but I'd never been there because of its remote location. Texas is a big state, and hell if I was going to road trip to some desolate cowtown just to see the sights. It made sense that a bunch of hermits would build their monastery out there, as the area was so damned remote nobody would go there without reason.

I turned off US-277, a four-lane death trap that barely qualified as a highway, onto a two-lane country road that split the flat, dry, sparsely wooded terrain like a part down a balding man's scalp. A mile or so later, I turned south on a barely-paved road that had so many potholes I thought I was driving in downtown Austin. A half-mile and a few lazy turns later, and I pulled up in front of a large, walled compound.

The place was bigger than I'd expected, easily ten acres if I had to guess, and larger than the junkyard almost by half. It was enclosed by a brick and stucco wall that was maybe eight feet tall—high enough for privacy, but not so tall as to be a serious deterrent to entry. The road I'd driven in on continued east through a large wooden gate into the compound, presumably so the monks could enter and leave without having to deal with pesky sightseers and looky-loos... like me.

That gate was closed, so I wisely parked the Gremlin in the gravel parking lot, activating my anti-theft wards before I headed to the visitor's center. The wards were probably unnecessary, considering the remote location. But after the reaction I'd gotten from Maureen on mentioning this Brother Carroll, I wasn't taking any chances.

I opened the large, heavy, weathered double-doors, which elicited a loud creak from their hinges. As my eyes adjusted to the gloom, I found myself in a sort of foyer with a few chairs, a handmade wooden reception counter, and various crosses and other iconography on the walls. Besides me and the spider living in an upper corner of the room, there was not a soul in sight.

There were two wooden doors with ancient, Victorian-looking door hardware leading out of the foyer, but both were locked. Temporarily stymied, I stood there for a few minutes listening for any signs that someone might be in the rooms beyond. I heard the faint tinkle of wind chimes in the distance, but other than that, the place was completely silent.

Another minute or so later found me weighing the pros and cons of climbing the walls and asking around for Brother Carroll. I'd almost convinced myself there'd be no harm in it, and that they wouldn't call the Tom Green County Sheriff's Department on me if I did, when one of the doors opened.

A frumpy, thin, middle-aged woman in an aqua long-sleeved blouse and ivory polyester pants shuffled into the room. The white rubber soles of her black canvas sport flats skritched and squeaked as she spun to bump the door shut with a bony hip. With her short, permed gray hair, she reminded me of the older ladies at my mom's evangelical church. The woman carried an office file box in her hands, and she had a large flower-print handbag slung over one shoulder, with the dark green neck of a corked and sealed wine bottle just peeking out the top.

Out of habit I stood still and silent, so she didn't even notice me when she entered the room. As she balanced the file box on a raised knee with her keys jangling in her hand, I cleared my throat, perhaps a bit more loudly than I'd intended. The woman jumped, a high-pitched yelp escaping her lips as she dropped keys and box both.

"Sorry, I didn't mean to startle you," I apologized.

She turned around, fixing me first with wide, startled eyes, and then flashing a smile that was all chagrin. She laid a hand across her flat chest. "Oh my, but my old heart can't handle scares like that no more. We don't get many visitors around here, at least not during the week. You here to see the meditative garden, or looking for the winery?"

"Um, neither, actually. I'm sort of looking for someone."

She tilted her head quizzically as she placed her wrists on her hips. "Well, no one's been here, not today. You're our first visitor of the day, and like I said, we don't get many except when the brothers are holding mass on Sunday mornings. Ain't many Catholics around these parts either, so even then it's pretty lonely in the chapel."

"Oh, I'm not looking for a friend—I'm here to see one of the monks."

The woman's brow furrowed with incredulity, then she gave me a limp-wristed wave. "Well, bless your heart. I don't know if anyone's told you, but the monks have all taken a vow of silence. They don't talk to no one, not even me, and I've been doing secretary work for 'em going on ten years now."

Rübezahl, you fucking dick.

THE LADY TOLD me her name was Dobbie, not Dottie, and it took everything I had to resist making a house-elf joke. Truth be told, the lady kind of looked like her namesake—I didn't want to be unduly cruel by alluding to the resemblance, even in a tangential manner. Dear Dobbie also informed me that the monks mostly remained cloistered in the confines of the monastery, and that they only communicated with her via handwritten notes, and only one day of the week.

Personally, I wondered how they got a fucking thing done without using verbal communication, then I remembered that millions of deaf people get along just fine without it. Still, it annoyed me to no end that someone who could speak would refuse to do so, simply because they wanted to be more spiritual or some-such.

After being gently but firmly guided out of the visitor's center—which was anything but, since apparently these monks didn't interact with the outside world at all, except for holding mass—I sat in my car, deciding what to do. Then, I drove into Christoval to get a bite to eat, noting the large SUV that tailed me about a quarter-mile back.

Amateurs. Keep your distance, and we'll get along just fine.

I ignored my tail and kept looking for a place to grab some grub and think. After driving around for half an hour, I finally realized the town didn't even have a Dairy Queen. I settled on a local BBQ joint instead, considering my options over a plate of pork ribs, potato salad, pinto beans, and a sweet tea.

Fuck it. I'm climbing that wall.

The sun was already going down by the time I left the restaurant. Strangely, as soon as I turned down the two-lane road that led to the monastery, my tail disappeared.

Weird.

By the time I pulled off the road, maybe a block or so from the monastery, it was after dark. I grabbed my Bag—I never left home without it, 'cause it was hella useful, and the damned thing followed me everywhere anyway—and softly closed the car door until it clicked shut. Then, I took off at a jog for the back wall of the hermitage.

Once I'd reached the outer perimeter, I squatted in the gravel and dirt at the base of the wall, listening for signs of activity. From the way it sounded, these monks went to bed super-early, because it was so quiet you could have heard a mouse fart. I watched a fat brown scorpion scuttle over the toe of my boot, then waited another minute or so, hoping a better idea would come to me.

Nope. May as well get this over with.

I felt terrible about the fact that I was breaking into a monastery, and that I quite possibly was about to shake down a monk. But I had good reason, and frankly if this guy knew anything about the Tuatha Dé Danaan, I was certain he'd understand. Standing up, I shook and lightly stamped my feet, just in case another scorpion had decided to hitch a ride. Then, I leapt up and grabbed the lip of the wall.

As soon as my fingers hit the rough stucco surface, I knew I'd fucked up. The hairs on the back of my neck stood on end, and I sensed a tiny pop of magic that indicated I'd just tripped an alarm ward. A slight smell of ozone filled the air, signaling that another, larger spell was brewing as well.

Fuck! Why didn't I examine the wall for wards?

Because Catholic monks aren't supposed to be using magic, that's why. The phrase "suffer a witch to live" came to mind, and I wondered what kind of hypocritical, self-righteous pricks protected their monastery with magic while masquerading as pious religious hermits. Since I'd already made my presence known, I decided to vault the wall, additional spells and magic-using monks be damned.

With a quick kick and a pullup, I landed on the balls of my feet on the other side of the wall. No sooner had I landed than I had the answer to my second question, because a group of five sandaled, clean-shaven, tonsured men wearing rough gray garb stood before me. Their robes were belted at the waist, not with rope but with thick, wide leather belts, and upon those belts hung a variety of medieval weapons. One of them bore a morning star, the next a mace, another a flail, the fourth a short sword, and the last had a shillelagh tucked in his belt.

Certainly, none of them looked like what I thought a bunch of wine-making, silence-vow-taking, cut-off-from-the-world monks should look like. While one of them had a slight paunch, it was apparent they stayed in shape. Each of the monks had thickly muscled calves and forearms, and their hands were strong and calloused. A not-so-silly, wild-ass guess told me those callouses were definitely not from garden work.

Weird. If these guys start smacking themselves in the forehead with scrap wood, I'm gonna lose my shit.

"Say, does anyone know the way to the confessional?" I said, flashing a smart-assed grin. They failed to respond, staring at me like I'd just pissed in the baptismal font.

Well, that went over like a lead balloon.

"Nothing? Seriously?" I stood up, nice and easy, raising my hands in the universal sign of friendliness. "Look, I'm not here to cause trouble or anything. I just need to speak with Brother Carroll."

The moment I mentioned his name, a frown crossed shille-lagh guy's face. He looked at the others, and all four returned his look and nodded. Then, the monks drew their weapons and attacked.

10

"Oh, come on... seriously?" I complained as I dove to my right, avoiding a rather vicious swing of a morning star that had been aimed at my head. I rolled smoothly to my feet, purposely angling away from the rest of the monks so I wasn't fighting more than one at a time. "Honestly, I don't want to fight, I just want to talk—"

An arrow zipped past my head, close enough to draw a thin line of blood from my cheek. I backpedaled, moving down the wall toward a largish stone building that I hoped would provide some cover. A monk I hadn't seen did a backflip off a nearby roof, slinging three wicked-looking throwing knives at me in midair. One of them buried itself point-first in the steel toe of my Doc Martens.

"Man, these Overlords are brand new. Now you're just pissing me off!"

I ducked behind a low stone wall, taking a moment to pull the knife out of my boot. More arrows and throwing knives zipped past overhead, clattering against the building behind me. A quick glance over my shoulder told me I hadn't yet been flanked, but it was only a matter of time.

A church bell rang from somewhere close by, obviously an alarm of some sort, and likely tied to the ward I'd triggered earlier. The spell had probably sent a silent signal first, followed by an audible warning at a predetermined interval. That was smart, as it would give the monks time to surprise an unwanted visitor with a security or strike team before the interloper knew they'd been noticed.

Silent or no, these monks were not fucking around. Moreover, they obviously expected intruders, and possibly on a routine basis. I had no idea what these monks were about, but it was becoming clear why their order was way the hell out in the middle of nowhere.

Across the central monastery yard, I saw robed figures with bows standing on cottage rooftops, silhouetted against the night sky. More monks emerged from various buildings around the hermitage, all similarly armed. Counting the five monks who'd initially confronted me, there had to be at least a couple dozen of the fuckers in play.

Briefly, I considered making my escape—the wall was right there, after all. But I hadn't come this far to get zero answers, and the magic-using ninja monks had definitely garnered my interest. I didn't want to freak them out, and I certainly didn't want to hurt them, because I was the intruder and they were just defending their home for all I knew. Still, I couldn't fight two dozen warrior monks in my human form.

Stealth-shift it is, then.

No sooner had I triggered my change than the ground beneath my feet began to glow with a faint golden light. Soon, distinct lines appeared in the soil and rocks underfoot, the light increasing in intensity as it coalesced into runes and other arcane symbols. Here and there, ancient Latin punctuated the runes and symbols—excerpts from an exorcism rite if my guess was correct. Somehow, using my shifter magic had triggered the monastery's latent magic defenses.

Ah, fuck!

Aiming for a nearby rooftop, I leapt off the ground just as the dirt and rocks exploded beneath me. The blast carried me farther than I'd intended, peppering my feet and legs with tiny bits of rocky shrapnel in the process. I landed on the other side of the building in an awkward three-point stance. As soon as my hand made contact with the earth, the ground began to glow with that same golden light.

This time, I'd anticipated the reaction. I leapt to my right, kicking off a cottage to land on a low stone wall that separated the garden from a dirt path that meandered through the yard. The glow that had appeared where I'd landed moments before faded away, although I could still feel the energy there, waiting to be triggered.

"Magic landmines? Are you flipping kidding me? Guys, I'm on your side!"

A baby-faced monk answered me from a nearby roof, not twitching a muscle as he held a longbow nocked with a cloth-yard shaft at full draw. "Liar! Thou art a beast, a therianthrope infected by the spirit of some foul demon from beyond the Veil."

Pfft. So much for your vow of silence.

"Be still, Brother Edmund!" a deep, mature voice commanded from across the yard.

"But he's an abomination," Edmund cried. "Our order was created to rid the world of his kind."

In the time that short exchange had taken, all two dozen monks had surrounded me, weapons in hand and bows at full draw, all focused and aimed on yours truly. My stealth transformation was now complete, and with near-vampire speed and strength, I was easily a match for a half-dozen of these chumps.

But four times that, and dodging their magical traps no less? It was time to de-escalate the situation.

"Abomination? I'm telling you, we're on the same side." I said as I stood to my full height on the wall, hands raised in the air. "You monks are hunters, right? Warrior monks who kill, what— demons? Malevolent witches? Rogue fae?"

"And worse than that!" Brother Edmund replied. "So, we're not afraid of the likes of you."

"I said silence—and do not attack," the older monk ordered.

He strolled across the yard, pushing his way through his brethren as they surrounded me. As he drew closer, I noticed he was one of the original five who had confronted me when I'd jumped over the wall. The monk eyed me curiously, like I was a difficult math problem he had to solve.

Shillelagh guy. So, you're their leader?

"The likes of me? Damn it, I hate those things just as much as you do," I said. "I mean, it wasn't long ago that I saved a woman from being eaten by a demon."

"He lies!" Edmund shouted. I had my eyes on their leader, but I heard the thrum of the bowstring as the monk released his arrow. I turned instinctively, pain erupting in my shoulder where the broadhead sank deep into my flesh.

Lucky that I had turned—that arrow had been aimed for my heart.

Somewhere deep inside me, a flicker of anger burst into a roaring flame. My Hyde-side had seen enough. I turned my head slowly, eyes locking on the young monk as I growled in a deep, inhuman voice.

"You'll pay for that insult, monk."

SOMETHING in my voice or gaze must've triggered an alarm in the young monk's lizard brain, that most primitive part of the mind where 100,000 years of survival instincts reside. He took an involuntary step back, eyes wide and mouth agape in horror, all while fumbling to nock another arrow. Meanwhile, the other monks readied themselves for battle, moving their weapons into offensive positions in some cases, or shifting their stances in preparation for a coordinated attack.

The older monk raised his hands overhead, holding the shillelagh like Moses raising his staff to part the Red Sea. He kinda looked like Moses—or, at least, how those old paintings depicted the man, with long grey hair and a beard to match, sun-weathered skin, a laborer's lean, muscled physique, and piercing blue eyes set deep beneath a furrowed brow. Not like Moses was a white dude, no matter how deep the tan, but whatever. This guy could've been Charlton Heston's twin, and that was a fact.

"Stop, every one of you," he said in a calm, low voice, lowering his hands slowly. "I know what he is, and while he is cursed, this man is not our enemy."

"But Brother Carroll," Edmund complained. "He has a demon in him. You heard his voice, and saw how he moves—not to mention that the ground in this holy place rejected him. He must be destroyed."

Zealots. Should've seen that coming from a mile away.

"Holy ground my ass—that's spell work or I don't wipe my ass in a north-south direction," I muttered.

Brother Carroll drew his mouth into a hard line as he closed his eyes and sighed. I took the hint. There was a lot more going on here than just a bunch of religious fanatics who hated supernaturals. And if I wanted to know what it was, and get answers about which of the Celtic gods wanted to mount my head on their wall, I figured I'd better play along.

Carroll opened his eyes again, addressing the trigger-happy

monk and his brethren at the same time. "Brother Edmund, might I remind you that in the past we have made alliances with those afflicted by magic, if only to further our cause? And, when we are able, do we not seek to free the willing and repentant from the bonds of evil curses and spells? Is that not also part of our mission?"

"Well yes, but—"

Brother Carroll raised a hand with his fingers and thumb pinched together, like a kindergarten teacher telling a child to shut their trap. "Enough. Brother Edmund, you will say one-hundred Our Father's and two-hundred Hail Mary's, then you will clean the latrines as penance for your insubordination."

One of the other monks snickered softly in the background. It looked like Brother Edmund wasn't well-liked around here. Brother Carroll's hawk eyes darted to the offending party.

"And, Brother Phineas, you shall join him." His eyes swept across the rest of the monks. "The rest of you, clean and care for your weapons, say your evening prayers, and get a good night's rest. There may be much to do in the morn."

Brother Carroll ignored the odd grumbling as the warrior monks dispersed. I couldn't tell if they were mad because they had to clean their weapons, or disappointed because they'd wanted to have a good scrape. Either way, it reminded me of the soldiers in my dad's unit—how they'd interacted when he'd take me to work, back when he was still alive.

"If I climb off this wall, is the ground going to zap me or blow me to kingdom come again?" I asked.

Brother Carroll gave me a rueful smile. "Interesting choice of words. Are you a believer?"

I shrugged noncommittally. "I sometimes attend the Eastern Orthodox church downtown, but it's more for the company than the religion."

He nodded. "Fellowship is a form of worship, and seeking is the act of a contrite heart."

"If you say so. Can I step off this wall now?"

"Yes, I've inactivated the wards," he said softly, glancing around to make sure none of the other monks were within earshot before he spoke. "As you might imagine, not everyone here knows the difference between power that comes from faith, and that which comes by other means."

"Do tell," I deadpanned, checking to make sure he'd done as he said.

My suspicions were warranted, and not just because of being attacked. He hadn't so much as snapped his fingers or uttered a single syllable of magic. Yet to my surprise, the wards had been inactivated, just as he'd said.

He chuckled. "The Lord works in mysterious ways, and He uses even the wicked to do His work."

"The wicked—does that include you as well?"

Brother Carroll's eyes dropped to the ground, and his voice grew somber. "Yes, without a doubt. Still, I'm doing my best to make amends." He shook his head, then flashed me a warm smile. "But enough talk of such matters. It's not often we get visitors inside the compound, and I'm sure you didn't come here to talk theology."

I held a hand out, wavering it back and forth. "Actually, I did —of a sort."

Blank-faced, he replied in hushed tones. "We should speak privately, then. Let's retire to my cottage, and I'll pour you a spot of wine while we discuss what troubles you."

MINUTES LATER, I sat inside one of the cottages that was farthest from the front gate and entrance. All the living quarters were identical on the outside, and nothing marked this one as being any different from the rest. Inside, it was nearly barren except for a small table, two chairs, a side table, and a small bed that almost qualified to be called a cot.

After pouring us both some red wine in a couple of wooden tumblers, Brother Carroll sat across from me and spread his hands apart. "The wine is one of the few creature comforts we allow ourselves. We purchase the grapes from vineyards across the country, and make our wine here in the hermitage. Most of it we sell to support our order, although we keep a few bottles from each vintage for ourselves."

I took a sip after casting a cantrip to ensure it wasn't poisoned. It was surprisingly good, light and fruity, a tad sweet but not cloyingly so, with just the slightest bit of spice at the end. If I'd liked drinking wine, it would probably be tops on my list.

"I'm not a wine drinker, but this is actually quite tasty."

He nodded to acknowledge the compliment. "I'm pleased to hear that. The brothers spend a great deal of time and care to ensure we produce the best wine possible."

"When you're not hunting supernatural creatures, you mean."

He frowned slightly. "Indeed. But from what I've heard, you've done a fair amount of hunting yourself."

I chuckled and inclined my head. "Colin McCool, pleased to meet you."

"Yes, the Junkyard Druid. I've known about you for some time, although I didn't think our paths would cross way out here."

"I'd have never known you existed, if someone hadn't told me to come here. Please, tell me about your order."

"Certainly. We tend to stick to the really nasty stuff no one else wants to handle. Possession, demonic hauntings, skin-walkers who get out of line, rogue vampires who hunt desolate places where no coven master cares to exert their will, that sort of thing. And there's more of it out here in the far reaches of the state than you might imagine."

I crinkled my nose in disgust. "Gah, skinwalkers. I had to deal with a couple recently. Let me tell you, it was not a fun time."

"The older ones can be... difficult, that is certain." He looked down into the depths of his cup, not meeting my eyes as he continued. "I understand you also dealt with the Fear Doirich on the same occasion."

"Nobody's supposed to know about that, except the people who were there."

He gave me a sympathetic look. "Yes, and one of them is no longer with us. I am very sorry for your loss."

I set my cup down on the table, hands gripping my knees as I tried to read his expression. He looked neither pleased with himself for surprising me with that bit of info, nor did he seem to regret putting me on guard.

"How do you know so much about me? And about the World Beneath?"

The old monk smiled, and that smile held both remorse and the weight of many years of pain and suffering. I'd seen the same look once, on my mentor's face when I'd asked him if he regretted living such a long life. His expression spoke volumes, and even without being aware of his knowledge of warding magic, I'd have suspected that Brother Carroll was much more than he appeared.

"I have been around a very long time. I followed Partholon to Éire, helping him defeat your kind, and I alone survived the plague curse they cast on us in retribution. I watched Fergus the Nemedian slay king Conand of the Fomori, and then saw the children of Nemed likewise fall to a curse of illness, with all but thirty drowning in a tidal wave raised by Conand's successor,

Morc, son of Dela. I witnessed the descendants of the thirty who remained as they returned to the Fair Isle, first as the Fir Bolg, and then as the Tuatha Dé Danann."

"Whoa—you mean to tell me you're *the* Tuan mac Cairill?" He nodded. "No offense, but I thought you were a myth."

"Hardly, although sometimes I wish it were so."

I took a few seconds to decide if he was telling the truth, because this was a hard pill to swallow. But there had to have been a reason Rübezahl had sent me to him. And who else would know which of the Celtic gods wanted me dead?

Brother Carroll sipped his wine, wiping his mouth with the rough sleeve of his tunic. "Take your time. I know it's a lot to digest."

I snapped my fingers and pointed at him. "If you're Tuan, that means you've been around longer than the Tuatha Dé Danann."

"As I said, I am older than the Tuath Dé, although none of us are older than the Fomori." Brother Carroll gave me a pointed look, like a college professor waiting for a student to work out the answer to a complex problem. A moment later, he gave a *hmph* and continued. "Had I pursued dark magics—and given service to forces far more evil than my kin—I too could have become one of the *little* gods. But instead, I chose service... and repentance."

"Repentance? For what?"

"You must understand, Colin—my people were descendants of those who survived the great flood. But instead of serving Y'weh, we intermarried with other races and chose other gods to serve. I believe that was why I was cursed with longevity, being reincarnated time and again to bear witness to the folly of my people and our descendants."

Like most clergy, the monk clearly believed the fae to be *nephilim*—the offspring of men and fallen angels. Or demons, depending on who you asked. Personally, I thought the gods might very well be worse than demons... but I wasn't buying the rest of it.

"C'mon, Brother Carroll. That's just stuff the church made up to scare people away from worshipping the Tuath Dé."

"Is it?" he asked as he arched an eyebrow. "Who do you think taught them the history of Éire, the land they sought to claim in the name of the Church?"

"I dunno. I mean, I've met some of the Celtic gods, and they're infinitely more powerful than any priest or pastor I've ever met."

"As you would be too, if you chose to cheat death, pursue dark magics, and dedicate your very long life to accumulating supernatural powers."

I rubbed one side of my face with one hand, because Brother Carroll was giving me a headache. "Whatever. Honestly, I couldn't care less where they came from, or how they came to be."

He gave me a look of long-suffering patience. "Believe what you wish."

"Yup, always have." I didn't have time to argue the origins of the Celtic pantheon. Honestly, who gave a fuck? If a tank was about to run you over, you didn't ask where it came from—you just got the hell out of the way. "Anyway, all I know is that at least one of the twisted fu—"

"Watch it—even the cottages here stand on holy ground."

"Sorry... um, twisted freaks?" I proffered.

"Thank you. They are that, and more."

"Right. So apparently one of the twisted *freaks*, and maybe more than one, wants my head on a platter."

He stroked his beard, considering my words. "And you know this how?"

"Before I closed the gateways, Finnegas did some sneaking

around in Underhill. The old man found evidence that some high-level fae were plotting against me. But he never did find out which of the Tuath Dé were involved." I paused, licking my lips. "I'd hoped they'd forgotten about me. But just the other day, they sent the Dullahan to my home."

Brother Carroll inclined his head. "Well, there you have it."

"Have what? Help me out here, because I haven't been around for four thousand years."

"When he's not collecting heads, the Dullahan is known to reside in the underworld. And what many do not know is this..." Brother Carroll leaned in close as he spoke. "... the Headsman serves Donn, the ancient darkness who rules over Tech Duinn."

11

Brother Carroll and I drank more wine and spoke well into the night. He wasn't such a bad drinking companion, and the more he drank, the more he divulged about the nature of the fae. Eventually, he revealed that while he thought of them as distant kin, he hated the Tuath Dé and their offspring, every last one. To the monk, they were evil incarnate, and it was his duty to destroy them.

He also expressed the opinion that, if Donn was indeed the one who'd sent the Dullahan, he was not working alone. "The Dark One rarely meddles in the affairs of mortal men," he said, "even one with your unique talents. Thus, I would suspect him to be in league with another of the little gods, or acting at the behest of one."

The last thing Carroll offered as he walked me out the front the gate the next morning was a warning. "Despite your curse, I see you have pure intentions. So, I wish you success in your endeavors against the fae gods. But if you wish to survive the schemes and machinations of the Tuath Dé, do not underestimate their ability to confuse and deceive. The Dullahan was merely a test, a probe, and not their final gambit. Expect them to come at you obliquely, and possibly from multiple angles. Prepare for the worst eventuality, and you might have a slim chance at surviving an encounter with their kind."

"Um, thanks—I guess. Any advice on weaknesses I might exploit?"

He arched an eyebrow. "Has the Seer taught you nothing? You cannot defeat them in an all-out battle—at least, not yet. Long ago, the Tuatha Dé Danann were bound by oath to never tell a lie, and by default, their offspring were held to that very same oath. If you wish to defeat them, you'll likely only do so by outwitting them."

"Hmm. You said 'not yet.' Maybe I just need to go hide out for a decade or so."

"Don't be juvenile. By the time you returned, everyone you ever loved or cared for would be dead, or worse. You would require hundreds of years to mature as you accumulated the knowledge, skill, and power needed to defeat them." His hawk eyes scrutinized me for several moments. "And if you could trade your humanity for the means to defeat the fae gods in mortal and magical combat, would you want to make that devil's bargain?"

"If it meant saving my friends and family, then yes," I said, meaning it.

The monk's expression grew somber as he shook his head slowly. "Then God help you, Colin, because no good can come from walking that path." He clasped my shoulder with a strong, calloused hand. "We may not see eye to eye, but I believe we're doing the same work. You are welcome back here, any time."

"And what would Brother Edmund say about that?" I asked with a wry grin.

"Oh, nobody listens to that turd anyway," Brother Carroll replied, immediately crossing himself. "Lord forgive me, but it's true. He's horribly foolish, a loudmouth, and a braggart—and for those reasons we pray for him daily."

I chuckled and extended my hand. "You've been a gracious host, and your advice will be most helpful in the difficult days ahead."

Brother Carroll—or Tuan, as I was coming to think of him—took my hand in his vice grip and shook it. "You are the Seer's apprentice, no doubt. Perhaps there is hope for you yet."

I smiled, saying no more, and headed down the road toward the Gremlin. When I looked back, the gate was closed and Tuan was gone.

Poor guy. To live four thousand years, being reincarnated time and again just to bear witness to all the evil things your progeny has done.

I considered how fucked up that was, if everything he'd said was true. I'd certainly seen stranger things, but I also wondered what kind of god would curse a man like that. Was it a just punishment? Did it make Brother Carroll's god any better than the Tuath Dé?

These were all fair questions, but ones for which I had no answers. And far be it from me to ponder theological and ethical dilemmas when I potentially faced a battle for my very survival. I cast those questions aside to focus on the real problems at hand.

One—the Celtic god of the underworld was quite possibly planning my demise.

Two—he was powerful beyond belief, and probably in league with another fae god.

Three—the gods played a long game, which meant they'd been scheming against me for much longer than I'd been aware. Their chess pieces were set and the game was already in motion. Yet I didn't even have a pawn on the board.

Four—the people I cared for were in danger, especially

Fallyn. It was well-known that we'd been dating since my battle with the Fear Doirich at Big Bend. Chances were good she'd be the first one they went after.

Of course, others could be at risk as well, but Finnegas, Maureen, Hemi, Crowley, and Luther could take care of themselves. Even in failing health, I suspected that few of the Celtic gods would risk taking the Seer on in a fair fight. And Maureen had been at odds with the fae for generations, so she was used to keeping her head down and avoiding that kind of trouble.

As for my own family, all I had left was my mother. Since that scare with Mei, the old man and I had been warding the shit out of Mom's house and vehicles; plus, Finnegas had somehow gotten Maeve to place my mother under her official protection. I'd considered taking her inside the Grove and leaving her there, but that would involve sleep spells and mind wipes. Finn said he wouldn't risk wiping her mind again, because she'd been mind-spelled one too many times over the years. Yet he assured me that no Celtic god would lay a hand on my mother, not while she was under Maeve's watchful eye.

Hemi was a power in his own right, plus he had two of the most powerful goddesses in the Maori pantheon watching his back. I doubted the fae gods wanted the kind of trouble they'd get for going after Luther—the Vampire Nations were no joke. And as for Crowley... well, he'd been raised in Underhill. If he'd evaded his mother's minions and assassins for this long, I was certain he'd be safe against the machinations of Donn and his unknown collaborator.

But Samson and the Austin Pack were all on their own. Sure, they'd give hell to anyone who jacked with them, but the 'thrope packs weren't organized like the vamps. Each pack was its own little fiefdom. Although individual packs were loosely affiliated with other, bordering packs, the nature of being a territorial supernatural creature meant that alphas and their followers mostly kept to themselves.

That meant the Austin Pack was vulnerable—that was my Achilles heel. That's why I needed to end things with Fallyn ASAP so Samson could get her far, far away from me. But to get her pissed or hurt enough to agree to leave Austin, I'd have to break up with her ugly.

I thought on it long and hard during the drive home. I hated to do it, because I really liked Fallyn. She understood me and accepted me for who I was. And when it came down to it, that was precisely why I wouldn't dare put her at risk.

But I couldn't lie to her either, and I couldn't bring myself to break her heart. I decided to tell her the truth, in person. I'd simply ask her to lay low and stay far away from me until all this shit blew over—problem solved. As soon as I hit Austin city limits, I picked up my phone and dialed Fallyn's number.

I WASN'T good at telling people how I felt, so my hands were already sweating when I placed my phone in the cradle and put it on speaker. All at once, I realized I was exhausted, semi-hungover, and a nervous wreck. Not at all keen on the idea of having an accident, I flicked my turn signal and took the next exit, pulling into a Whataburger while the phone rang. Bacon cheeseburger and chocolate shake therapy sounded like just the thing about now.

The ringing stopped and someone picked up on the other end.

"Hello, this is Fallyn." She sounded oddly formal, which was very unlike her usual smart-assed, perky self.

"Fallyn, hey—it's me, Colin."

"Oh, I didn't see your name on caller ID—got distracted. I

did have something I wanted to speak with you about, though—"

"Sorry to cut you off, but I need to see you, like right now. Is that possible?"

Silence. I was almost ready to hang up and call her back when her voice came on the line again. "Actually, no. That's what I wanted to talk to you about. Colin, I think we need to see other people."

"Okay, gr—huh?"

"I said I think we need to see other people."

I froze like a deer in headlights, fingers gripping the steering wheel like a drowning person grabbing a lifebuoy. "Come again?"

"Look, I know this is sudden, but I met someone. And besides, we haven't exactly said we were going to date exclusively."

But we didn't exactly say we were in an open relationship, either.

"Colin, are you there?"

"Yeah, I'm here." It was sort of what I'd wanted, but not like this. My heart was sinking like a lead balloon.

"I'm sorry, Colin. I never wanted to hurt you, but I really think this is for the best."

Someone spoke in the background, low enough so I couldn't make out what they were saying. A man's voice, smooth and... well, *manly*. Fallyn giggled and muffled the phone with her hand, but I could still hear what she said.

"In a minute. Would you stop already?" she said playfully, before coming back on the line. "Colin, I have to go. I, um, have company."

"Sure. Fallyn, I—"

"Yes?"

Quite uncharacteristically, I found myself at a loss for words.

"Colin, honestly, I really do have to run."

I hit the steering wheel with my hand, silently raging for a several seconds.

"Hello, Earth to Colin? Still there?"

"I—I'll see you around, Fallyn."

"Yeah, of course. Maybe we can get some coffee next week and catch up."

"Coffee. Right." What was I supposed to say to that? She'd just been warming my bed a few days ago.

"Sounds like a plan. Oops... gotta go."

More giggling and muffled speech.

"Wait—!"

Click.

Well, that was totally fucking unexpected.

It felt like my heart had just been ripped from my chest. Not like I didn't have experience with getting dumped. Thanks to Bells, I was familiar with the feeling. Still, that had not gone as planned.

And who was that guy? Had Samson taken the initiative on our plan and hooked her up with some studly male werewolf from another pack? Or had I simply thought our relationship was more serious than it actually was? I'd be the first to admit that I was clueless when it came to women, and horrible at reading social cues. Again, the time I'd spent dating Belladonna had proven that fact, over and over again.

I thought about the years I'd spent with Jesse, back before my *ríastrad* had surfaced. Things were just so easy with her, so natural. We'd practically grown up together, and each of us knew our partner's likes and quirks... heck, we'd even finished each other's sentences.

Looking back, I was certain it must've been disgustingly cute, but things sure in the hell had been less complicated with Jess. At least before she'd died and became a dryad, that is. But Jesse was gone, and now so was Fallyn.

Shit, this doesn't make sense!

The Alpha's daughter wasn't the wishy-washy type... and what was up with all that giggling? Could it be a spell of some sort? Had Samson hired a witch to lure her away from me? I wouldn't have put it past him. He'd never liked the idea of me dating his daughter, and for good reason.

Still, you'd think he'd consult me first.

I dialed the clubhouse. Mitzy answered.

"Hey, it's Colin. Is Samson around?"

"Naw, he's out dealing with some sort of Pack business. Anyway, you know he doesn't like to take calls here at the clubhouse."

Samson was paranoid as all hell. He had people in law enforcement and government, locally and at the state level, some Pack members and others that he paid off. According to the Alpha, the government was *always* listening. He and Hemi were two peas in a pod when it came to the topic of conspiracies.

"Right. When he gets back, just tell him I need to speak with him about Fallyn."

"Colin, I like you and all, but I'm not stepping in that pile of shit. If you need to talk to Samson about his daughter, you do it yourself."

"Mitzy, this isn't—"

"Did she dump you or something? You sound upset."

"Yeah, but that's not—"

"Sorry kid, it's still none of my business. I have enough to deal with, being one of the few humans around here. You're on your own, but I will tell Samson you called."

I beat my forehead with my palms. "Alright. Thanks, Mitzy."

"You got it."

Click.

Once I got over my initial shock, I considered the strange timing of this breakup. Never mind that it was just plain odd.

Again, Fallyn wasn't the fickle type, and she didn't warm up to just anyone. Add in the fact that Samson almost never got involved in "Pack business" unless it was something serious, and I started to wonder if he really had paid a witch to make Fallyn fall for another guy.

Was it his style? I couldn't say. Samson was hard to get a read on. One minute he'd be chewing my ass, and the next treating me like a son. I chalked it up to his age, because old 'thropes were known to be mercurial. Normally I wouldn't spend two seconds trying to figure him out, but in this case, I really wished I knew what was going on.

Whether Samson was involved or not, something about the whole thing wasn't right. The situation stank of fae meddling, because this was just the sort of fucked up shit they would do. And everyone knew no species was better at using charm spells and glamour magic than the fae.

When it came to those twisted fucks, there was one person I could go to for reliable intelligence and advice—although I hated the thought of asking. Asking a favor meant being indebted to her, and since I was still on her shit list, she'd really make me pay for it. But considering what I'd recently learned—and what was potentially at stake—it was worth owing a favor to someone I despised.

Ignoring the gnawing sensation in my gut, I put the car in gear and headed for Maeve's house.

IT'D BEEN ages since I'd been to Maeve's house. Well, months, anyway—if you didn't count all the time I'd spent in the Grove. Sadly, those months had not been kind to Maeve's abode. Before it had looked run down, but now?

The formerly stunning Victorian mansion looked

completely abandoned, with missing roof shingles, broken windows, plywood nailed over the front door, floorboards rotted through on the front porch, and graffiti inside and out. A powerful "look away, go away" spell had been cast on the house and grounds. I could get past it, but it was easily strong enough to run off the average human passerby. An official-looking sign on the front door warning of "black mold" or some-such was the icing on the cake.

Sheesh, this place is a total wreck. Or is it?

You never knew with the fae, and in Maeve's case I'd never been able to pierce any illusion she cast. She was a fae god, albeit a minor one, so her powers were beyond my skill to negate. An educated guess told me the place wasn't as bad as it looked, and this was all camouflage to keep people away. How she kept the neighbors from complaining to the city and HOA was anyone's guess—I figured she had them charmed, or in her pocket via other, more mundane, means.

Abandoned—yeah, right. They're here for sure. Just have to find out how to get in, or how to get someone's attention.

The last time I'd visited Maeve was with Finnegas. On that glorious occasion, he'd freed me from any and all obligations to Maeve. Shortly after, he'd wrangled the factions into making me their justiciar, which pretty much made me a free agent and somewhat of an independent power as well.

Yay, me.

Since then, I hadn't felt the need to return. When Maeve had justiciar work for me, she communicated through her flunkies, and I was fine with that. I did the work, the pay hit my account soon after, I never had to deal with Maeve directly, and everyone was happy.

Unfortunately, I couldn't get the answers I needed over the phone, and it wasn't like Maeve would speak to me over the phone anyway. I couldn't recall her ever using modern technology—she had *people* for that. Answering phones, sending texts, and other such mundane tasks were beneath her. Like any queen, if you wanted to speak with Maeve, you had to request an audience.

Sure, I could've crawled through a broken window, but I knew better. Back when the fae still had ready access to Underhill's magic, the place had been a death trap. Shifting walls and rooms, halls that seemingly went on forever, hidden dungeons accessed by stairways that descended for miles—I had frequent and recurring nightmares about getting lost in that place. Such magics had been intended to protect Maeve's palace, contents, and occupants. Without an endless supply of magical energy to power those protections, I suspected the Queen had resorted to simple wards and traps... a deadlier, if less elegant, solution to palace security.

Violate a bunch of wards that Maeve had cast? That was a whole bucket full of nope right there. Uh-uh, no immolation or getting turned to stone for me. I'd be invited in, or not enter her house at all.

I walked around the side of the house, making plenty of noise as I tromped through knee-deep weeds. "Hello, anyone home?" I shouted, cupping my hands to my mouth for effect. "I need to speak with Maeve. Anyone care to let me in?"

I was already being watched—of that, I was certain. The question was, would the flunkies on guard duty bother to tell Maeve I was here? Or an even better question, would Maeve—who almost certainly was aware of my presence—deign to have said flunkies let me in her spooky-ass house of horrors?

No one answered, and the only sounds I heard were the whisper of the wind in the weeds, the rattle of a loose shutter as it banged against the house, and the occasional dragonfly or bee as it buzzed past. Having almost reached the back garden, I was tempted to give up and head back, but the thought of Fallyn being in danger spurred me on. I'd lap this house a hundred times if I had to, just to find out what Maeve knew.

I rounded the back corner of the house and abruptly found myself face-to-face with one of Maeve's pet gargoyles. It sat like a foo dog statue outside a Chinese imperial palace, resting on its haunches but ready to leap into action at a moment's notice. The gargoyle's creepy stone eyes nearly crossed as they focused on me, and it leaned in to sniff me warily.

"Ahem. Hello there, Lothair. How's the guard creature business been?"

The gargoyle chuffed indignantly, dusting me with a light coating of powdered stone as it did. Then, it stood on all fours, turned its tail up in the air, and trotted toward one of the back entrances of the house. I wasn't certain if I was being escorted or shunned, so I held my ground. If I hulked out I could whoop one of Maeve's gargoyles, but it wouldn't be a fun time.

Lothair stopped mid-stride and glanced over its shoulder.

"Alright, hint taken," I said as I jogged to catch up. "Don't blame me for not wanting to be your between-meal snack. What do you gargoyles eat, anyway? River rock? House bricks? Precious stones?"

The gargoyle snorted before taking a sharp right turn down a short garden path that led to an ancient-looking well. The beast leaned its head over the edge, sniffing disdainfully and then stepping aside. Curious, I approached the well and leaned over the waist-high stone wall, scattering a cloud of flies that had been hovering inside and just out of sight.

The first thing I noticed was the stench—a combination of stagnant water, decomposing flesh, and sewage. After stepping back to get a lungful of fresh air, I held my breath and looked into the well a second time. At first, I couldn't see much, but as my eyes adjusted to the gloom I saw a variety of bones and skulls floating in the water at the bottom. Some were humanoid, but not human, while others were definitely more monstrous in appearance.

So, gargoyles are carnivores. Who knew?

"I take it those are the visitors who weren't welcome? Next time, I'll make sure I have an invitation."

I swear I heard Lothair chuckle as it loped off toward the house.

12

Lothair led me to one of the back entrances, which had been boarded over with plywood as well. He sauntered over to a concrete pad a few yards from the door, turning in a circle like a dog before plopping down with his head resting on his forepaws. With Maeve's guardian now ignoring me, I assumed I had carte blanche to enter the premises.

As I reached for the plywood covering the entrance it disappeared, revealing a rather formidable wooden entry door. The door was dark-stained oak banded in iron, and it had a porthole at head height covered by a wrought iron grate. Before I could knock or try the handle, the door swung open. I was greeted by a massive creature, easily eight feet tall. The beast was roughly human-shaped, but covered in thick, black, matted hair. Its eyes shone like coals from within the overhang of its bangs, and two large tusks jutted from its fur-covered mouth.

Buggane. Maeve is branching out in her choice of security.

As a species, bugganes were a sort of cross between an ogre and a troll. They were known for their brutishness, their foul odor, and a general lack of manners. As with trolls, when hired for domestic work, bugganes were usually spelled so their smell wouldn't overwhelm their employer. Thankfully, Maeve had done everyone the courtesy of erasing this brute's musk. In the wild, however, that smell almost always preceded a buggane attack.

As experienced hunters were aware, almost every reported sighting of a "Bigfoot" type creature could be chalked up to buggane activity. The fiends were fond of scaring humans, abducting them, and, on occasion, killing and eating them. But for all their drawbacks, they were cheap and incredibly efficient muscle. If Maeve had hired bugganes for security, it meant either her resources had been spread thin, or she was expecting serious trouble. Or both.

The huge creature lifted its nose slightly as it took a deep whiff. Then, it spoke in an unexpectedly high, nasally voice. "Ye smell like a MacCumhaill. Cowards are ye, the whole lot."

Fionn MacCumhaill was never known to be a coward, so I wracked my brains trying to determine why the buggane would say such a thing. Finally, the answer dawned on me. Manx legend had it that Fionn had fought a massive buggane, not once but twice, and ran off before succumbing to defeat—meaning death—both times. As I recalled, the story ended with my ancestor cursing the buggane for winning a fair fight.

Honestly, Fionn was kind of a dick, and the grudges that many of his enemies still had against him caused me no end of grief.

"I'm not Fionn," I said. "Are we going to have trouble?"

The creature slowly rocked back and forth as it considered my question. "Oh, the neck of you fella, ta' say sumthin' like that. No, not while I'm inna Queen's service. But after, we might, ya' wee pile o' keck."

"Whenever you're ready, I'm game, Stinky."

"*Traa dy liooar*, MacCumhaill—in good time." He opened the door wide with a hand that was the size of a dinner plate, spitting a huge gob of phlegm on the floor at the same time. "C'mon, Herself awaits."

I followed the massive pile of matted fur into the house, shutting the "door" behind me. As soon as I passed the threshold, the appearance of the home's interior changed drastically, becoming much the same as the last time I'd been here. Shabby and a bit timeworn, but livable. And, thankfully, no shifting walls and corridors. Even so, I didn't care to get lost inside this place—it was still massive and much larger inside than out, so I dogged the buggane's heels the entire way.

We walked for what seemed like an eternity, although I knew instinctively it had only been a few minutes. It was a simple illusory effect, but one that could easily trick most unwelcome visitors. By altering one's perception of time and distance, you could trick someone into moving in slow-motion, which in turn would provide ample time for defense or escape. My minor and recently-acquired talent for chronomancy allowed me to perceive the nature of the spell, but I lacked the skill to negate the effects completely.

After walking down several long corridors and through a number of rather interesting rooms—one had been dedicated entirely to Nagel paintings, an investment I was certain that Maeve must have regretted—we came to a set of large wooden double-doors. The entrance had once been painted white, but that paint had since been stained yellow by time and neglect. Still, the doors were quite elegant and regal-looking, finished with brass hardware, glass door knobs, and bolection moulding in the classic Victorian style.

"G'wawn in," the buggane said, stepping aside with a combination belch-fart that would've made Peter Griffin proud. "An' mind yer manners."

I held my breath as I opened the doors, not trusting Maeve's anti-odor smell to eradicate such eruptions. Upon entering the room, I realized that I shouldn't have worried, because the space consisted of a huge conservatory—no, an arboretum—filled with all manner of trees, flowers, ferns, and other visually-pleasing plant-life. It smelled of freshly-turned loam, exotic flowers, and rainforest. I walked a few steps inside, marveling at the place, at which point the doors slammed shut behind me.

Sparing a glance over my shoulder, I made note of the fact that the doors had vanished. Somebody wanted privacy for this meeting, no doubt. Or they wanted to keep me here. I'd been at Maeve's mercy from the moment I'd stepped through that back door, so I was more intrigued than perturbed.

Bugganes, time distortion spells, disappearing doors... Time to find out why Maeve is taking such peculiar precautions in her own home.

THE ARBORETUM WAS EASILY fifty by one hundred feet, which made it more of a concert hall than a room. An arched glass ceiling high overhead revealed a star-filled sky. Considering it had still been daytime when I'd entered Maeve's house, either the time-distortion spell had been more effective than I'd realized, or I'd been transported to another place and time since my arrival.

There was a single, flagstone path that ran from where I'd entered toward the center of the space, so I followed where it led. Some of the plant species looked rather unfriendly—brightly-colored things with strange spiked leaves shaped like snapping jaws, or spiny thorns that dripped with what was almost certainly toxin-laden sap. I didn't need my druid powers to know they were deadly, so I kept to the center of the walkway.

A few twists and turns later, Maeve came into view. Although her back was turned, I could see she'd shed her wealthy MILF disguise, likely because maintaining it had become a superfluous waste of magical power. Now that she remained sequestered inside her palace instead of mixing with the local socialites, disguises were unnecessary.

Despite appearing in her true form, she wasn't nearly as overwhelmingly beautiful as she'd been on my last visit. On that occasion, she'd tried to both glamour and cow me, and thus had been in full faery queen bloom. Now, she definitely appeared to be one of the fae, with her long, lithe figure, flowing golden tresses, and petite elfin ears on display for all to see. But she looked less resplendent than before.

Clearly, Maeve had decided to tone down her natural Tuatha radiance. I took it as a subtle communication that there would be no subterfuge between us, no attempts to influence me via glamours or other fae magics. I'd still be on my guard, however. The fae were as fickle as Texas weather, and I saw no reason to do otherwise.

"Colin, how generous of you to honor the grace of our presence."

Golden shears in hand, she was carefully trimming leaves and stems from what looked to be a bonzai tree. As with everything in Maeve's home, looks could be deceiving, and upon closer inspection I noticed that the little shrub had eyes. Every so often, the plant would hiss and shake when she snipped something away.

"Hush," said Maeve, "or I'll feed you to the bugganes."

The little bush went still.

"Don't you mean, 'grace us with your presence'?" I replied, maintaining my distance.

"I said exactly what I intended to say," Maeve said as she set the shears down on the table, examining her work as she spoke. "You killed the jötunn. You will suffer the consequences of that injudicious act."

"Are you threatening me?" I said, sounding a lot more like a certain cartoon character than I'd intended.

"No, merely stating the obvious. There are powers other than the Tuath Dé, you know. And like my kin, they do not care to see their children murdered."

She turned to face me, and for a moment her gauzy white dress was backlit by a lamp that sat behind her on the table. I tried not to notice that her naked body had been perfectly silhouetted through the nearly sheer fabric. The faery queen smiled slightly as she noticed the flush on my face, then she slowly stalked toward me.

Keep it together, McCool. She may not be using magic, but she is trying to throw you off balance. And she's basically your grandmother.

That thought alone cooled my engines considerably. I stood stock still, forcing myself to relax while maintaining eye contact as she drew close. I was taller than Maeve, but not by much in her true form. The Tuatha Dé Danann—and their immediate progeny, the high fae—were by nature a tall race. The faery queen returned my stare, sapphire and seafoam eyes looking into my soul as she got in my space. She laid a hand on my cheek, spreading warmth through my entire body with her touch.

Finnegas believed that while Maeve might not want me sexually, she likely wished to possess me in other ways. In her twisted fae mind, I would serve as just recompense for the loss of her human lover, my ancestor Oisín. When Oisín had wished to return to Earth from Underhill to see his friends and family, Maeve saw it as a sin tantamount to infidelity. And Maeve—or rather Niamh, as she'd been known then—had killed him for that trespass.

For that reason, my mentor had intervened on my behalf to extricate me from Maeve's machinations. Before he had, I believed the faery queen had seen me as a sort of pet, a dog brought to heel. When I'd tricked her, retrieving the Four Treasures of the Tuatha Dé Danann only to use them to seal the pathways to Underhill, well—I could only imagine what she wanted to do to *me* now.

As gently as possible, I pushed her hand away. "Maeve..."

Her eyes narrowed slightly as she withdrew, and somehow her brow furrowed without causing a single crease in her porcelain skin. "It is fortunate that you remind me of Oisín. But do not mistake my fondness for weakness, Justiciar. I am a queen, and I will have my way in due time."

"I came here for information, not an argument," I said in a calm, firm voice. "And if at all possible, I'd like to keep this civil."

She tsked and turned her perfect, celestial nose up at me, as if examining a cut of meat gone bad. "I am not some strumpet who remains at your beck and call, druid. You've done admirable work for me in your capacity as druid justiciar, and have been paid in kind. I owe you nothing."

Actually, she was supposed to cooperate with me, providing intelligence and resources if it helped me do my job. But I didn't want to play that card yet. Since I was clearly already annoying her, I decided to prod a little harder. Maybe she'd tell me what I wanted to know, just to get me to leave.

"Strumpet? Who's a strumpet?" My eyes darted up and to the left. "Okay, at face value Bells sort of qualifies, but in reality she's a lot more of a prude than you'd guess. Fallyn is an open book, and that girl certainly won't just bed anyone. Janice and I aren't even a thing, although we did go on that one date—Brigid still hasn't forgiven me for that. And as for Sabine, you already know how that went."

Maeve stared at me like a statue of Athena, all regality and imperiousness. "Are you quite done defending your inamoratas and detailing your failed relationships?" she asked. "Because the more you carp, the more I prefer the company of the hissing shrub yonder."

Hmph. Didn't take much to crawl under her skin, did it?

It took everything I had to keep a smirk off my face. "Alright, then. I'll get to the point. Why is Donn after me, and which other Celtic god is working with him?"

THE QUEEN TILTED HER HEAD, smiling slightly as she clapped her hands softly. "Well done, Justiciar, well done. I hadn't expected you to get much from your visit to the Mountain King—except Van Winkle's curse, perhaps. Tell me, how did you manage to enter his hall and exit again of your own free will?"

I wagged my finger at her to express my displeasure. "Tsk, tsk, Maeve—you've been keeping tabs on me."

"Do not flatter yourself. A queen knows what goes on in her own demesne, as well as in bordering territories."

"I thought Rube's Icehouse was inside your territory? Did your borders shift?"

She smiled sweetly, like a kindergarten teacher correcting a particularly slow child. "You should well know, not every land obeys the physical laws of your world. Where the fae are concerned, demarcations of power and property are not delineated by geography alone. The Mountain King's demesne is where he wills it to be, and his borders begin at the entrance to his hall."

"Kind of like your palace, eh? Once you're past the front door, you ain't in Kansas no more."

"Just so. And you still haven't answered my question," she replied.

"I'll answer yours, if you answer mine."

She turned her back and picked up the shears again. "I'll

discover the truth in due time. What else can you offer in exchange for what I know?"

I leaned my butt against the table and crossed my arms, facing her while staying just out of reach of her pet shrub. Being this familiar with a faery queen was playing with fire, but then again, we'd played these games for some time now. If I started showing her the respect her station demanded, she'd see it as weakness.

"You've already confirmed Donn's involvement," I said, changing tack. "Although for the life of me I can't understand why he'd be interested in taking me out."

She snipped a leaf from the shrub, pausing to give me a disinterested sideways glance. "Surely you're joking. Once you defeated their druid, you became of extreme interest to my people. Upstart heroes and demigods tend to attract their attention eventually, as did Fionn and Cú Chulainn both."

"And, like Oisín, both men met with tragic ends."

Maeve frowned. "Oisín made his bed. But you're wrong about Fionn, druid. He isn't dead, but instead sleeps awaiting the day when the Isle has need for a hero of his ilk once more."

"Okay, so two out of three of those men died due to the meddling of the Celtic gods."

Maeve stabbed the shears into the table. Her lips were drawn in a line, and her voice was hard and cold. "Watch your tongue, Colin McCool. I will not be insulted in my own home."

I held a hand up in supplication. "Apologies, I didn't mean to offend, but merely to establish precedent. Like you said, heroes tend to attract the wrong sort of attention from the gods."

Like that, her expression softened and her voice became sweet and smooth as honey. "Just so. Consider who was involved in the Hound's death."

I chuckled. "It has not escaped my notice that, according to legend, a certain Queen Maeve was behind that conspiracy."

Maeve snapped the shears closed and held them up for emphasis, while still examining the shrub with a studied eye. "Ah, but back then I still went by my given name. I only took up the mantle when I came to Earth to get away from my family. The subterfuge served a purpose for a time, and over the years it stuck. But other goddesses have born the name before me."

I hopped up and sat on the table behind me, the better to look Maeve in the eye. "You're saying another goddess had Cú Chulainn killed."

"And I will say no more on the matter. But it is not goddesses you need fear at the moment. I've been sworn to secrecy by one who remains superior to me even after all these centuries. Again, I can offer nothing more, but suffice it to say that Donn does not act alone, and in truth he likely bears you no ill will."

"Meaning?"

She gave me a pointed look, her supernaturally beautiful eyes shifting from cerulean blue to sea foam green and back again as she weighed me on the scales of Anubis. At that moment, I didn't feel like a cocky-assed kid chatting up the MILF next door, although that was the game I'd been playing for the last several minutes. Instead I felt insignificant, an ant crawling across the palm of a giant, staring up at an all-seeing eye that blotted out the sky.

One false move, and I'd be squished.

After several agonizing moments, Maeve grabbed her shears and turned her attention back to her shrub. Internally, I breathed a sigh of relief.

"Meaning, gods are more like mortals than you know. They feel loss, and pain; they long for those they love, they hold grudges, and they seek revenge on individuals who've wronged them. They fear many things. Growing old and feeble, diminishing in power, losing the adulation of their worshippers—and most of all, death, which comes to us all eventually."

She snipped a branch from the shrub, causing it to squeal in pain and anguish. "Make no mistake, druid—there are those gods who see you as a threat to their continued existence. That alone is reason for many to want you dead, but some feel they have more reason than others. I can say no more."

"But—"

Maeve cut me off, just as a very large someone stepped out of the foliage across the patio. "Dufgal, please show the druid out."

I wasn't surprised that the buggane had escaped my notice, since I'd been mostly focused on Maeve—she was the biggest threat in the room, after all. But hell if those huge hairy things weren't creepy fuckers. Put them in a forest or a deep, dark cave, and they'd sneak up on you without so much as kicking a pebble or cracking a twig.

"At yer pleasure, Highness," the buggane said with a stiff bow. "C'mon, you. She ain't got no more time fer yer natterin'."

I'd only taken my eyes off the queen for a second, but when I looked back, she was gone.

13

The first thing I did when I left Maeve's house was call Fallyn. While the faery queen hadn't been clear on exactly who was after me, I didn't have to be a mindreader to know it was bad. After getting Fallyn's voicemail for the third time, I started calling the clubhouse every five minutes, hoping that Samson would get back before I lost my mind.

I hit redial again, and someone picked up on the other end.

"For the last time, Colin—he's not fucking here!"

"Mitzy, wait—"

Click.

I called back but got a busy signal, which meant that Mitzy had taken the phone off the hook. They still had old school phones at the clubhouse, since Samson was about as tech-savvy as an Amish farmer with an EMF allergy, and twice as cheap. The last time any technology had gotten updated at Pack HQ, Ronald Reagan was still eating jelly beans in the Oval Office. At a loss for what to do, I dialed Maureen.

"So, how'd yer visit with that fecking monk go?"

"I'll have to give you the details later. Maureen, I think Fallyn is in trouble, and I can't get a hold of Samson to find out if I'm freaking out for nothing."

"Trouble ya' say—as in fae trouble?"

I briefly explained what had happened, painting the situation in broad strokes for brevity's sake.

"Aye, lad, that sounds fishy. Hang on." I heard talking in the background. "The Seer says to come back to the junkyard so we kin figger it out. 'Sides, ya' got company, and frankly I don't like the look o' the bastards. One's clearly daft and the other—well, just get back quick 'afore they scare off our customers."

"Shit, I forgot Hideie was coming today. Alright, I'll get there as fast as I can."

Minutes later I pulled up to the junkyard, only to find Hideie and Click squaring off in the parking lot. Hideie had glamoured himself to look human, thankfully. The amused expression he wore said he was taking things a lot less seriously than the quasi-god standing across from him.

Oh boy, he's in one of his moods. Time to defuse this situation, before he sends Hideie back to feudal Japan.

Click had the sleeves of his leather jacket pushed back, and he was dancing around with his dukes up like an old-time boxer. "Take it back, ya' feather-brained, top-knotted dimwit, or I'll knock yer block off!"

Thankfully there were no customers around, but there were a few unfamiliar cars in the lot, which meant we had people in the yard pulling their own parts. Maureen had stormed off toward the stacks as I pulled in, presumably to keep any visitors away from the parking area until I defused the situation. And Finnegas? The old man was kicked back on a plastic lawn chair, a cigarette in one hand and a cold longneck in the other, enjoying the show.

Click circled the tengu, all the while hurling the most ridiculous insults—"sheep-headed fuck-funnel" had to be my favorite.

Hideie appeared to take it in stride, but by the way he had his arms crossed, I knew he was ready to draw his katana from thin air at a moment's notice. My erstwhile magic tutor might have been a minor god of sorts, but even he couldn't recover from getting beheaded by one of the World Beneath's greatest swordsmen—er, sword-birds? Sword-ravens? Whatever. I just needed to make sure they didn't come to actual blows.

I slammed the car door, giving Finnegas the stink eye as I tromped across the parking lot. "Seriously, Finn? You were just going to sit there and let this play out?"

He blew smoke out his nostrils and grinned like a jack-o-lantern. "I'm fairly certain their talents cancel each other out. Still, I can't say I'm not eager to see your fencing instructor cut that crazy little prick down to size."

"Damn it, Finnegas—I have bigger problems to deal with right now," I growled. "You could've at least tried to deescalate the situation."

The old man chuckled. "Live as long as I have, and you'll come to realize that scenes like this don't happen every day. Gotta take your entertainment where you can get it, kid."

I gave him a look that could curdle milk as I stepped between the mountain goblin and the ancient magician. Once I stood between them, I shook a finger at Click.

"You, behave yourself!" I turned a disapproving eye on Hideie. "And you—what did you say to get him riled up like this?"

The old tengu's dour expression belied the mirth in his voice. "I merely implied that the tutelage I've been providing you in kenjutsu is vastly more practical than instruction in magic. And many times more likely to save your life."

Click jumped at the yōkai, forcing me to stiff arm him to keep them separate. "Take it back, ya' cock-swabbing feather duster! I'll clobber ya'—nay, I'll send ya' back in time is what I'll do. Take ya' back ta' when ya' were just a wee egg in yer mam's rookery, then crack ya' into a frying pan and have ya' fer an omelette. See how ya' like that!"

"The magician might find that very hard to do once his head has been separated from his shoulders," Hideie replied with a bemused smile.

"That's it!" I roared, letting my anger bring a bit of the beast out. My voice deepened several octaves, and veins popped out all over my arms and face as my Hyde-side began to surface. "There will be no cracking of eggs, no beheadings, and definitely no supernatural battles at my place of work."

DESPITE THE FACT that he was basically a god, Click took a few steps away from me. I glared and pointed a finger at him. "You, sit your ass down and chill out, or I'm cancelling today's lesson." I frowned at Hideie. "And you—honestly, I'd have expected my kenjutsu sensei to refrain from starting fights in his student's front yard."

Hideie's expression darkened at being chided by a pupil. Then, he bowed slightly, stiff and formal. "My apologies, Colin-san. It will not happen again. But, if I might make a suggestion? Please do not schedule our lessons at times when the magician is expected."

"Actually, he wasn't expected today." I palmed my forehead. "Gah, our lessons. I'm so sorry, but I don't have time right now. There's been a bit of a crisis—"

Finnegas cleared his throat. "Has my apprentice forgotten that within the Grove he has all the time in the world?"

"The Seer makes a fair point," Click interjected.

I turned on him, snapping my fingers and thumb together like a mouth closing. "Nobody asked you."

Click screwed his mouth sideways as he rubbed his chin. "True, but since when have I kept my opinions secret? Anyways, ya' wanted me ta' settle down, and now that I think of it, the birdman's shit breakin' has got me curious. Tell ya' what—I'll cool my heels fer a bit, if I get ta' watch yer sword lesson with old featherbrains."

"I really don't have the time—"

Finnegas cut me off. "Colin, maybe a few moment's distraction is exactly what you need right now. Since we had our unexpected visitor earlier in the week, you've done nothing but run around like a headless chicken. Getting a workout in will calm you down, and a few hours of rest in the Grove after would go a long way toward clearing your head."

I rubbed a hand across my face, noting the two-day stubble on my cheeks and face. Honestly, I probably didn't smell too great either, so a long swim in the Grove's pond sounded like just the ticket.

"Alright, alright," I said to the old druid. "But I want you working on a plan while I'm gone."

He looked at an imaginary watch on his wrist. "Right, I'll be doing that for the whole five minutes you'll be away."

Click shared a look with Finnegas. "They're so cute when they start learnin' that time is a construct."

Finnegas scowled. "Don't think this means we're friends. Personally, I'm hoping the tengu slips and accidentally skewers you during the lesson."

The Welsh magician nodded enthusiastically. "Aye, me too!"

I addressed the tengu and the godling as I headed for the Druid Oak. "C'mon, you two—the sooner we get this over with, the sooner I can find Fallyn."

Click tapped a finger on his chin. "Fallyn, fallen, fall in... damn it, I had somethin' ta' tell ya', but it's slipped my mind."

"Not the only thing that's slipped," Finnegas muttered as we walked away.

Minutes later, we were inside the Druid Grove. I instructed Click to sit quietly on a bench in front of my Keebler cabin, on pain of banishment from the Grove should he do otherwise. Meanwhile, Hideie had dropped his glamour, having no need for subterfuge here in the Grove. Currently, we faced each other across a forty-foot clearing—he with a wooden bokken in hand, and me holding a blunt metal facsimile of Dyrnwyn.

As usual, our first exchange had not gone well for me. My hand stung almost as bad as my pride, and it was all I could do to hang onto the sword while my healing factor dealt with the damage. Hideie shook out his wings, then folded them across his back and nodded to me.

"Attack, Colin-san. And this time, do not hold back."

I obliged, sprinting across the clearing at vampire speed. When I'd first begun training with the tengu, he'd insisted that I practice fighting him in all my various forms—human, partially-Fomorian, and full-Fomorian. That last one had been a mistake, as I soon lost my temper due to not being able to score a hit on the mountain goblin. Things had escalated from there, and since then, we'd been sticking with my human and stealth-shifted forms.

On closing the distance, I faked a high horizontal cut to my teacher's eyes. He raised his wooden sword with almost casual disinterest to block the attack. However, my attack had been a feint, and I changed the direction of the cut mid-stroke, turning it into a downward slash at his wrist.

Yet even at this speed, he was able to step back while bringing his blade down and to his left, parrying the cut and following up by sliding his blade down mine. He finished by wrapping up my arms on his weak side and drawing his wooden sword across my throat as the coup de grace.

"Shit! Again," I said, backing away as soon as he released me.

I loosened my shoulders, drawing attention away from the fact that I'd slightly adjusted my grip. Circling my instructor, I attempted to set up my next attack.

As I moved in, I kept the tip of my sword pointed at the tengu's eyes to make it that much more difficult to see my blade coming. Choking down on the hilt with my right hand, I slashed at his eyes again, hoping for the same response. Instead, he leaned away, which was fine because it would leave him slightly off balance, helping to set up my next move. At the last moment, I changed the angle of the attack again, seemingly going for the exact same attack on his wrist.

I was clearly about to score a cut on Hideie's sword arm, but oddly, he made no move to deflect my blade. Instead, his beady raven's eyes watched with curiosity as I brought the blade around in a tight circle, coming around his guard as I stepped into a deep lunge to perform a one-handed thrust at his face. Hideie pivoted like a salsa dancer, with perfect posture and moving only from the hips down. The tip of my blade passed his face with millimeters to spare. While I was busy missing his eyeball, Hideie glided past me as he landed a hard forehand blow across my ribs.

The tengu stepped away, relaxed but poised with his sword held in a low guard. I cradled my bruised ribs and wounded pride, waiting for my Formorian genetics to handle the injury. Meanwhile, Click looked on with interest.

"Your blade work improves, Colin-san! Had you been the slightest bit faster, I would be wearing an eye patch for the next few days."

I bowed slightly to acknowledge the compliment, resisting the urge to wince at the twinge of pain that accompanied the movement. Standing upright once more, I held my sword in a neutral guard, blade tip once more pointed at the sword master's eye.

"Again."

TWO HOURS OF "GROVE TIME" and innumerable bruises later, I bade my fencing instructor farewell. After walking him to the Oak, I gave a formal bow.

"Arigato, Hideie-sensei."

"*Oyakunitatte yokatta*, Colin-san. Always a pleasure."

I walked him to the tree and mentally instructed the Oak to drop him off downtown as he preferred. Like many visitors to Austin, Hideie had grown fond of our city, and he'd recently purchased a high-rise condo off 4th Street. I'd been avoiding the downtown area since the disaster, so I'd yet to visit his place.

In truth, though, he'd yet to invite me over—which was fine, since we had little in common besides swordsmanship. Tengu were basically Japanese fae, and rather aloof by nature. After spending some time with Hideie, I seriously doubted that we'd ever develop a close friendship. A shame, really—I found him to be intriguing, and he'd make for one hell of a backup in a fight.

After the tengu had gone, I sniffed my pits and immediately regretted doing so. It was definitely time for that swim, as I was dog tired and felt like yesterday's trash. But despite my weariness, there was no way I'd take that nap Finnegas had suggested—not with Fallyn's peculiar behavior weighing heavily on my mind.

Click popped into view beside me, just as I was stripping out of my sweaty clothes on my way to the pond.

"Gah! Damn it, Click, I told you to stop doing that."

He frowned as he smacked a fresh pack of cigarettes against his palm, top side first. "Aren't ya' the master of this grove? How could ya' not see me?"

"I'm, uh—still getting used to it."

I glanced around, looking for a place to change, then I realized who I was dealing with. Click wasn't exactly the type to respect personal boundaries. He'd probably pop out of nowhere and start talking to me no matter where I hid.

"Hope you don't mind, but I swim in the buff," I warned.

"As would any druid," he replied.

I shrugged and stripped down to nothing, then I dove into the pond. The waters of the Grove were cool and invigorating, and just the thing to sooth sore joints and tired muscles. Recently, I'd discovered that almost any time I spent here was recuperative, but bathing in the waters of the pond and streams was almost as good as taking an hour-long nap.

When I stepped out of the water, I willed the droplets to evaporate and roll off me until I was dry—a feat that was quite a bit easier without clothing. Then, I tromped over to my little tree-cabin to grab a clean pair of jeans while Click busied himself by chatting up a few birds. My curiosity got the best of me, so I tuned in with my druid senses to see if the birds had anything to say. Of course, the conversation turned out to be one-sided, which further solidified my opinion that Click was ninety-nine percent batshit crazy.

A few minutes later, I stepped out of my treehouse, barefoot and shirtless so I could enjoy the soft grass underfoot and the "sunlight" on my skin. Click was deeply engaged in explaining Alhazred's third axiom of summoning to a hummingbird. Since it was a subject I knew little about, I listened in for a few minutes for fun. But when he started to draw a summoning circle in the dirt, I decided it was time to interrupt before he invited some horror from the Void into my druid grove.

"Ahem."

"Oh, there ya' are! I was startin' ta' think you'd decided to take a nap after that beating ya' took. Meant ta' ask ya'—why'd ya' let him whip ya' like that?"

I scratched my head and shrugged. "Because, Click—he's better than me."

The mad trickster godling once known as Gwydion shook his head vigorously. "No, he's not. Not by a long shot, lad."

I sat on a stump, temporarily amused by Click's argument and curious to know where he was going with this line of thought. "Okay, I'll play. If he's not a better swordsman than me, why is it that I've yet to score a hit on him—even after hundreds of hours of sparring?"

Click crossed his arms as his boyish, James Dean-like face split in a broad grin. "Oh, that's easy. S'because he cheats."

"Come again?"

"He cheats, and like a damned card counter, ta' be sure. Mind ya' now, lad, he doesn't do it intentionally—I suspect his kind exert their magic by instinct. He's likely not even aware of his talent, nor of how it facilitates his supernatural expertise at fencing."

I scratched my nose with a knuckle. "This whole time, he's been using magic to beat me?"

"O' course. How d'ya think he was able ta' beat ya' so easily?"

"Huh. So, what's his secret?"

Click tapped his temple with an index finger. "He sees the future. Not far ahead, maybe a moment or two. It doesn't take much magic ta' do—just a bit o' skill—which is why ya' never noticed him doin' it. But, it's enough ta' allow the birdbrained prick ta' anticipate yer moves, and then counter 'em almost before they happen."

"Shit, then I'm never going to beat him," I said.

"Oh, I would'na say that. He is teaching ya' ta' handle a blade like a pro, and that's the truth. But ye'll have ta' learn his trick if ya' wanna best him."

"Wait a minute—I can learn how to do that? To anticipate my opponent's moves?"

"Why, o'course ya' can. Anyone with enough talent at chronourgy and chronomancy could, if they only had someone ta' show them."

I stared at Click expectantly. "And?"

He stared back in confusion, then his eyes lit up. "Oh, ya' want me ta' show ya' now? Sure, why not? But I didn't come here fer a friendly visit. There's somethin' I meant ta' tell ya', but I can't think of what it was fer the life of me. Hmm..."

He tapped a finger on his chin, muttering softly. I waited patiently for what seemed like an eternity while the semi-immortal magician talked nonsense under his breath. I was pretty sure he was talking to himself, and answering back like a damned schizophrenic.

Sheesh. If this is what immortality looks like, I'll pass.

"Click..."

"Keep yer pants on, I'm gettin' there."

"Look, I'd love to hang out, but Fallyn is missing and I—"

The boyish wizard's head snapped around. "What was that ya' said?"

"Huh? I said I'd love to just chill out, but—"

"Nah, the next part."

"—but Fallyn's missing."

He snapped his fingers. "That's it! That's what I came ta' warn ya' about. Ah, damn it—it's gone again. Somethin' about falling, fall in..."

Yup, nutty as a fruitcake.

"Click, how about you just show me how Hideie anticipates my attacks?"

He squinted and looked up at the sky. "S'pose I could. But it'll take centuries fer ya' ta' learn ta' do it consistently. First, ya' have ta' learn ta' detect the flow o' time..."

14

I skipped the nap, but my dip in the pond seemed to have done the trick. Finnegas was waiting for me when I emerged from the Grove, roughly two minutes after I'd entered.

He scowled. "You didn't sleep a wink, did you?"

"No, but I feel refreshed just the same. So, what's the plan?"

The old druid finished off his beer, then wiped his mouth on the rolled-up cuff of his long-sleeved Western shirt. "Been thinking about it since Maureen filled me in. First off, you don't even know if something has happened to Fallyn. Could be she really did get sick of you and she's decided to play the field. Or, she just got cold feet. People do that sometimes, you know. Love can be a scary thing."

"No, it's not like her. You don't understand, Finn—Fallyn is a rock. She doesn't take up with people easily, and she's not the fickle type. It may seem like I'm overreacting, but I'm fairly certain I'm right."

Finnegas pulled out his tobacco pouch, filling a folded piece of rolling paper with tobacco as he spoke. "I didn't say you were overreacting. I simply want you to consider the most likely possibilities before you take the next step."

"Which is?"

Finnegas expertly rolled the tobacco and paper between his fingers and thumbs until he had a nice, thick, tightly-packed cylinder. Then, he licked the paper and sealed his cancer stick. Once he'd lit up, he took a drag and pointed at me with the ciggy between his fingers.

"I think you're right about the Tuath Dé being involved. Only reason I brought up the other stuff is because I don't want you to be blindsided if we're wrong." He took another puff and spat a fleck of tobacco as he exhaled a cloud of smoke. "Something also tells me that Samson was deliberately distracted by some manufactured crisis, just to make it easier for them to charm Fallyn, or whatever they did to her."

"'Them' meaning the fae?"

"If they're working for the Tuatha who are after you, yes. But I have a feeling we're dealing with one of their first-stringers, not just some run-of-the-mill fae magician." He chewed stray piece of tobacco as he considered the situation. "Either way, your first move is to locate Fallyn and make certain she's not in danger."

"And if she is?"

"Contact me through Maureen, then Samson, and wait for us to arrive before you confront this Tuath Dé agent. We have no idea who it is or what powers and talents they possess. Consider it a given they'll be dangerous."

"If Fallyn's in immediate danger, I won't be able to wait."

He pushed his straw cowboy hat forward to scratch the back of his head. "As I'm well aware. If you must go in with guns blazing, then you'd better send that damned tree to come get me. You cannot face these beings without back-up, especially if we're dealing with one of the Celtic gods. Is that clear?"

"Crystal," I said, knowing I was going to end up disobeying him the minute I decided Fallyn was in peril. "But what's

Samson going to do against a god? I know he's an alpha and all, but still—"

"Samson has connections, the sort that could come in handy should you run afoul of Donn and his mysterious accomplice."

"You think it really is Donn who's behind this?"

Finnegas gesticulated with both hands, leaving the cigarette to dangle in his mouth as he spoke. "All clues seem to point to him, don't they? You saw some sort of underworld scene in the portal that brought the Dullahan here, as well as in the one he escaped through. Tuan seemed to think he's involved, and that old fart knows more about the Tuath Dé than anyone alive. I can think of more than a few reasons why Donn might want you dead."

"Besides the fact that I present a threat to the Celtic gods?"

"In addition to that, actually. Fionn always was a spiteful shit, full of himself and too prideful to let a slight go unanswered. He did Donn's son wrong, even though they'd once been friends and the boy had followed Fionn loyally as a member of his fiann. It stands to reason that, at least in part, Donn could be seeking revenge on you in Fionn's stead as recompense for that evil act."

"Why is it that every time someone is after me, it's because of something Fionn MacCumhaill did to them?"

Finnegas flicked ash from his coffin nail. "Told you before— Fionn was a hero and a jackass, and he made a lot of enemies by way of being both. You just happen to be his only living heir, and whether you like it or not, you're stuck carrying his mantle. It's why I trained you, so you may as well accept it and train like hell to deal with the next threat that comes along—because it only gets worse from here."

"You speak as if from experience."

He rubbed the back of his neck. "Generations of it. I've buried plenty of your ancestors before their time, and I'd not care to repeat the experience with you." The old man paused to drop his butt to the ground, grinding it out with his heel. "One thing those folks didn't have, though, was your *ríastrad*. It gives you a distinct advantage the others never possessed."

"It's also brought a lot of unwanted scrutiny. I can't help but think that if I didn't have it, I'd never have attracted the attention of the gods."

"And if dogs had ziplock asses, no one would ever get shit on their shoes. Trust me—if you hadn't inherited Cú Chulainn's warp spasm, you'd have been dead by now for sure. Curse it may be, but consider it a blessing that it's kept you alive this long."

I nodded, noticing again that Finnegas was looking a little thin. "I'm about to go find Fallyn. Can you hold down the fort while I'm gone?"

"Pfah. I was outsmarting the Celtic gods long before you were a dirty thought in your daddy's mind. Don't need you wet-nursing me. Worry about finding your girl instead."

"Got it. Tell Maureen to keep her phone close."

AFTER A TRIP to the Pack clubhouse—and getting yelled at by Mitzy for being a pest—Guerra told me where I could find his alpha. They'd had a break-in at the Pack's second clubhouse, a ranch that sat on land adjacent to their hunting grounds on the Balcones Canyonlands National Wildlife Refuge. According to Guerra, the evidence suggested that another Pack might be edging in on Samson's territory. Samson had taken the threat seriously, heading out there with Sledge and a few more 'thropes to investigate.

When I arrived at the ranch house, Sledge, Trina, and a few other 'thropes were picking through an assortment of smashed furniture, clothing, and household goods in the front yard. The place was a disaster area, with broken windows, claw marks on the exterior walls and porch columns, and the strong smell of urine everywhere. I didn't even have to cast a cantrip or shift to smell it, because the place reeked of wolf urine.

I noticed a lot of clenched jaws and tense shoulders among the 'thropes working through the detritus in the yard, so I made sure to approach slowly and with my eyes down. Trina acknowledged me first, so I walked toward her instead of Sledge. She was sorting clothing into boxes, discarding items that were shredded and torn beyond repair and keeping those items that were still serviceable.

"Trina," I said by way of greeting.

She tsked and ran a hand over her close-cropped hair as she exhaled heavily. "You come to help?"

"Sorry, but no. I'm looking for Samson. Is he around, or..." I let the question trail off.

"Or, should you even be bothering him at the moment?" she responded while keeping her eyes focused on her task. "Normally I'd say you should leave him alone, but you wouldn't be here unless it was important. What's up?"

"It's about Fallyn, but I'd rather discuss it with Samson."

Trina chuckled humorlessly. "Yeah, I heard she dumped you. Tough break."

"Huh? No! Er, I mean yeah, she sorta did. But..." I took a deep breath, gathering my wits before continuing. "How'd you hear about that?"

Trina frowned at me. "You kiddin'? Everyone in the Pack knows. Pack bonds, right? Anyway, she stopped by the clubhouse and we could tell something was different. So, we asked, and she told us."

"You don't think it's weird that she broke up with me all of a sudden? After sweating me for months?"

Trina shrugged. "Meh. No offense, but you're not really her

type. 'Thropes tend to stick with their own kind—wolves with wolves, bears with bears, snakes with snakes, that sort of thing. After she took up with you, we had a pool going on how long it would last."

I stared at her for a moment, pushing my luck and not caring. "That's cold."

"C'mon, you know how it goes. You might've been all 'hero of the hour' and shit after that dust-up with Sonny, but you're still the odd duck around here." She spread her arms, surveying the destruction around us. "Plus, when there's grunt work like this to do, you're never around."

"I just found out what happened here, Trina."

"See? That's exactly what I'm talking about. If you were involved in Pack business on a day to day basis, you'd have known about it hours ago. You only come around when you need something." She wadded up a pair of granny panties and threw them in a cardboard box. "No offense, but you're Pack by association only. Nobody really sees you as being one of us, and that's a fact."

I threw my hands up in the air. "I know that—"

Trina cut me off with a shake of her head. "Uh-uh, let me finish. You're a shifter, everybody knows that, but you're not a 'thrope. That automatically makes you an outcast. Add in how you've been banging the Alpha's daughter—when she wouldn't give any of us the time of day—and it's easy to see why you're not exactly the most popular motherfucker around. Sledge, me, and a few others might like you, but we're in the minority—and even we think you're weird as shit. So, don't get all offended if you're still getting the cold shoulder from the Pack."

Trina had a point, but I didn't want to admit it out loud. Officially I was a Pack member, but I'd never really been part of the Pack. Still, hearing it stung a little, because I'd been there for them when it mattered. I tongued a molar and counted to ten before answering. Meanwhile, Trina continued packing clothes into boxes.

"Anything else?" I asked, with only a slight bite of sarcasm in my voice.

"Nope. Samson's out in the woods tracking spoor and figuring out who did this. We all think it's wolves from a neighboring Pack trying to flex, but nobody can recognize any of the scents. Anyways, you'll find him out there—but I don't recommend sneaking up on him right now."

"Got it," I said, still smarting from her words. I was already heading for the trees when Trina called after me.

"No hard feelings, druid. But you needed to know where you stand."

Yeah, thanks.

Without another word, I headed into the woods to find Samson.

INSTEAD OF CATCHING up with the Alpha, he caught up with me. I was walking down a deer trail, not making any effort to be stealthy, when he dropped out of a tree behind me. I'd known he was near, but he'd still managed to remain hidden from me, which was impressive. Of course, he knew these woods much better than I did—but if I'd have been using my druid senses, it would've been no contest.

I turned to face him while keeping my eyes on his chest, which was awkward considering the circumstances. Samson just looked at me, armed crossed and naked as the day he was born. That meant he'd either recently shifted, or he'd been preparing to when I'd approached. Or, he didn't want any other scents on him while he was sorting out the various tracks and trails left by whoever had trashed the clubhouse.

Either way—*awkward.*

Finally, I gave up and turned my head away, blocking the view with my hand. "I've got some shorts in my Bag, if you need them."

The Alpha ignored my weak attempt at humor. "What are you doing out here, Colin? I know you're not here to help"—he raised his hands defensively—"and wipe that hurt look off your face, because we both know it's not your style. You only get involved when things get violent, but when there's actual work to do, you're generally nowhere to be found."

"Gee, thanks. First Trina, then you. What, is it 'shit on Colin day' or something?"

"Boo-fucking-hoo. Want to tell me why you're out here laying scent all over the trails I've been trying to decipher for the last four hours?"

I was tired of looking away, so I figured *fuck it* and looked him in the eye. According to what Fallyn had taught me about dealing with dominant wolves, so long as I looked away every three seconds or so, I should be fine. *Should* being the operative word.

"Fallyn broke up with me, and now I can't get a hold of her."

He actually rolled his eyes. "Holy shit. Isn't that what the plan was all along? Sounds like the problem just sorted itself out."

"Yeah, but..."

Samson chuckled. "I know this might seem like the end of the world to you, but from where I stand, it's a huge relief. This pack has more than two dozen male members, mostly wolves, and half that number in female 'thropes—and almost half of them are non-wolves or lesbians. So, when my daughter takes up with a druid with a serious identity complex, you can imagine it created some friction in the Pack."

"Hey, she's the one who pursued me. It's not like I chased after her or anything. Hell, she didn't even like me at first."

"That's not the point." He rubbed a hand over his mouth, exhaling in exasperation. "Look, kid, I like you, but you attract trouble like shit attracts flies. Add in that the Celtic gods want to shut you down, and you're a father's worst nightmare. Nothing personal, but hearing Fallyn broke up with you—well, it was music to my ears."

"Yeah, but I was supposed to break up with her—not the other way around."

"Like I said, sounds like the problem solved itself. Now, if you can just manage to stay away from her and the Pack until your little dust-up with the Celtic gods blows over—"

"Blows over? They're gods, Samson. Weren't you the one who was just telling me that they hold a serious grudge?"

"Not my problem. That's druid business. So, if you could just stay away for a while, and steer clear of Fallyn until you work things out, that'd make my life a hell of a lot easier."

I stared at him with my mouth agape—now *Samson* was the one acting strange. I'd figured for sure he'd be concerned about Fallyn's weird pivot regarding our relationship, because it really wasn't in her character. With Samson acting so nonchalant about the one-eighty his daughter had done, I was seriously starting to suspect foul play on a broad scale.

"Samson, Fallyn could be in danger. You realize that, right?"

He frowned, crossing his arms again. "Not if you're not around. So, why don't you get lost before you bring the Tuatha Dé Danann down on our fucking heads? I have enough on my hands right now, dealing with this incursion."

"But Fallyn—"

"But nothing!" he roared, his eyes turning pale blue as he glowered at me. His voice dropped to a near whisper, dripping with menace as he continued. "Now get your ass out of here, and let me protect my Pack."

I knew better than to argue with him when he was like this, especially if he was under a geas or some other form of mental enchantment. Dropping my eyes, I backed away, not wanting to risk turning my back on a dangerous predator like Samson when he was on edge. I kept him in sight as I backed off, until he shifted and bounded into the trees.

Fuck.

Once I was nearly back to the clubhouse and well away from Samson, I knelt and placed a hand on the pine needles and leaves of the forest floor. Slowing my breathing as I reached out with my druid senses, I probed the area for several acres around, searching for anything that might be amiss. Other than the werewolf spoor and wanton destruction of the property, I detected nothing out of order.

Frustrated but undeterred, I shifted my vision into the magical spectrum and headed back to the front yard and parking area. Casually, so as not to arouse suspicion, I examined the house and surroundings for evidence of magical tampering. At first, I sensed nothing out of place, but I soon noticed something weird about a print near the driveway.

It looked like a werewolf's rear paw, and a smaller one at that. However, there was something about the depth of the print that wasn't quite right. A print that size would belong to female werewolf, and therefore it should've been much shallower than it was. Looking at it in the magic spectrum did nothing to reveal whether it was a legit track or not, so I knelt down to see what my other senses told me.

The ground was hard and firm, indicating that whatever had made it was much heavier than it should have been. I cast a cantrip and leaned in, sniffing the track with druid magic and my enhanced sense of smell.

There.

On the surface, the track smelled like a werewolf. But underneath it there was another, fainter scent—one only someone with my combination of skills could detect. The track smelled of magic. Fae magic.

Although I couldn't pierce it, my other senses told me that the werewolf print had been an illusion—one that subtly altered the appearance of the larger, canine paw print that was actually there. After examining some claw marks and other evidence left from the attack, it became clear that this had all been a cleverly-staged distraction.

Shit. Something tells me things are about to get very, very interesting.

15

"What're we doing, bro?"

Hemi was sitting in the front passenger seat of my Gremlin, and not comfortably. Even with the seat pushed all the way back, his knees were pressed against the dash and glovebox, and he had to tilt the seat back to avoid contact with the headliner. In short, my big Maori friend was not a happy camper.

My hands gripped the steering wheel as I leaned forward, squinting as I scanned the mass of people hanging out at Pecan Grove in Zilker Park. I'd parked as close to Barton Creek as possible, ensuring I had a good view of park visitors heading down to hang out near the water or picnic in the sun. It was a popular hangout, and since it was a warm day, there were tons of people enjoying what fall in Austin had to offer.

Nothing.

"Shit," I said as I banged the steering wheel in frustration. I glanced over at my friend. "I told you, Fallyn is supposed to be here on a picnic date with her new boyfriend."

"Going full-on stalker, aye?" He frowned. "Not your style, mate."

I pulled out a pair of binoculars, knowing full-well it made me look like a creeper. Hopefully, with the obfuscation wards activated on the druid-mobile, nobody would notice.

"Like I said, I think she got glamoured."

Hemi scrunched his lips sideways and squinted at me. "Sure she didn't just find a better-looking bloke to shag?"

I huffed at him. "Seriously? C'mon, you know that's not like her. I mean, she worked me for months. Months, Hemi!"

"Happens to the best of us, bro. So she took you for a ride. No need to go wobbly over it." He stretched his hoodie up to cover his eyes and leaned his head back. "Wake me when you come to your senses."

"Thanks for the vote of confidence. Sheesh."

Hemi ignored me, obviously intent on taking a nap. I continued to scan the parking lot as new visitors arrived. A brand-new Jaguar sports coupe pulled in, a sleek silver dagger of a car with dark tinted windows and vanity plates that said "NVYGLR." It pulled into a space a row over, and a tall blond dude with blue eyes, chiseled features, and a $500 haircut got out. With his cream-colored, cable-knit sweater and designer jeans over suede chukkas, his whole look said, "I have a personal fashion stylist."

I watched as he walked around the back of the car to let his passenger out. Holding the door open, he extended a hand to assist his companion as she exited the vehicle. Sure enough, it was Fallyn.

"Son of a bitch."

Hemi pushed his hood back far enough to glance at me with one eye. "Finally realize you've gone bonkers?"

"Nope. Take a look—that's Fallyn and the fucker who glamoured her."

I pointed at the couple, who were now headed into the park. Fallyn had a wicker picnic basket slung over her arm, while her "date" carried a soft-sided cooler. The she-wolf had traded her standard motorcycle boots, tattered t-shirts, and faded jeans for a floral print sundress, a white denim jacket, and blue canvas slip-ons.

"You sure that's her, bro?" he asked, grabbing the binoculars off the dash. "Huh. That's her alright. Outfit threw me off."

"Now do you believe me? Fallyn would never dress like that, not in a million fucking years." I grabbed the binos back, staring at the couple as they strolled through the park. "And a picnic date—are you serious? That girl wouldn't be caught dead doing bougie shit like that. She's a burger and beer date, one hundred percent."

Hemi rubbed his moko. "Hmm... you might have a point. Don't know her that well, but it's weird."

"Hell yes, it's weird. No, 'weird' doesn't even begin to cover it. It's... insane, that's what it is. And I don't think this asshole just glamoured her—I think somehow he spelled the whole fucking Pack."

"Aw, c'mon, mate. Now you're grasping at straws. Who could glamour a whole werewolf pack?"

"Hemi, you grew up around gods and demigods."

He shook his head. "Not really. I spent some time around them, but Mum sent me away when I was just an anklebiter."

"Okay, but you know how dangerous the gods can be. I'm not aware of a single fae who could cast a spell that powerful—but a god? Admit it, dude, there's almost no limit to what some of them can do."

He stared across the park at Fallyn and her date. "I dunno. You could be wrong. See any magic on them?"

I'd already checked them in the magical spectrum and pulled up jack squat. "No. But that doesn't mean it's not there. It could just be that he's using a form of magic that I'm not familiar with, or he's hiding it somehow."

The big Maori sighed. "Or she's just keen on this bloke. More than you, I mean." I gave him a look that could peel paint, and he held his hands palms up. "Just saying, bro."

I tossed the binoculars on the dash. "Fuck it, I'm confronting them."

As I reached for the door handle, Hemi laid a hand on my arm. "Whoa. You sure about this? Could get ugly."

"You mean if I'm wrong and everyone else is right?"

"People get dumped all the time. And jealousy does make people do stupid things."

I hung my head. Was I the only person in the world who could see what was happening? "I'll be right back, alright? And I promise—I'm just going to talk to her, that's all."

"Sure, get some closure. If the plod shows up, I'll call Borovitz."

"I'm not going to get arrested, Hemi."

"Just saying."

AFTER SLAMMING THE CAR DOOR, I pushed my sleeves up and marched toward Fallyn and the man I saw as her seducer. I was fuming inside, and determined to do something about it. Not just because some asshat who dressed like an *Esquire* cover model had stolen my girl, but also because no one saw what was going on but me.

One wrong word, and I'm going to clobber this fucker.

I was about halfway across the park when I started thinking about how stupid this was going to look. If I walked right up on them, it would be apparent that I'd followed Fallyn here—and then I really would look like a stalker. And the more I looked at them, the way they talked, laughed, and stared at each other, I couldn't help but think that maybe Hemi and Samson had it right.

Maybe she did just get tired of me.

I stopped mid-stride.

Wait a second—is he doing it to me, too?

Suddenly, I was having a hard time separating what was real from what was in my head. Had Fallyn and I really been that serious? Or was that just my imagination? Was this guy an agent of the Tuath Dé like I'd first thought? What if he was just better-looking and more charming than me? The fucker definitely looked a whole lot richer, that was for sure.

Gah!

I hid behind a tree about fifty feet away, watching as they reclined on a picnic blanket with wine, cheese and pâté spread out before them. They sat facing one another and were wholly focused on their conversation. Fallyn raised her glass to take a sip, then *Esquire* boy said something funny and she laughed so hard she nearly spilled it.

Wait a minute—Fallyn hates wine.

None of this was making any sense, not a damned bit of it. Reality was warping itself around me—or rather, around the guy who was sitting with Fallyn. And while I still felt a twinge of doubt, the longer I thought about the facts and not how I felt, the fishier the whole damned thing smelled.

Only one way to find out, but I need an excuse—in case I really am just crazy with jealousy.

A quick glance around the park revealed what I needed. A couple of skinny white stoner kids were tossing a frisbee to their dog. The dog was fat little bull terrier mix, and by the way it ran sideways as it chased the frisbee, I was pretty sure it was stoned too.

I reached out, sensing the ebb and flow of the air around me. When the wind shifted toward Fallyn and her plus one, I gave it the barest nudge. Wonder of wonders, the frisbee flew past me and beaned Mr. Wonderful on the head.

Couldn't have planned that better.

"Got it!" I yelled as I ran out from behind the tree to retrieve the frisbee.

I ran up to the couple as Fallyn's date stood up with the errant flying disc in hand.

"Sorry, I believe that's ours—oh, hi, Fallyn." I looked back and forth between them, as if noticing them for the first time. "Fancy meeting you here, and... whoever this is."

Fallyn bounced to her feet, straightening her dress as if self-conscious of how she looked. The anxious look she stole wasn't directed at me, however, but at *Esquire* boy. I forced a smile on my face, but what I wanted to do was—

I blanked out.

"Colin, did you hear me?" Fallyn was snapping her fingers in front of my face. "This is my friend, Dermot. Dermot, this is Colin."

Dermot smiled warmly, extending his hand. "Ah, you must be the McCool boy I've heard so much about. A pleasure, I'm sure."

Boy? Who you calling—

As soon as I made eye contact with him, I blanked out again. When I came back to my senses, I was shaking hands with the chump.

Wait a minute, how'd I get here?

I let go of his hand like it was a live wire. When I touched him, I couldn't detect any magic per se, but this creepy, oily feeling came over me. Quite honestly, it gave me the willies.

"Dude, can we have our frisbee back?" I looked over my shoulder at the stoners and their dog, who was now giving me puppy dog eyes.

I waved them off. "I'll be right there, Slater. Cool your heels."

"Yeah, but the dog really wants his frisbee, man."

Dermot looked straight at them. "Give us a moment, will you boys?"

Their faces went blank, then the stoners nodded their agreement. "Oh, sure, man, take your time." They mumbled amongst themselves as they walked back to their spot. "He seems nice. But how'd that other dude know my name was Slater?"

I decided to keep my eyes on Fallyn, who was now leaning against Dermot and fawning all over him. "Hey, can I talk to you for a minute? Alone?"

"Oh, Colin. I knew you were going to do this. You're so— needy. That's why I broke up with you, honestly it is. I want someone who knows what he wants, someone I can depend on." She looked up at her date with a dopey smile, like he was her own personal savior. "And Dermot here is just what I was looking for, all long."

"Would you listen to yourself? This isn't you—you're not into silly, romantic shit like this, picnic dates and wine and crap. Hell, the only time I've ever seen you in a dress is when we went undercover in New Orleans. This guy has you glamoured, Fallyn. I need you to shake it off and come with me, right now."

"No, that can't be," she replied. "Dermot's wonderful, the perfect—"

The she-wolf tilted her head, squinting as if working out a difficult problem. I was starting to get through to her, finally.

"Ah, ah—we can't have that now," Dermot said. Her "date" snapped his fingers, and instantly Fallyn turned to stare at him with a dopey expression on her face.

I didn't dare look at Dermot again, because I was starting to figure out his trick. With my eyes on Fallyn, I kept track of him with my peripheral vision as I reached in my Bag for Dyrnwyn. From what I could tell, he was grinning ear to ear.

"I'll knock that smarmy grin off your face right now, motherfucker, and deal with the consequences later," I snarled.

"Look, darling," Dermot said with an amused laugh. "It appears our boy here is a sore loser. Well, we can easily fix that."

Dermot stepped in front of me. I shut my eyes until they were lowered, then opened them just enough to make sure I knew where he was.

My voice was a low growl as I responded to his taunt. "I'm warning you, Dermot. Let her go."

I had my hand around Dyrnwyn inside my Bag, and I was about to pull it out and cut this fucker down like the dog he was.

Just as I was about to strike, Fallyn stepped between us, preventing my attack. "Colin, you need to leave. Now."

"No way, not unless you're coming with me," I replied with steel in my voice.

"Oh, I think not," Dermot trilled. "The young lady will stay with me, and you can go. I'll deal with you directly, when the time is right."

He reached around Fallyn to snap his fingers in front of my face, and everything went white around me.

"COLIN. HEY, YOU IN THERE?"

I blinked a few times before things came into focus. Hemi was shaking me by the shoulders, his brow knitted with concern. From the looks of it, I was still standing in the same place, but Fallyn and Dermot had gone.

"What happened?" I asked.

"Dunno. Fell asleep. When I woke, you were standing here."

"How long?" I said, frantic.

"Maybe twenty minutes?"

"They could still be here. Hemi, we have to find them. I don't know what powers this guy has, but he's dangerous. And if something happens to Fallyn, I'll never forgive myself."

"Okay, okay. Relax, cuz—we'll find her." Hemi was a lot more nonchalant about the situation than he should've been. Just how extensive were Dermot's powers?

I looked around and saw the stoners with the dog. "Hey, did you guys see where those people went?"

"Who?" they said in unison, chuckling at the coincidence.

"The couple that was here. You know, the guy you hit with the frisbee?"

"Oh yeah, him. They packed up their stuff and left, man."

I ran over to him, grabbing him by his Baja hoodie and lifting him off the ground. The dog growled, and I growled back. It pissed itself and hid behind the other hippie's legs.

"Where. Did. They. Go?" I said between clenched teeth.

He pointed upstream, toward Barton Springs Pool. "Th-th-that way, man."

I set him down, gently, and took off in the direction he'd indicated. "Sorry about the dog. C'mon, Hemi."

"Yeah, yeah, I'm coming."

Soon the big Maori was plodding along beside me at a jog. His legs were longer so he didn't have to run as hard. "Guy zapped you, huh?"

"Yup."

"So, what're you going to do? If you find them, I mean. Get zapped again?"

I shook my head. "I can't face him, not until I get a handle on his magic. Might have to sneak up and shoot him with a cold iron bullet. It won't kill a god, but it might stun him for a second —long enough to get Fallyn away from him."

"If he's fae."

"I don't actually think he's fae, because I don't know of any fae who can cast a glamour that powerful so easily. I'm pretty sure he's either a Celtic god or a demigod."

"Think a bullet will hurt him?"

"You're a demigod, so you tell me."

Hemi clucked his tongue. "Our powers vary. Depends on who your parents were. Me? I'd rather not take a bullet. Hurts, and you have to dig it out before it'll heal."

I grabbed a fresh magazine from my Bag, palming it for the moment. "A cold iron bullet might not kill him outright, but I'm gambling that it'll ruin his day. The fae descend from the Tuatha Dé Danann, so they more or less have the same vulnerabilities."

The Maori warrior slammed a fist into his palm. "And if not? Beat down it is, then."

My eyes darted around as we passed Barton Springs Pool. Finally, I spotted a flash of Fallyn's dress, moving down the trail away from us. "There!"

We sprinted after them down the Barton Creek Greenbelt trail, past upper Barton Springs. The trail was packed with people jogging, hiking, and biking, all of them making the most of this warm and sunny fall day. The mass of bikers and pedestrians slowed us down considerably, but thankfully they thinned out about a half-mile down the trail. But no matter how fast we ran, it seemed that Fallyn and Dermot were always just around the next bend in the trail.

"This ain't right, bro. Think we're being had."

I glanced over at Hemi, who to his credit was staying neck and neck with me even though I'd already stealth-shifted. I wasn't running at full speed—too many people around. But I was doing my best Usain Bolt impression, that was for sure.

"It's them, Hemi."

"I know that," he huffed. "But it's a trap."

"Agreed. What choice do we have, though?"

My friend nodded once, and we ran on. We passed Campbell's Hole, a popular swimming spot, and there the trail forked. On instinct, I took the left fork down to the creek. Sure enough,

Fallyn and Dermot were disappearing into the woods on the other side.

I waved to catch Hemi's attention, then glanced around to see if any mundanes were around. Satisfied we were alone, I pulled my Glock and switched out the mag.

"Time to gear up," I said, "because I'm pretty sure once we go into those trees, it's going to get ugly."

Hemi hmphed, then began chanting under his breath. Most of his body was covered, but a faint glow at his wrists told me he'd activated his battle wards. He reached out, his hand disappearing for a second. When he pulled it back, he held a long polished wooden club with an axe-like head.

"Ready," he said with a nod.

All pretense aside, I leapt across the stream, moving at near-vampire speed. Hemi couldn't keep up with me when I moved like this, but I could scout ahead and be back at his side in seconds. I stopped in a small clearing, listening for movement.

There was plenty of it, in all directions. From what I could tell, whatever was out there was big, and there were at least four of them. I heard a loud, ominous growl, then five pony-sized cu sith jumped out of the trees at me.

"Contact!" I yelled as I emptied my magazine at the nearest black-furred, red-eyed monster.

16

Cu sith were giant, black, wolf-like canids bred and raised by the fae as guard dogs. They were often very intelligent, and some could be friendly, but it depended on their training and upbringing. Unfortunately, the unseelie fae loved using them for hunting humans. I'd killed a fair number of wild and rabid cu sith over the years, but never a pack of four at once. And never a pack made up of cu sith the size of Shire ponies.

The first one skidded to a halt at my feet after I placed eight rounds in its face in rapid-fire succession. My Glock 19 held fifteen rounds in the mag and one in the barrel, so that left me another eight rounds to even the odds. Rather than waste all eight rounds on a single cu sith, I decided to follow the advice of one of my firearms instructors.

When outnumbered, put a round in everyone who's a threat and see what happens.

I dove over the dead dog at my feet, coming up in a kneeling stance with my pistol in the Combat Axis Relock extended shooting position. CAR was a shooting system created for close-quarters gun fights, and the extended shooting position actually meant that the pistol was held high, closer to my face, and canted slightly. This allowed for quick sight picture acquisition and rapidly switching from target to target.

As I'd expected, the remaining dogs were close, within ten feet or so. I fired a shot into each, head shots all, then repeated the process. *Blam blam blam, blam blam blam!* The demon dog on my right took one in the eye, whining and batting at its face with one paw. Brain damage, for sure.

But the other two remained unfazed, continuing to rush me. Before I'd finished the second volley, the middle cu sith was leaping over its dead packmate, while the final one moved around to flank me. With two rounds left, I popped both off at the dog that was in midair, hitting it center mass. Then, as it tackled me, I grabbed it by the throat with one hand, using my other hand to punch it in the eye with the barrel of the pistol.

The dog had me pinned with its forepaws, claws digging into my chest. It snapped and slathered at me, but I managed to hold it away from my face as I continued to use the Glock like a set of brass knuckles. Despite my enhanced strength, I didn't seem to be doing much to deter it, and unless I held out until it died from blood loss, I was going to lose this fight.

I didn't think I'd last that long, though, since the fucker's buddy was growling from somewhere behind me. It was so close I could smell its fetid breath, which smelled like a mix of rotted meat and blood and dog shit. I was about to see the inside of a giant wolfhound's mouth, up close and personal.

Ah, fuck. I'm not even up to date on my tetanus shot.

Just before the damned thing bit my head off, Hemi came crashing out of the trees, yelling like a madman and swinging that war club like Babe Ruth. He smacked the cu sith that was about to use my skull for a chew toy upside the noggin, sending it rolling across the clearing. The Maori warrior glanced at me and I nodded, so he bounded after it with a look of wild, violent glee on his face.

My dog was temporarily distracted, so I took that opportunity to shove my pistol down its throat, leaving it there. The dog started hacking like a tiger coughing up a fur ball, backing up as if to escape whatever was choking it. I kicked the cu sith and sent it skidding, but somehow it managed to stay on its feet. Reaching into my Bag, I rummaged around for Dyrnwyn so I could cut this thing down and be done with it.

But I'd forgotten about dog number two.

I realized I hadn't done such a great job of killing that one when it latched onto my leg and shook me like a chew toy. That. Fucking. Hurt. I felt my hip pop out of socket, and figured I was about to lose the leg if I didn't do something fast.

Time to see what Finn's spell can do.

Pulling my hand out of my Bag, I shoved it in the dog's eyes and said the magic words. A ball of fire and lightning sprang into existence in front of my hand, and while I didn't have time to spool up a huge one, it didn't matter. At 28,000 degrees Celsius, the combined fire and lightning fried the cu sith's head like an egg in a microwave, and the resulting pressure caused its head to explode in a shower of bone, blood, and grey matter.

Unfortunately, much of that bone shrapnel ended up in my leg, along with some of the heat from the spell. I screamed in agony, but still kept my eyes open as I scanned for the final threat. Fifteen feet away, the final cu sith coughed up my gun in a pile of dog vomit and saliva, then it turned its eyes on me and bounded across the clearing.

Going to be hella fun to clean that.

It was either go for the sword or cast another spell. I didn't know if I'd have time to find the sword, so spell it was. I was still extending my hand as the words came out of my mouth, so my arm was down the cu sith's throat when I released the spell. The heat lightning exploded the cu sith's torso from the inside out, tossing blood and guts and dog shit and who knows what else everywhere.

When the bloody mist and smoke cleared, Hemi was standing about ten feet behind the dog's remains, wiping dog guts off his face. I had the cu sith's mouth and neck wrapped around my upper arm, and the damned thing was still gnawing on me, not yet realizing it was dead. My friend looked at me, and I at him as I ripped the lower jaw from the demon dog's skull.

"Fucking hell, mate. Next time, just throw a steak on the barbie."

A chuckling groan escaped my lips, then I passed out.

It would be nice to say that reality slowly faded back into existence. But actually, I came to my senses screaming in pain when Hemi popped my hip back into its socket.

"Motherfucker!"

"Watch it there, aye? Mum's not keen on that talk. And she looks in on me from time to time."

"Sorry," I replied through clenched teeth. "But fuck, man, give a guy a warning next time."

"Naw, bro. Best to fix it while you were out. Easier that way."

I glowered, nodding my acquiescence. "Thanks. Any sign of Fallyn and Dickface?"

"None. Illusion, ya' think?"

"Those cu sith sure in the hell weren't," I said. I grabbed onto a nearby tree, grunting as I pushed myself to my feet. "We'll have company soon. Help me put their remains in a pile so I can get rid of them."

We dragged the bodies together in silence. Hemi was still covered in guts, so I was pretty sure he was pissed at me. And as for me, I was focused on ignoring the pain in my hip and leg while my Fomorian DNA healed the injuries. My healing factor worked a lot slower in this form than when I was fully shifted, so it would be a while before I was back to my usual self.

Once we had the bulk of the carcasses and body parts in a pile, I reached out with my druid senses, coaxing the soil to swallow up the lot of it whole. I'd have preferred to burn it all to ash, but there were sirens in the distance so we were out of time. Gunshots weren't exactly a common occurrence in Zilker Park, so folks were bound to have noticed it when I'd emptied a full mag into those cu sith. I didn't want to draw the cops right to us with a big cloud of smoke, so it would have to do for now.

I pointed at the remains as they disappeared under the earth. "Druid magic tends to speed up natural processes, so the soil bacteria and insects will take care of the flesh. I'll come back later and get rid of the bones."

Hemi chuckled. "Or you could leave it. Some bloke or bird from the local uni would flip over this."

"Yeah, that's the last thing I need, to have Maeve up my ass over exposing a fae creature to the scientific community."

Shuddering at the thought of suffering a lecture from the faery queen, I cast a concealment spell over the burial spot. As an afterthought, I borrowed a little power from the Grove, using it to coax a thorny acacia bush to grow there as a final precaution.

"Neat trick, that," Hemi remarked drily. "Say, I thought you closed up Underhill. How d'ya think that drongo got 'em here?"

"I was wondering the exact same thing. Your guess is as good as mine."

The last time Hemi and I had seen a pack of cu sith had been on our excursion to Underhill. Single cu sith were a rarity earthside. The fae tended to keep them penned up so as to avoid unnecessary human deaths—that sort of thing tended to draw unwanted attention. Thus, to have a whole pack roaming around was a million-to-one occurrence.

"The cops will be here soon, Hemi. I'll tell the Oak to get us out of here."

"Forgetting something, mate?" he said, holding my pistol up by the tip of the barrel. "Be a shame for the plod to find that, aye?"

"Thanks." I grabbed it from him, shaking cu sith guts off it before tossing it in my Bag. "So, you still think I'm crazy?"

The Maori warrior rocked back on his heels. "Naw. Mixing it up with those pups cleared my noggin'. That bloke definitely used magic to mess with our heads."

"Agreed. The question is, how in the hell did he cast a glamour that influences everyone known to the spell's target? You hadn't even seen the guy, and you were affected by it."

"You too. Mebbe you ought to speak with Finnegas about it, aye?"

"I intend to. We're going to need a plan of attack for the next time we run into him." I chewed my thumbnail, letting Fionn's magical insight wash over me. "He definitely uses eye contact and line of sight to exert his powers. But there has to be some sort of trigger for the spell besides that."

"Could be anything, eh?"

"Let me ask you this—before I mentioned *her*, did you feel different at all?"

"Her? You mean..." Lights came on in Hemi's eyes. He might look big and dumb, but he was anything but the latter. "Yeah nah. Guess I did start getting muzzy about then. Dreamy and sleepy, sort of."

I snapped my fingers. "Bingo. Just to be safe, don't mention that name at all until I see you again."

"Again? Where you off to?" He crossed his arms over his

chest. "You'd best not ditch me when you give this bloke a hiding."

"Not to worry. So long as you don't mind mixing it up with the Celtic pantheon, that is."

"Piece of piss, mate."

"Okay then. Still, I don't think we should confront this shit-bird until I figure out a way to counteract his glamour."

"Eh, Maki might have a clue. I'll ask."

Someone shouted from the direction of the creek. "Stop, police!"

"Oops, that's our cue," I said with a snicker.

Hemi knew the drill by now, and he followed close on my heels as we ducked behind some trees. I called the Druid Oak to me, laying one hand on the rough surface of its trunk, and the other on my friend.

Take Hemi home. Then, I need to see Finnegas.

WHEN I ARRIVED at the junkyard, Finnegas was nowhere to be found. That wasn't unusual, as the old man had ways and means about him that he kept to himself. He could do a disappearing act like nobody's business, and I was pretty sure most of the Celtic pantheon were afraid of him—or, at least, they had a healthy respect for the old cuss. Still, it made me nervous that I didn't know where he was.

I was headed toward the office to find Maureen when I got flagged down by one of our shop hands.

"You look like shit, *Jefe*."

"Mountain biking accident, Jesus. Not as bad as it looks." His eyes narrowed, and I realized I probably should have changed before I'd gone looking for Finnegas. Lacking alternatives, I quickly changed the subject. "So, what'cha been up to?"

"Nothing, just school and here. Still working on that Supra. I'll bring it by when it's done, give that ugly old antique of yours a run for its money."

Due to a serious sport tuning addiction, Jesus was a whiz with electronics and computers. He'd started out working the yard, pulling parts like any other wrench monkey. But once my uncle had learned about his knack for electronics and computer systems, he'd brought him into the shop. Not surprisingly, Jesus held old-school hot rods in contempt, and he was always razzing me about my Gremlin.

"We'll see about that. Anyway, what can I do for you?"

"La Roja said if you were looking for her, to remember your training. No idea what she meant. She's fine as hell, but a little weird, ya' know?"

"She is at that. Guess I'd better go find her. Thanks, Jesus." I spun on heel and headed back to the Oak at a jog.

He hollered after me. "You keep leaving that Gremlin around, I'm gonna' swap that engine out. Drop in something with fuel injection and a chip. Then maybe you'll have a chance against the Supra!"

I laughed and hollered over my shoulder. "You touch my car and I'll have you degreasing engine blocks for weeks, Jesus."

"You're joking, right? Because I might have set aside a turbo four from a totaled Raptor."

"Don't even think about it!" I yelled, just before I ducked around a stack of crushed cars.

Knowing I had little time to waste, I sprinted to the clearing where the Oak normally resided. Moments later, I was in the courtyard behind Eire Imports.

The back door was locked, but I still had a key. I walked inside and found Maureen in the office, cleaning, oiling, and sharpening a variety of weapons and armor spread across an oilcloth that covered the desk. The collection included swords, daggers, throwing knives, a mace, a small buckler, some fine chainmail armor, and a crossbow.

But what really caught my eye was the saber in her hands. It had a basket hilt decorated in fine filigree, mated to a long, slender blade with a slight curve and sharpened one-third of the way from the tip along the back. The sword was definitely of fae make, as the handle was well-worn, yet the blade was mirror-polished and free from any blemish, scratch, or nick.

"Wow, Maureen—you preparing to storm a castle?"

"After all the shite you've kicked up, it might come down ta' that." She smirked, keeping her eyes on the blade. Her nose twitched as she caught wind of me, then she wrinkled her nose in disgust. "Oh, boyo—what in Lugh's name have ya' been in? Ya' smell like last week's beans."

"Cu sith. Pack of 'em jumped me and Hemi."

She set the sword down on the desk very, very carefully. "There hasn't been a cu sith sighting in Maeve's demesne fer some time now."

"Right, because we hunted all the wild ones down or chased them away. And since I locked all the gates to Underhill, there haven't been any new arrivals. Whoever sent them after us must have a lot of juice, to portal four fully-grown cu sith from Underhill to Earth."

She gave me a knowing look. "Yer' playin' in the big leagues now, Colin. And whoever's after ya', they'll be playin' fer keeps."

"Speaking of which, I was looking for Finnegas. I needed to ask him about this guy I saw with, er..."

"Fallyn? This is the bloke who stole yer lass?" Maureen's eyes hazed over as she slumped into a nearby chair. "Feckin' hell, but I feel jaded all o' sudden."

I winced, knowing that the mention of Fallyn's name would likely trigger Dermot's spell. A cloud of confusion descended over my thoughts, like a layer of gossamer-thin spider silk.

Before my mind could fuzz over completely, I made a conscious effort to shake the spell off. Instantly my head cleared, but I doubted Maureen was even aware she'd been glamoured.

"Yes, Maureen—and he's our Tuath Dé agent. He's been holding her hostage with some sort of love spell. Not only that, but he's glamoured everyone who knows her so they don't suspect anything is amiss."

"C'mon now, lad. Just because some fella' nabbed yer girl, it doesn't mean he's workin' fer the gods."

Damn it.

"Maureen, think! We've been dating seriously for weeks, and before that, she worked me for months while things were up in the air with Belladonna. You know her—no way would she just up and dump me for some random guy."

The half-kelpie pinched the bridge of her nose, obviously struggling to reconcile what she remembered with what Dermot's spell was telling her to believe. "I—that doesn't make sense."

"Think it through. She isn't the flighty type. You're just feeling the effects of the spell Dermot cast to abduct her."

Maureen stared at me intently, brow furrowed even though her eyes were still glazed over. With some effort, she stuttered out a few words in old Gaelic, words of power. She repeated those words, stronger the second time, and with even more conviction the third time round. Suddenly, it was like a cloud lifted and she was herself again. She leapt to her feet, slamming her fist on the desk.

"Gods damn it! This chancer's cast a foul spell, lad—the darkest sort o' enchantment. Strong magic, too. If he's not a god, I'd say he's borrowed a bit of a god's power." Her expression darkened. "Yer lass is in it deep, boyo."

"I know, Maureen. That's why I need to find Finnegas."

17

Minutes later, I was standing in the warehouse bathroom in my boxers while Maureen tended to my remaining wounds. She'd insisted I clean up before going after Dermot and Fallyn, saying that I was likely to get arrested if I went out in my current state. The half-kelpie pulled a strip of gauze tight around my leg, tying it off securely as she spoke.

"I'm sorry, lad, but I've no way ta' get hold o' the Seer. As ya' know, the old man's a right dodgy sort when he has ta' be. So fer now, yer' on yer own."

I glanced at Maureen in the mirror as I wiped a bit of dried cu sith goo from my forehead. "I don't suppose you'd have any suggestions on how to fight a glamour or charm spell cast by a Celtic god?"

"None, sadly. I've some natural resistance to it, being half-fae. As Hemi does, I suspect. You were able ta' shake it just now —perhaps ya' can do it again, now that you're aware of what this wanker's doin'."

"I don't know, Maureen. All he had to do was look me in the eye, or snap his fingers in front of my face, and I was under his spell. It took a supreme act of will to fight it, and by the time I broke free, they were gone."

Maureen crossed her arms as she leaned against the bathroom doorframe. "Sounds like it's line o' sight. So, ya' need ta' find a way ta' see the maggot without lookin' at him."

My phone rang for the fifteenth time that day. I checked it, just to be certain it wasn't Fallyn, but it was Mendoza again. I knew it was him because the caller ID was completely blocked, name and number both. Out of frustration, I put it on speaker and answered.

"Damn it, Mendoza, I already said I'm not interested."

Silence for one beat, then another. "Rumor has it you're in a bit of a bind right now. Something about a girlfriend, and a mysterious stranger?"

I looked at Maureen, who was shaking her head emphatically. "It's nothing, Agent Mendoza. Just a sudden break-up, is all."

"Colin, we've had you under surveillance since Big Bend, and her as well. There's obviously something weird going on, for the—er, subject—to drop you like a hot potato. Every agent I've put on her lately ends up going MIA and losing a few hours of memory. Any idea why that is?"

"Wait a minute—you figured out the name thing?" I asked, seriously curious.

"Our HQ has some pretty powerful anti-magic protection on it. Techno-magic, I believe you'd call it. Our experts noticed the defenses going haywire every time we mentioned the subject's name. Wasn't much of a leap from there to determine that she's the focal point for a powerful charm spell."

I tsked. "Agent Mendoza, I thought you were supposed to be relatively clueless about magic."

"Compared to people like you, McCool, we are. But we've learned through trial and error how to protect ourselves—

despite being forced to work with second-rate SMEs on the matter." He paused and exhaled heavily. "So, are you ready to cut a deal? Your expertise for our help?"

I glanced at Maureen, who shrugged. "Honestly, Agent Mendoza, even I'm out of my depth here. I'd hate to bring your people into it, and be responsible for their safety."

He chuckled humorlessly. "Son, every single one of my people knows what they signed up for. Most of them have had brushes with the supernatural, many have lost family members or loved ones, and all of them realize they are expendable. In the eyes of Cerberus, supernatural creatures are the greatest existential threat to the United States of America since Communism, and my agents are willing to do what it takes to fight that threat."

Maureen rolled her eyes and flipped the bird at the phone.

Personally, I didn't know what to say to that. Mendoza had basically admitted that he and his superiors were scared shitless about the World Beneath. And, by extension, me.

Did I really want to get in bed with this outfit? What was going to happen after they got what they needed from me? Would they decide I was too much of a liability to keep around —a threat to their continued existence? No, I wasn't quite desperate enough to make a deal with this particular devil. Not yet.

"I'm not your man, Mendoza. Don't call me, I'll call you." *Click.*

I turned off the phone and smashed it underfoot. Then, I pulled the battery out, tossed the rest in a metal trash can, and fried it with a bit of static electricity. My Bag held about a dozen burner phones, so it was no great loss—one of the perks of being the Druid Justiciar.

Maureen frowned. "Couldn't ya' just switch out the card thingy? Money doesn't grow on trees, ya' know."

"Too risky. For all I know, they'd already planted a stealth-ware packet on it. They've probably been listening to all my calls for days now. Bad enough to have the fae trying to eavesdrop on me without having Cerberus listening in as well."

"So, boyo—what's yer plan?"

I wiped off the worst of the dirt and blood with a wet rag before pulling a clean t-shirt on—one of many I kept in my Bag for such occasions. "What you said about line of sight, were you sure about that?"

"Sure as I can be. Plenty o' fae require it ta' cast their glamours."

"Good, because something Mendoza said gave me an idea." I slipped into a clean pair of jeans and sat on the toilet to pull on my boots. "I know someone who can locate F"—I winced at the slip-up, biting my lip—"I mean *her*, if I can get him what he needs to cast a tracking spell."

"Yer' callin' Crowley, then," she said, giving me a hard look. Maureen still saw the wizard as a plant, a double-agent who was likely working for his mother, the evil Tuatha sorceress known as Fuamnach. The half-kelpie knew the fae well, and to her there was no amount of subterfuge or deception that was beneath them.

"I am. The guy hasn't let me down yet."

"Aye, lad. But give him time and he will, just as sure as my mam was a waterhorse."

CROWLEY'S PLACE was on the outskirts of town, and for the most part, he rarely left the grounds. Since he'd betrayed his evil faery stepmother while helping us rescue a bunch of abducted kids from Underhill, she'd been sending assassins to capture her adopted son. From what I'd gathered, she wanted to bring him back to Underhill so she could brainwash him again.

Mother of the year, right?

Once you knew the backstory, it made sense. She'd abducted Crowley from his human parents when he was a very young boy. Then, she'd wiped his memory with mind magic and used him as her own personal slave and whipping boy until he was old enough to be of greater use. About the time he'd hit puberty, Fuamnach had experimented on him using who knows what kind of sorcery, turning him into her own personal magical hitman and lackey.

The ironic thing was, she'd trained him a little too good. Crowley might have been a young wizard, but from what I'd seen, he was a match for practitioners who had centuries of training. Thus far, I didn't think Fuamnach's flunkies had even managed to scratch the paint on his wards, never mind getting close enough to attack the guy.

And honestly, I think he kept himself sequestered on his farm more out of personal preference than a desire to avoid a fight. He didn't seem to see his adopted mother's efforts as more than a minor annoyance, which must've really burned her britches. Crowley might have been more of a frenemy to me than friend, but I had to admit I admired the hell out of his style.

When I pulled up to his place, I noted that the illusions that had previously obscured the empty farmhouse, burned-down barn, and formerly wrecked grain silo were gone. Crowley was standing in the middle of his driveway, staring up at the converted silo that served as his wizard's tower, rubbing his chin as if pondering the great questions of our age.

I parked my car in front of the farmhouse and sauntered over to stand next to him. The guy looked like a young Jeff Gold-blum—with dark and curly hair, a lean muscular frame, and olive skin. Except for some faint scarring on one side of his face and hands, he appeared to have completely recovered from our first encounter. On that occasion, he'd tried to use Balor's Eye against me and failed miserably. Although he was self-conscious about the scars, rather than detract from his good looks they merely added a roguish factor he'd previously lacked.

The young wizard ignored me—not unusual for someone who'd learned their manners in Underhill. I stared up at the tower, trying to figure out what he was searching for up there. After a few minutes, I got bored and broke the silence.

"Um, what are we looking for?"

He scowled slightly, not at me but at the problem he faced. "I'm trying to decide on a color for the window shutters. It's very industrial-looking, so I thought some shutters would make the place feel more like a home."

I stifled the urge to blurt out the reason why I'd come. Even though I had an urgent mission, you couldn't rush Crowley. He was going to do things in his own time, and when he was on a roll, you kind of had to let it run its course.

Tilting my head, I framed one of the windows in my outstretched hands. "Does look kind of plain, now that you mention it. Kind of like a big silver dildo pointing up at the sky. Not very homey at all. But do you really think some shutters are going to remedy that sitch'?"

"Yes, it is rather phallic," he said, ignoring my question. "At the moment, I'm torn between Tudor Brown"—he waved a hand absently and a set of illusory shutters appeared at every window —"and Deep Forest Green."

Another wave of his hand changed the color of the shades yet again. "I'd go with the green," I offered.

He squinted at the tower for a moment before clucking his tongue. "It is the obvious choice. If I go with the brown, it'll merely look like a great big silver phallus, post-anal coitus. Rather tawdry. No, it simply won't do."

I would've laughed if the situation hadn't been so dire. "Great. Um, now that we've settled that..."

He cut in with a chop of his hand. "Say no more. I've already cast a tracking spell to locate your canine paramour, or at least her last known location as of an hour ago. I ran into quite a bit of interference, which obviously means that the person who abducted her is making it difficult for you to find them. But the fact that I could complete the spell would indicate he is merely playing hard to get."

I scratched my head. "How'd you know what I came here for?"

"Let's see..." he said, counting off on his fingers. "First, your skills at augury are dismal at best. Second, despite our mutual respect, neither of us can stand the company of the other for longer than is necessary to accomplish the odd shared goal or task. And finally, earlier today, I detected a mass glamour spell, of which I determined that your current concubine was the focal point."

"Wait a minute—were you keeping tabs on her?"

Crowley gave me his patented "are you really that dense?" look. "Hardly. I noticed the enchantment when her name came up in casual conversation. As soon as I felt the tendrils of the spell settling in the recesses of my mind, I knew what was going on."

"And how were you not affected? This guy is throwing around some serious, god-level mojo. Even Maureen felt the effects of his spell."

Crowley gave the slightest of eye rolls. "I was raised around the Celtic gods. Fuamnach taught me defenses against such magics at an early age."

"Anything you care to share? I could use some help in fighting this guy's glamour."

"No offense, but currently you lack the magical aptitude to

master such spells. If we had several months to practice, perhaps..."

I knew what Crowley was getting at, and there was no way I was letting him inside the Druid Grove. You didn't just give a wizard like Crowley access to the source of your power. I liked him, but when it came to magical power, he was like a recovering crack addict in a drug dispensary. No matter how much he wanted to resist, he simply couldn't help but pocket some of the goods.

"Uh-uh, nope. Not gonna happen."

He smiled like a kid caught with his hand in the cookie jar. "It was worth a try. You'll find your female friend at McKinney Falls State Park. Or, at least, she was there an hour ago."

"Thanks, Crowley," I said, already heading to my car.

"It's the least I could do," he hollered after me, cupping his hands to his mouth. "To keep you from reconciling with Belladonna, I mean."

"Yeah, I know," I yelled back as I hopped in the Gremlin and cranked the engine over.

Just to be an asshole, I fishtailed through a U-turn, kicking up gravel and a cloud of dust that enveloped the entire driveway and Crowley as well. Chuckling, I kept my eyes on the rearview mirror so I could see how he reacted. The dust cloud parted around the wizard, just as a rock pinged off my windshield. By the time my tires hit county pavement, I had a spiderweb crack covering half my windshield.

Oh, you fucking douche.

That was one good thing about Crowley—we always knew where we stood with each other.

———

McKINNEY FALLS WAS A REALLY cool and very popular state park located in the heart of Southeast Austin. Home to the oldest bald cypress tree in the state, as well as one of the most popular swimming holes in town, the park was typically overrun with locals and tourists alike. It was definitely not the place to get into a supernatural showdown with a Celtic god. Too many witnesses—and way too many opportunities for collateral damage.

Why Dermot had brought Fallyn there was anyone's guess. He had to know that I'd be tracking them, and that eventually I'd manage to catch up with them again. If I had to take a stab at his motives, I'd say he was taunting me by cavorting all over the city while she was under his spell.

Quite obviously, it was another trap.

If I found them, there'd be a ton of people around, and if I didn't, I'd be back to square one. Either way I was fucked, but I felt I had little choice but to pursue Fallyn and her abductor and hope for the best. Now that I was aware of his glamour, my intention was to attack him in order to interrupt the spell so Fallyn could break free. She was incredibly headstrong, and I couldn't help but think that she was fighting his control over her with every last bit of willpower she possessed.

I drove around the park looking for Dermot's prick-mobile, finally finding it in the Onion Creek Trail parking lot. The trail ran the circumference of the park, so he and Fallyn could be anywhere—but I had a feeling that Dermot would make it easy for me to find him. He wanted me to see them together, and to know there was nothing I could do about it. This whole charade was all about humiliating me and putting me in my place by taking away the things I loved.

Then, when I was completely broken, they'd either end my life or let me wallow in my misery. The folklore was full of stories like that, tales of heroes and demigods who crossed the gods and were then punished to a completely asymmetrical extent out of sheer spite. I could kick myself for letting Fallyn get caught up in it, but what was done was done.

Now, it was up to me to make Dermot pay, and the gods behind him as well. I parked my car and reached into the glove box, grabbing a pair of polarized wayfarers. Dermot's magic worked by sight, which meant it was carried by electromagnetic waves. Polarized sunglasses filtered out light waves, and I was pretty sure that with a bit of warding, these shades would diminish the effects of his magic considerably.

I grabbed a magic marker and drew a couple of runes on the lenses, then spoke a simple phrase to activate the magic.

"*Cloigeann a ghlanadh.*"

I doubted that my Gaelic was spot on, but it was the intention and will that mattered in magic, not the methods one used to focus it. The runes on the glasses would block my field of vision somewhat, but at least I wouldn't turn into a total space case when I saw Dermot. Once I was satisfied with my handiwork, I stealth-shifted and headed down the trail toward the Upper Falls.

Upon arriving at the falls, I spotted them immediately. Fallyn stood at the water's edge on the opposite side of the creek, blankfaced, with Dermot behind her, his hands on her shoulders. People all around were ignoring the couple, despite how creepy the two of them looked. I had no doubt they'd been standing in that exact spot for some time, waiting for me to arrive.

Dermot spotted me at the same time I noticed them. I clenched my fists as he leered at me, gloating and clearly enjoying my anger. Placing a hand on each side of her face, he turned Fallyn's head so she was staring right at me. Fallyn's abductor whispered in her ear while keeping his eyes on me. Despite the background noise made by the running water and swimmers, I heard every word he said.

"Look, here comes your rescuer. See how dashing and fearless he is, love! Oh, what a sight fer sore eyes he must be right now. And he's figured out a way ta' protect himself from my talents. Tsk, tsk... now this is certain to end in blood."

"If you touch her," I snarled in a low voice, "I'll fucking rip you to shreds."

"Oh, we've done plenty of touching, no doubt. But don't you worry, MacCumhaill—I'd never sheathe my spear in a she-wolf's backside."

I ignored the jibe, trying to catch his captive's attention. "Fallyn, just hang on, and do what you can to resist. I'm coming for you, I promise."

A tiny bit of recognition crept into her eyes, although it took several seconds before she recognized me. Fallyn attempted to speak, but all she could do was stutter and drool. Her eyes filled with tears, and she cried out in frustration and rage through the Pack bonds. That cry brought me to my knees.

It was a cry for help.

18

I wanted to leap across the water and attack the prick, but I didn't have the benefit of his glamour to distract the crowd. All I needed was to have video of me jumping thirty feet and running at vampire speed plastered all over social media. So, I did the next best thing: I ran across the edge of the falls, leaping from rock to rock until I reached the stony plateau beyond.

As I ran, I was forced to take my eyes off Dermot and Fallyn while navigating my way across. It was no more than a distance of forty feet, but they were gone when I reached the other side. There was no path on this side of the creek, so they'd either headed downstream toward the lower falls or to the public golf course above the creek.

My guess was that Dermot wanted as many people around as possible. Obviously, he wasn't ready to face me yet, and his intentions were to draw out my suffering—and Fallyn's—for as long as he could. Whether it was due to sheer cruelty, or because he was under orders to do so, I had no idea. Clearly, he was avoiding a showdown, which meant he'd take her to a public place.

Golf course.

There was a deer trail that led up the creek bed, and I headed for it at as quickly as possible without drawing attention. Their tracks were evident in the dry, soft clay along the path, so I had to assume that Dermot wanted to be followed.

Another trap. Why not.

How he moved so fast with her in her current state was a mystery to me, but they'd traveled at least fifty yards in the blink of an eye. I had to wonder, was he portaling to stay ahead of me? If so, he was a lot more powerful than I'd initially suspected.

Sure, the super-glamour thing was a dead giveaway that this prick wasn't your run-of-the-mill demigod. But if he could portal... that was flirting with deity-level power. The only entities I'd seen who could cast portals at will were gods, or close to it. Maeve, The Dark Druid, Click, Lugh, and so on. Finnegas could do it too, but it took a hell of a lot out of him these days.

The more I thought about it, the more I worried that I wouldn't be able to save Fallyn—not alone, anyway. Chastising myself, I pushed those thoughts from my mind, putting on superhuman speed in an effort to catch up to them as quickly as possible. I zipped out of the woods and onto the fairway, casting left and right for some sign of her.

There.

She and Dermot were zipping across the golf course in an electric golf cart, which certainly traveled a lot faster than someone could on foot. But it was nowhere near fast enough to get away from me in my partially-shifted form. I could hit fifty miles an hour easily in this state, and more when I had fully shifted.

Either Dermot was fucking with me again, or he wanted to be caught. I was betting on the former rather than the latter, but I dashed across the greens toward them just the same. They were well ahead of me, but I rapidly gained ground on the cart.

Within seconds, I'd almost reached them, just as they passed a rather large water hazard.

Dermot looked over his shoulder at me with a wicked grin on his lips. "Sorry, druid, but ye've not yet earned the right ta' challenge me in battle. Pass this test, and there'll be just one more hurdle ta' leap before I allow ya' ta' fight me for the bitch's freedom."

He snapped his fingers, and directly ahead of the cart, a large clear oval appeared in midair, framing a scene both familiar and unknown to me. On the other side was a nearly-empty parking garage, complete with oil-stained concrete and painted parking berths running along either side.

"You son of a bitch—I'm going to fucking kill you!"

He winked at me. "Doubtful, and I've been dead before. So, that's hardly a threat from where I'm sitting. See ya' soon, druid."

I put on a burst of speed, reaching desperately for the cart as it sped through the portal. My fingertips barely brushed the rack on the back of the cart, but I was just short of gaining purchase. The portal was already winking shut, and although I was sorely tempted, I doubted I could make it through without losing about two feet in height the hard way.

I skidded to a stop, snatching my lead leg and arm back. As the portal closed, it severed the tip of my middle finger and about half an inch off the toe of my boot.

"Shit!" I yelled at the sky. "Mother-fucking ever-loving cock-sucking Celtic wannabe god assholes!"

Leaning forward, I placed my hands on my knees, more in frustration than due to exhaustion. Blood dripped down my jeans from my severed finger, but I didn't even care. All I could think about was the tortured look in Fallyn's eyes, and the feeling of sheer despair that had come over me through the Pack bonds.

I rarely felt such messages, since I was not truly a 'thrope and for all practical purposes a Pack member in name only. Maybe it was because we'd been in close proximity, but I couldn't help but think that desperation had amplified her mental cry for assistance.

And I'd failed her.

A racking sob escaped my lips. I knew that crying wasn't going to do anyone any good, especially not Fallyn, so I took a couple of deep breaths to gather myself. Just as I was about to head back to my car, a chittering, feral voice spoke up from behind me.

"Aw now, don't cry. It'll all be over shortly, lad. And I promise —when I'm done, ya' won't feel a thing."

I SPUN IN A CROUCH, nearly doing a double-take as I identified the speaker. I'd seen some weird shit in my time, but this was a new one to me. The thing facing me was roughly humanoid, about five-and-a-half feet tall with a thick neck, webbed, clawed hands, and the round, cherubic face of a stuffed animal. It stood about waist-deep in the pond, shedding water in rivulets from the short, sleek, brown fur that covered most of its body.

Muscles bulged underneath its furry skin across its short arms, thick shoulders, and round stomach, yet it lacked the V-shaped torso common to most 'thropes when in their hybrid, half-human form. If I had to describe it, the thing was shaped more like a torpedo than a man. Beady, dark-brown eyes stared at me beneath a backward-sloping brow, and its whiskers twitched as it scented the air with a wide leathery nose.

"What are you?" I asked, honestly curious to know what the hell I was looking at.

"Yer death, lad—an' that's a fact."

In the blink of an eye he was on me, biting, scratching, and clawing as we tumbled onto the sloping, muddy bank of the pond. The were-thing moved faster than any 'thrope I'd ever seen, and faster than most vamps as well. I attempted to grapple with it, but it was like wrestling greased quicksilver. Each time I grasped at a limb or tried to wrap my arms around its body, the creature would slip free. Then it'd be gone, attacking me from another angle before I even had time to process the previous failed counter.

Within seconds, I stumbled and fell, having nearly been hamstrung by the creature on its third pass. I bled from a dozen wounds, and hadn't even managed to land a single solid blow. The thing slunk on all fours just out of reach, stalking me in circles as it spewed insults at me.

"This is hardly sporting. I was told you were a tough one, that you'd put up a fight. Wrong they were, so very wrong. Yer' weak, like the rest o' yer ilk. Won't be long 'afore I'm feastin' on yer flesh in yon' pond o'er there."

I looked around us while keeping him well within my peripheral vision, hands clamped on my ruined thigh. "Lots of spectators here today. Aren't you worried about ending up on the news?"

"Don'cha worry about them, lad. Thanks ta' Dermot's magic, we're not even here as far as they're concerned." He licked his lips with a short pink tongue that was well-matched to his Beanie Baby face. "Yes, there's plenty o' time fer me ta' play with my food, that's fer certain. Plenty o' time."

The way he'd chewed up my leg, there was no way it was going to heal in time for me to beat him hand-to-hand. And if I could, it was clear that even with near-vampire speed and strength, I was no match for this character—at least, not without a way to slow him down. That meant it was time to pull out the magic.

I drew on some of the Oak's power, leaning on our bond to

magnify my innate druid powers. Resting my hand on the ground, I ignored the wet, sticky blood between my fingers and focused on controlling the grass beneath the weird were's feet. As I pushed my magic and intentions through the soil and toward my opponent, blades of Bermuda grass thickened and lengthened, grabbing onto his ankles and anchoring his webbed feet to the turf.

The 'thrope smiled, displaying a neat row of tiny, sharp, bloody incisors lining the top and bottom of his mouth, framed by some rather nasty-looking canines. His odd little pink tongue darted out to lick his lips again, then he leaned down and severed the grass vines with a deft swipe of his claws.

"Good try, but yer' gonna hafta' do better'n that ta' nab the Otter King, drood."

Ah, he's a were-otter. At least it explains the speed.

With a growl I poured more magic into the soil, coaxing the grass to attack the were-otter's feet and legs. Much to my frustration, the damned thing was way too quick for me to catch. After a minute or so, all I had to show for my efforts was a spilled pint of my own blood and several patches of exceptionally long, lush grass scattered around the pond.

The pond—of course.

Changing tactics, I fired up the old hand cannons and shot several fireballs at the thing. If there was one thing water fae hated, it was fire. Even if I couldn't hit him, I could certainly get a reaction—and that might be enough. As expected, I wasn't quite fast enough to nail him with a fireball, but that didn't matter.

"Lad, d'ya' think yer' the first person ta' lob fire at me?" he taunted as he zig-zagged around the pond. "Dodging these things is child's play—I could do this all day!"

Smirking, I queued up my next surprise. "Sure, you can dodge one at a time... but what about a wall of fire?"

I spread my fingers wide, extending both hands toward the were-otter. Gouts of fire shot from my fingertips, fanning out in broad arcs that covered most of the ground between me and the pond. As I'd suspected, his legs weren't long enough to jump over the flames. Instead, he backpedaled into the water, sinking beneath the surface.

When the flames died out, his head popped out again.

"Come now, ya' don't think such tricks are gonna stop me, do ya'? Why don't we stop all this nonsense and end this game, 'afore ya' embarrass yerself some more?"

"Yes, let's," I whispered, reaching out until my druid senses were in contact with the entire pond.

DRUID MAGIC WASN'T NEARLY AS flashy or fast as other forms of spell work. But what we lacked in speed, we made up for in efficacy. Druids formed fireballs by concentrating the ambient heat in the air and compressing heated gas molecules into a very small space. Once they ignited, you simply used your will to send them toward your intended target.

Creating ice was much easier, because water molecules were closer together so it took less effort to pull the heat out. I drew all the heat energy from the pond with a thought, shooting it out of my left hand in a geyser of flame twenty feet tall. Instantly, the pond water crystallized into a tight matrix of ice crystals, solidifying the pond—and my foe—into one huge were-popsicle.

Were-creatures were incredibly hardy, and this one was no exception. Otters were quite comfortable swimming in freezing waters that would send the average human into hypothermia in minutes. For that reason, I didn't expect my spell to kill the Otter King, but that wasn't the point. I just wanted to slow him down so I could cut his ever-loving motherfucking head off.

Reaching into my Craneskin Bag, I slid Dyrnwyn out as I limped down the bank and onto the now frozen pond. The sword could be finicky when it came to who I chose to attack, and sometimes it would refuse to light up if the person or creature I intended to kill wasn't truly evil. It blazed into flames as soon as I stepped onto the ice, which told me in no uncertain terms that the creature I'd captured possessed the blackest of hearts.

The Otter King's eyes widened as the sword lit up from hilt to tip with pure white fire. "Now, now, lad—let's not do anythin' rash. I'm sure we can come to some accommodation here."

With each step I reopened the slowly-healing wound on my leg. Warm blood ran down my right leg, pooling in my boot. I stopped a few feet away, taking care to keep the sword away from the ice. The last thing I needed was to let this thing loose, because there was no way I was going to fight it in this condition.

The were-otter had done a number on me, and upon reflection, I was lucky that he'd been overconfident. If he'd wanted to end it quick, he'd have killed me. Or my Hyde-side would be picking his teeth with otter bones—take your pick.

I knelt down on my uninjured leg, holding the tip of the blazing hot sword a few inches from the otter's eyes. He winced away, shutting his eyes to avoid the bright light and heat emanating from Dyrnwyn.

"First off, between the portal and all the bleeding, I just ruined a perfectly good pair of boots. I might've gotten the toe repaired, but once you fill these things with blood, there's no cleaning them, because it soaks into the lining. No matter how much you disinfect them, they stink to high heaven every time you put them on." I wiggled my toes inside the boot, feeling the congealing blood squish between them. "Fucking shame."

"I can get you new boots—finest otter skin ya' can imagine.

Keep yer feet warm and dry in driving snow or freezin' rain," he countered.

"Otter skin? Seriously?" I said as I rubbed the side of my face, instantly regretting it upon realizing I'd just wiped blood all over my cheek. "Isn't that sort of, I don't know —cannibalistic?"

The were-otter smiled, which only served to make him look even more creepy. "I'm the Otter King. My subjects will gladly sacrifice their lives in service ta' their king."

I coughed and spat bloody phlegm onto the ice near his head.

Bastard must've busted one of my ribs. Either that, or one of his claws pierced a lung. Fantastic.

"Not interested. Unless you have something better to trade..." I pushed myself fully erect and drew the sword back in preparation for a full swing, golfer style. When in Rome, after all.

"Wait, wait, wait!"

I paused with the sword held in both hands over my right shoulder. "Hmm... bet if I did this right, I could make your head bounce up on the green. I wonder if they give away hole-in-one trophies for decapitations on this course."

The were-otter's face was ashen, and his eyes were two large, black orbs. "Stop, fer the love o' Balor! Let me live, and I can tell ya' where the lass is bein' kept."

I lowered the sword, extinguishing the flames. "Now we're getting somewhere. Speak."

"She's in a house in the hills, a big mansion-like place."

"Go on," I coaxed.

"It's all made o' glass and concrete and steel, a monstrosity 'tis."

Resting Dyrnwyn's tip on the ice with a hiss, I stared at the were-otter. "I need an address, Whiskers, or no deal."

"A-all I know is it's in some place called Hudson Bend," he stammered. "That's the best I can do, as I went there by portal and left the same way. Otters are no good fer rememberin' numbers, anyway. Any druid worth his salt'd know that."

"Now, that wasn't so hard, was it?" I asked as I slid Dyrnwyn into my Bag.

"It wasn't at that," the Otter King replied. "Now, if ya' can just thaw this ice, I'll be on me way."

"Nope, don't think so," I said as I pulled my Glock from the Bag.

After rustling around for a bit, I found what I was looking for. Taking my time, I hit the mag release and dropped a magazine full of iron-tipped rounds into my palm, pocketing them. Then, I slammed one full of silver-tipped bullets into the mag well, leaving a single iron-tipped round in the chamber, just in case. The thing was fae, but it was also a 'thrope. At this range, I figured if one type of bullet didn't work, the other one would.

"Whassat? Wh-what're ya' doin' with that?" His teeth chattered, and it wasn't from the cold.

"Your death, and that's a fact," I said as I pointed the barrel at his forehead.

"I'll curse ya', ya' feckin' double-crossin' drood—"

I pulled the trigger once, watching with detached interest as gray matter, fur, and bone blew out the base of the were-otter's skull. Although black blood leaked out onto the ice, his eyelids were still fluttering, so I pulled the trigger twice more. Then, for good measure, I stood over him and emptied the rest of the magazine into the top of his skull.

"That otter teach you," I said to no one in particular.

19

By the time I'd picked up all the spent shell casings, my leg had nearly healed. But based on the attention I was getting from passing golfers, Dermot's spell must've lifted the second I killed the Otter King. Cops were a forgone conclusion at this point.

Time to go.

I tossed the pistol and shell casings in my Bag, where no one would ever be able to find them unless I allowed it. The were's head was now a bloody pile of pulp, so I didn't think any passerby would realize they were looking at a murder scene. However, I needed to dispose of the body and get back to my car fast, before someone called the cops. Still walking with a slight limp, I stepped off the ice.

Using my druidic powers to force heat back into the pond, I flash-thawed it. Steam rose from the surface, which helped hide what I was doing from golfers who happened by. I watched with satisfaction as tendrils of pondweed pulled the Otter King's body under the surface. With a final push of magic, I coaxed the muddy earth at the bottom of the pond to bury the 'thrope's corpse so deep it'd never be found—at least not in my lifetime.

Just as I was finishing, an older couple pulled up in a golf cart. They were decked out for a day of golf in matching visors and Hawaiian shirts, pastel-yellow and pink pants, and white leather golfer's gloves. They stepped out of their cart, walking over to me with concern on their faces as they took in my battered and bloody appearance.

"Good heavens, son—what happened to you?" the old man asked.

I pulled a fake badge out of my pocket and flashed it at them, tucking it away before they could identify it. "Animal control, sir. I was off-duty today, but we're shorthanded and we got a report of a rabid, er, otter on the course. But not to worry, it's been handled and disposed of properly."

"An otter?" the old lady said, clapping a white-gloved hand over her mouth. "How on earth would such an animal show up here, in Austin of all places?"

"Oh, they're native to East Texas, and they've been making a comeback. I expect we won't see this one again anytime soon, though," I said with a wink. "Now, if you'll excuse me, I need to go get a rabies shot."

"Of course," the old man said, not buying a word of it. "Come on, Ethel. The Burkes are waiting on us."

I left the couple bickering over whether or not they should have helped me, and took off at a limping jog for the Upper Falls and my car. On the way, I called one of Maeve's fixers.

"Brandon, it's Colin McCool."

A snarky, nasally male voice replied. "Thanks for ruining my day, druid. Tell me what you need, so I can tell you to fuck off."

"I need you to get rid of a dead 'thrope."

"Hah! Told you I wouldn't do it. That's Luther's department. Get one of his goons to help you."

I clucked my tongue. "Hang on now, I wasn't finished. This stiff is one of yours, some sort of were-otter... otter-thrope..." I struggled to find the right word, scratching my head. "What the hell do you call those things, anyway?"

"A lutrinathrope, if you want to be specific." Brandon paused. "There are only a few of those, you know. Which one did you kill?"

"I dunno, a male I guess. Never caught his name, but he referred to himself as the Otter King."

There was a sharp intake of breath on the other end of the line. "I'll need to inform the Queen. The Otter King's wife will want to recover the body—and she'll want to know who killed her husband."

"Meaning, she'll be coming after me."

He tsked. "As soon as she finds out you were involved, yes."

"She can get in line." I almost hung up, then I changed my mind at the last minute. "Brandon, do me a favor, will you?"

"Oh, for you? Anything," he replied sarcastically.

"Tell Maeve to give me some lead time on this one. I kind of have my hands full right now."

"No promises," he said before hanging up.

By the time the call ended, I was back at the creek. Avoiding the crowds at the falls, I headed upstream until I found a spot that was relatively private. I stripped down to my Jockey shorts and dove into the cold, clear water, washing off all the blood and gore from the fight. Then, I got out and toweled off with a clean t-shirt and changed clothes, tossing my dirty stuff inside the Bag.

What's my next move?

First, I needed to find that house. Hudson Bend was a big neighborhood, located on an isthmus that extended out into Lake Travis, north and west of the dam. The area was a strange mix of multi-million-dollar waterfront homes, condos, and middle-class ranch houses and two-stories in areas that lacked a view of the lake. While some of the homes on the waterfront had large lots, much of the area consisted of the sort of standard-sized lots you'd find in any middle-class neighborhood. And that meant people and witnesses.

However, I expected that Dermot's magic would keep nosy neighbors from prying. Thus far, he'd seemed like the type who enjoyed privacy and flying under the radar. It remained to be seen whether that propensity for stealth and anonymity would persist once I confronted him. The gods were simply not known to care very much about collateral damage, and frankly any rescue attempt could devolve into a shit-show very, very quickly.

That meant I needed to do this quiet, and I'd need back up in case things got nasty. At the very least, if I had help, they could pull damage control while I took care of Dermot and freed Fallyn. The only problem was, almost everyone I knew was under Dermot's super-glamour.

Which left only three people to call—Hemi, Crowley, and Maureen. Each of them qualified as a power in their own right, but I was potentially dealing with the gods themselves. I only hoped we four would be enough.

A LITTLE ONLINE sleuthing narrowed the potential addresses down considerably. I doubted very seriously that Dermot owned a glass and steel mansion in Austin, Texas. Not that a member of the Celtic pantheon couldn't afford it—far from it—I simply didn't think he'd own local real estate. I'd never seen the guy around town, and Maeve wasn't exactly keen on letting potential rivals hang out in her demesne.

And if that was the case, the creep was likely either renting a house or using an empty place that was on the market. Maureen and I checked a couple of short-term home rental and real estate sites and found three likely candidates in the Hudson Bend neighborhood. I marked them on my maps app, and we were good to go.

Hang on, Fallyn. We're coming for you.

Crowley had reluctantly agreed to help—after bitching about being in the middle of an important experiment—but he said he'd meet us when we verified the location. Maureen and I decided to borrow a late-model SUV from the junkyard, one of our fix-and-flip rides, figuring we'd blend in a hell of a lot better than if we took the Gremlin. Sure, the druid-mobile wouldn't get a second glance from any humans, not with all the wards I had on it. But to a Celtic god or demigod, it'd stick out like a sore thumb. So, the SUV it was.

We were just pulling out of the junkyard parking lot when I heard the distinctive rumble of a V-twin roaring in the distance.

"Maureen, stop for a second. I think Samson finally broke free from the spell."

She gave me a funny look, then put the vehicle in park. Seconds later a chopped-out Harley came screaming up Congress Avenue, doing at least two digits over the posted speed limit. The bike came to a screeching halt in front of us, and a short, bald biker with a lumberjack beard and a pissed off look vaulted off the saddle.

"Well, he's about half a pint from shiftin' and goin' rogue," Maureen said casually.

I figured he'd have heard Fallyn's cry for help, but doubted it'd be enough to break him out of his spell-induced fugue. Apparently, I'd been wrong. The good news was, we'd have one more person storming the castle. The bad news? Samson might just eat us if I didn't play this right.

The Alpha stalked up to the truck, grabbing the hood with both hands and crinkling sheet metal with his fingers. He stared at us menacingly through the windshield as his razor-sharp nails scraped the paint down to the metal. Although still in human form, his eyes had a crazed look that said he was a gnat's ass hair away from going full-on 'thrope.

"Oh, he's payin' fer that bodywork," Maureen said.

Cars were already starting to slow down as they drove past. In a few minutes, we were going to have cameras on us—or guns, if someone called the police. Either way, this was not what I needed right now.

"Lemme talk to him," I said, stepping out of the truck.

"Where. Is. My. Daughter?" he half-growled, half-roared at me.

I kept my eyes on his chest as I walked toward him, stopping while I still had some fender and bumper between us. "That's what we're going to find out, right now. You can either come with us and help, or you can freak out on one of the busiest streets in Austin. Then, you and I can tussle live on social media while the fucker who took her has time to go on the move again. Up to you."

When I said "took her," veins popped out on his forehead and neck. For a second, I thought he was going to change. I still wasn't making eye contact with him, but I had eyes on him in case he flipped out. Just as quickly, the tension in his face and shoulders relaxed, and when he lowered his head and took his hands off the hood, I let out an audible sigh.

"Who took her? And how?" he said in a tortured voice that started in a growl and ended in the closest thing to a whine I'd ever heard from the guy.

"Are you calm enough to be in an enclosed space while we discuss this?" I asked. He nodded. "Alright. Hop in and I'll tell you on the way."

We were a couple of miles down the road before I began to speak. If he lost control inside the truck, we'd all be fucked, and it'd likely cause an accident. I couldn't have that, so I waited until Samson's heart rate had slowed down before I addressed the topic. Once I started explaining, I didn't stop, quickly bringing him up to speed as we headed to pick up Hemi.

When I finished, Samson was livid but under control. "Wait a minute—you mean this asshole has the whole Pack under this spell?"

I nodded. "And anyone who knows her. As soon as her name comes up in conversation it triggers the spell."

"So, don't say it," Maureen admonished while keeping her eyes on the road.

Samson was clenching his jaw so hard, he looked like he was ready to crush rocks between his teeth. "He's a minor god, or close to it—has to be. No regular fae could wield that kind of power."

"That's what we've been thinking," I said.

Samson tugged on his beard for a few seconds, fuming. "What's the old man have to say about all this? And where is he?"

"No idea on both counts," Maureen said. "He told me he was goin' ta' find answers, and we haven't heard from 'im since yesterday. Ya' know how he is, Samson. He'll show up after things have gone pear-shaped, naked and fartin' thunderclaps with his wee bits flapping in the wind, no doubt."

"We can hope," I said under my breath.

Samson scowled at me, having heard me perfectly clearly. "So, if the old man is MIA, then how do we deal with the glamour?"

"I have a solution for that," I said. "But you're not going to like it."

AN HOUR LATER, Maureen, Hemi, Samson and I were slinking along the lakeshore under a gibbous moon, headed toward the last house on our list. Each and every one of us wore cheap drugstore store sunglasses that I'd spelled up to deflect Dermot's magic. Because I'd been in a rush, I'd grabbed whatever I could —with mixed results. Or course, I kept the wayfarers I'd spelled up earlier, while everyone else took whatever I had on hand.

Hemi was rocking some John Lennon-looking things, with gold wire frames and purple lenses. Maureen had a pair of sunglasses that would've made Iris Apfel proud. And Samson? Well, let's just say he was giving Anna Wintour a run for her money.

He futzed with his sunglasses as his expression went from frown to snarl to grimace, and back again. "I still don't understand why you couldn't enchant my own shades," he groused.

"Because, they're not—it's a science-magic thing, alright?"

"Gimme yours," he said in a voice that brooked no argument. *Think fast, Colin.*

"I can't, because... uh... they're tuned to my aura."

"Bullshit, kid. Hand 'em over."

Maureen chuckled. "He's got yer number, boyo. Might as well oblige him, or else we'll be here til' the rooster crows."

"Fine, take them," I said, tossing them over.

He caught mine like Blade in a movie fight finale, slipping them on with a smirk. I eyed the pair he tossed back to me, wondering why in the hell I hadn't been more selective during my shopping spree earlier. After slipping them on, I had to admit that they provided better coverage. Still, I couldn't help but look at myself with my phone.

"Fuck," I declared.

Hemi slapped me on the back. "Meh, you look good bro. Like Elton John, aye?"

Maureen snickered. "All ya' need is a bit less hair and a mink stole."

I was about to say something snarky when Crowley

appeared and beat me to it. "Getting the band back together? Or was there a group discount on eye exams today?"

"Har fucking har," I replied. "Wait 'til you see the pair I saved for you." All I had left were fairly hideous pair of Donna Karan knockoffs. Despite that, I wondered if they'd look better on me than the current set I wore.

"No thank you, Sir Elton," he replied. "I have spells for that."

"Then spell me up," Maureen, Samson, and I said in unison.

"Sorry, doesn't work that way. My magic is uniquely attuned to my own physical and spiritual bodies."

Samson chuffed. "Where have I heard that line of bullshit before?"

"Enough!" I hissed. "I'll wear the fucking sunglasses, if it means we can get this rescue mission started. Or have we forgotten that a certain someone who we care about is waiting for us up there?" I pointed up the hill, across a lush green lawn that sloped up to a backyard pool and entertainment area that made the Hyatt Regency hotels look tawdry.

Samson got in my face, his mouth set in a sneer. "I haven't forgotten for a second. That's my little girl up there, and she's everything on this tired, cursed fucking planet that means anything to me. And after this is all said and done, you and I are going to deal with the fact that you're the reason her ass is in a sling in the first place."

I held my ground. "Fine. But I want my glasses back later."

Samson scowled. "Your fuck up, your show. Scout it out, druid *apprentice*. And if you get my daughter killed, I'll mount your head on the clubhouse wall."

He stormed off into the shadows, probably to shift and gear up for the coming fight.

Hemi pumped his fist in the air. "Way to stand up to him, mate. Fight the power!"

"Movement, back of the mansion," Crowley said calmly as he faded into shadows of his own making.

I ducked behind some shrubbery, peeking between branches to see who it was. Dermot stood at the edge of the pool wearing a bathing suit with a towel draped around his neck.

"Well, we have the right place," I said. "That's Dermot."

"Naw, that's Diarmuid!" Maureen exclaimed under her breath.

I looked at her like she was crazy. "That's what I said, Dermot."

"Not when ya' say it like that, ya' didn't," she replied. "Colin, that's Diarmuid O'Dyna, the son o' Aenghus Óg."

"The Celtic god of love?" I asked.

"Yep."

"Well, that explains a lot," Samson replied. He'd already shifted and had snuck up on me, breathing hot, fetid dog breath over my shoulder as he peered through the bushes at the guy who'd taken his daughter.

"It explains we're fecked, that's what," Maureen said. "He's a right bastard, that one, and no pushover in a fight."

"I've killed demigods before," I said, with minimal conviction.

"Not like this, ya' ain't," Maureen replied. "He's as close to a god as ya' can get, without being full Tuatha."

Crowley whispered from concealment nearby. "Moreover, if he's wielding Gáe Dearg and Moralltach, we'll all certainly die if we face him directly."

"Red Spear and Great Fury? I'll assume those aren't inappropriately-named sex toys," I quipped.

Hemi looked at me, and I at him.

"Sneak attack?" I asked.

"If you still got that choice-as cloak," he replied with a sly grin.

20

Gunnarson's cloak of invisibility was a semi-sentient magical artifact that still held a grudge against me for killing its former master. Sentient magical objects tended to bond with their owners, and that bond was generally passed down from generation to generation. Since Commander Gunnarson had been the last of his line, it was to be expected that the cloak and I would have our differences.

I'd come to an understanding with the damned thing while in the Hellpocalypse, but I still didn't trust it enough to use it in dire situations such as this. Hemi, on the other hand, got along with the damned thing quite well. Apparently, it held him in high esteem due to his demigod heritage. Irish mutt that I was, the cloak saw me as little better than gutter trash. So, Hemi got the cloak, and we got to wait until he snuck up on Dermot and cold-cocked him.

"Here, dude," I said, handing him said item.

"Ah, there's my little buddy." He grabbed it in his meaty hands, draping it around his massive shoulders. It fit, but just.

"Looks better on you than it does on me," I said.

"That's exactly what the cloak said, mate." He had the good manners to look abashed. "Aw now, I'm sure it doesn't mean anything by it."

"Whatever. Go mess that guy up. We'll be right behind you."

Hemi took off while I stayed behind with Maureen and Crowley, whose head was now draped in a dark, semi-opaque fog. Samson was off hiding somewhere near the house, the plan being that he'd jump into the fray as soon as Hemi made his move. Then, Maureen would sprint to the house and grab Fallyn while Hemi, Samson, and I kept Dermot busy. Crowley was there for crowd control, of course, just in case Dermot had more friends waiting in the wings. Say, a were-otter assassin or another pack of cu sith.

Currently, our target was swimming laps in the massive pool behind the mansion, a seven bedroom, ten bath monstrosity that probably cost more than the yearly budget of my home-town. I couldn't detect Hemi at all, even with my druid senses and magical sight—small comfort now that we knew what we were up against. Dermot was the son of Donn, and the adopted son of Aenghus. Maureen and Crowley had both speculated that he may very well be wielding the powers of two different gods. If that was the case, this fight could be very, very interesting.

My eyes were fixed on the pool, and as the minutes dragged on, I wondered if Dermot might also be the related to Manannán mac Lir, because I'd yet to see him pop up for air. Finally, his tall, lean frame emerged from the water, walking up the steps with slow, deliberate movements. He certainly didn't look like he was on the lookout for trouble, so I hoped that Hemi had remained undetected and our plan would go off without a hitch.

The Celtic demigod stretched like a cat, then bent over to grab his towel from the lounger he'd draped it over before diving into the pool. Just before his hand touched the towel, he tensed visibly. Yet, it was too late. First I saw Dermot's head snap back with tremendous force, and a split-second later, I heard the loud crack of Hemi's tewhatewha connecting with his face. Blood sprayed out in an arc as he flipped end over end, landing in a heap on the far side of the pool.

"Go time," I growled, already sprinting out of hiding and up the hill.

Earlier—after realizing I couldn't shift into my full-on Fomorian form because the glasses wouldn't fit on my huge bulbous head—I opted for going Fomorian, but human-sized. Thus, I'd have all the speed, strength, and durability advantages of my fully-shifted form, except for the size and weight that my nearly ten-foot-tall frame provided. For the umpteenth time, I hoped it would be enough.

I moved hellaciously fast when in my shifted forms, yet somehow Maureen managed to pass me on the way to the mansion. That was fine by me, as she had the most important job of all, which was breaking the spell and getting Fallyn to safety. The half-kelpie was hell on wheels with a sword, a fact I could readily attest to after having felt the sting of her waster during many a training session. Yet she was still only half-fae, and had readily admitted that even an older, full-blooded fae would be no match for a demigod.

As I ran up on the scene, my eyes scanned the area for additional threats. By the time I got there, Samson had pounced on Dermot's unconscious form, and he was currently ripping and tearing at him for all he was worth. Hemi stood by, now fully visible, smacking his war club into his open palm. I watched through the floor to ceiling glass windows that ran the length of the house as Maureen zipped from room to room, searching for Fallyn.

An uneasy feeling crept over me, like we'd missed something important while casing the house and grounds.

"Something's wrong," I quietly said to myself.

"Naw, mate," Hemi replied. "Whacked that bloke into the wops. Doubt he'll come round soon."

Maureen skidded to a stop at the mansion's back door, sticking her head out. "She's not here, Colin. We've been tricked."

My head swiveled from the house to Samson and the bloody mess he'd made of Dermot. The Alpha was still in werewolf form, straddling the demigod with his head down and shoulders slumped, chest heaving as he recovered from the exertion required to murder a demigod. The corpse's face, throat, and chest—because it couldn't possibly be alive at this juncture—was completely unrecognizable, nothing but bones with strips of bloody flesh hanging off.

I turned to address the others, intending to tell Maureen and Hemi to split and regroup later while I disposed of the body. Before I could speak, Samson flew over our heads, crashing through the second-story glass facade of the mansion. Dermot's high, maniacal, laughter echoed behind me, and that's when I knew things were about to go to hell in a hand-basket.

THAT LAUGH CHANGED in pitch and intensity, even as I spun to face the threat. And a threat he was, if he'd survived what Samson had done to him. Dermot stood in a puddle of his own blood on the other side of the pool, but as I watched, he began to change. What little skin was left on him split, and he shed that and the bones beneath like a moth shedding a chrysalis.

The person who stepped from that shell—fully dressed in a colorful, belted tunic and breeches, no less—was a man I did not recognize. Although unknown to me, he was obviously one of the Tuath Dé. This one was tall and fair like Dermot, with shoulder-length golden hair, ruddy cheeks, and that permanent look of youthfulness that nearly all the Celtic gods possessed. Athletic in the way of a hunter, he had long, graceful limbs and legs that were well-suited for slinging spears and chasing down prey.

But his eyes were his most distinguishing feature, two amber orbs that flickered and shone like clear marbles lit from within by a candle's flame. Both eyes lacked a sclera, iris, or pupil, being one contiguous gleaming ball of fire that stared unblinkingly from each eye socket. When he smiled, that very same glow shone from the back of his mouth, like he had a fire stoking deep inside his belly.

Yet, that wasn't the scariest thing about him. Worse than his creepy eyes and glowing mouth, he was growing before my eyes. That's how he'd shed the shell he'd worn seconds before —by expanding physically to ten, fifteen, and then twenty feet high.

"Colin—run, lad!" Maureen whispered urgently behind me.

I considered it for a second or two, but then I figured, "Fuck it." If Dermot and Fallyn weren't here, this guy would be the only lead we had on their whereabouts. For that reason alone, running wasn't an option.

Besides, I was in my Fomorian form. My Hyde-side might have been hobbled in size, but not in attitude. Not finding Fallyn here had our blood up, and both sides of me were sporting for a fight.

"You must be my third trial," I rumbled.

"Aye, s'wot Diarmuid said," he replied in a sweet, strangely soothing voice. "An' if ye best me, he'll give ye a chance ta' save that she-wolf. But I doubt ye'll manage it. None have, an' not for two millennia."

"We'll see about that," I said, adjusting my glasses on my face. "Others have said the same, and I'm still here."

"What's wrong with yer eyes?" the giant asked, ignoring my verbal posturing. "Are ya' blind? I saw a singer on that strange augury cube, an Egyptian lad with bronze skin and the voice of an angel. He wore the same coverings over his eyes. Diarmuid said 'twas because he was blind."

He seemed earnestly curious rather than purely confrontational, so I decided to play along. "Nope, just a fashion statement."

"Hmph. Might have to take some back ta' Mag Mell. Tethra and Manannan would find them most amusing." He stared more closely at my shades, then a smile crept across his face. "I see what ye've done. Ye can take them off, Fomorian. My magic doesn't work that way."

"I'll keep them on, if you don't mind," I replied.

The giant shrugged. "Have it your way. Shame they should perish with you, though. I'd like to take them home, as a trophy."

"This bloke seems pretty sure of himself," Hemi said.

Just then, Samson darted out of the second story like a missile aimed at the giant's head. Without even looking the giant batted him away, sending him sailing over the lawn and into the lake. He skipped like a stone a few times, then landed with a splash and sank as if he had lead shoes on.

"Mebbe for good reason," Hemi remarked grudgingly.

Older werewolves were not good swimmers—their bodies were way too dense. Someone needed to fish him out. No matter fast they healed, werewolves had to breathe to survive, and they needed even more oxygen due to their high metabolisms.

I cupped my hands and yelled down the hill. "Crowley!"

"Consider it done," he said in a conversational voice, knowing I would hear him.

I spoke over my shoulder at Maureen, keeping my eyes on the giant. "Mind telling me what we're dealing with here?"

"Oh, I'm more than happy ta' tell ya' that, descendant of Fionn mac Cumhaill," the giant said. "Áillen is my name."

"Otherwise known as The Burner, lad," Maureen said.

"Ah, the terror of Tara," I said, sharing a look with Hemi.

The big Maori nodded in recognition of that brief flash of oratorial brilliance. "I see what you did there. Top work."

"The same," Áillen said, ignoring our aside. "I can spare yer companions if ye like. This can be a fair fight between us two, and no other—if you so choose."

Hemi began to step forward, but I reached out to stop him from volunteering for a suicide mission on my behalf. "I so choose."

I heard Maureen groan behind me as my Kiwi friend got up in my face. "Bro, reconsider. If this fella's as tough as Maureen lets on, you'll need our help."

"Hemi, if this guy is as tough as I think he is, your help won't matter." His expression soured, and I raised my hand in a placating gesture. "Hear me out. He breathes fire. The legends say he burned down entire fucking towns. Towns, as in multiple. Are you fireproof? I didn't think so. Neither are any of the rest of you. And if we all die here, who's going to rescue you-know-who?"

He chewed his lip while trying to think his way around my argument, but finally relented. "Gah, you're right. Don't get killed."

I kept my eyes on Áillen as I gave my final instructions. "Maureen, get everyone out of here. When I'm done, I'll meet you all at the junkyard."

Maureen gave me a disapproving look, then the hard lines in her face softened. The half-kelpie, who'd helped raise and mold me into the person I was, had tears in her eyes. She walked up

and squeezed my face between her hands, not gently by any
stretch.

"Don't get feckin' killed, or me and Tiny here'll be chasin' ya'
down in Tír na nÓg ta' kick yer ass back here."

I didn't have the heart to point out that, if I died, I was pretty
sure I'd end up somewhere else.

"I promise," I said, knowing I might not be able keep it.

AFTER MY COMPANIONS HAD LEFT, I squared off with my opponent across the swimming pool.

"So, you're Áillen." I gestured at him, head to toe and back
again. "Don't you think you're a bit conspicuous? Maeve doesn't
like letting the mundanes in on our little secret, you know."

"Diarmuid gave Niamh his word that the locals would'na see
anythin' unusual. 'Twas one o' her conditions fer lettin' him face
ye in her demesne. I have magic sufficient to keep that promise."

*So, Maeve allowed this to happen. I wonder, is this her way of
paying me back for betraying her?*

I sucked air through my teeth and crossed my arms. "You
seem much more reasonable in person than they made you out
to be in the folk legends."

His fiery eyes blinked, then he chuckled with merriment.
"An' ye've much better manners than yer forebear. It'll be a
shame ta' burn ye ta' cinders."

I loosened my neck up and worked the kinks out of my
shoulders as I replied. "Yeah, I've heard that Fionn was a real
dick. Not as bad as Cú Chulainn, I guess, but still a prick."

Áillen placed his hands on his hips. "Oh, now, historians
have been much harder on some of us than others. Take me, fer
example. I had done service fer the King at Tara, and he refused

ta' pay me. I warned him what'd happen if he failed ta' be true ta' his word, but the hateful cunt would'na listen. Now, the fables make me out ta' be a murderer and a monster, but I only wanted what was rightfully mine."

"Geez, man—the 'c' word? What'd he owe you, anyway?"

"Ten-dozen head o' sheep, eighteen cartloads o' hay, a side o' smoked beef, and a keg o' ale." Áillen paused, seemingly deep in thought, tapping the side of his cheek with a finger. "Oh, and I almost fergot—one o' his daughters, as well."

"To wed?" I asked, perfectly serious.

"Nay, ta' eat," he said with a straight face, before rolling his eyes. "O' course ta' marry. I'm a fire-breathing giant, not a feckin' lunatic. Don't be a dullard, just fer spite."

"Um, sorry. Had to ask." I tapped my foot, wondering if I should stall for more time. So far, I had no idea how I was going to beat him. It was one thing to kill a giant like Snorri, but a fucking fire-breathing giant was another matter. "So, should we get this show on the road, or what?"

"If yer' askin' should we start this fight, I'm ready when you are."

"First, what are the rules?" I asked, knowing that I'd immediately break them.

Áillen gave me a puzzled expression. "Rules? T'isn't a formal duel. Been sent here ta' kill ye, and that's what I intend ta' do. The only rule is ta' survive."

"Kill or be killed, got it." I looked him in his weird, flickering eyes. "Gotta' say, though, it's a damned shame we had to meet this way. It's not often that the people trying to kill me are polite about it. So, good knowing you, Áillen."

He crossed his arms, thrusting his lower lip out as he considered my words. "Same. I'll speak well of ye, druid, when yer' gone."

"Enough talk. Let's do this."

The giant nodded. Closing his eyes, he opened his mouth wide like a snake ready to strike. Air rushed into that huge gaping hole he called a mouth, and as it did, his chest and gut expanded to twice it's normal size. I briefly wondered if the neighbors would notice a twenty-foot fire-breathing giant tromping around next door, then I realized I should be running.

I took off like a bullet toward the lake, just as Áillen spouted fire from his mouth like a geyser. He tracked me as I ran, incinerating everything around me with the massive cone of flame that spewed forth from his mouth. Although I managed to stay ahead of his deadly breath, the heat seared my backside, burning off my clothing and melting the rubber soles from my boots.

By the time I reached the lakeshore, my clothes were smoldering scraps, my sunglasses were drooping off my face, and my boots were nothing more than leather spats held on by a few scorched laces. Based on the pain I felt, I figured that one half of me was probably burned and blistered, but that would quickly heal in this form. On the bright side, I hadn't been incinerated on Áillen's first pass.

Well, it's a start.

As I discarded my now ruined sunglasses—no great loss there—I glanced over my shoulder to see that the giant was striding down the hill at a leisurely pace. When you were twenty feet tall, you really didn't have to run to get anywhere in a hurry. For a moment I considered shifting to my full size, but that would just make me a bigger target.

No, to beat Áillen it was best that I stayed small and quick. He might be able to breathe fire, but he was bound to run out of whatever fueled those flames at some point. I doubted his flaming breath worked via any mundane means, as the physics simply didn't work out. If anything, that fire was magical in nature, and no one had an endless reserve of magic—not even a god.

Thus, my plan was simple. I'd get him out in the open where I could move fast and change direction quickly, to see if I could wear him out. It was a good plan—so long as I didn't get incinerated first.

21

Áillen was hot on my heels—in more ways than one—and spitting fire like a dragon with hayfever. To avoid getting fried to a crisp, I was zig-zagging all over the place, usually just a few steps ahead of where the giant was aiming. His breath was starting fires everywhere we went, so I headed toward a large swathe of unoccupied land near the marina. I didn't want any innocent bystanders to get caught in the crossfire—not on my watch.

After playing cat and mouse with Áillen for several minutes, I started to understand how Fionn had been able to defeat him. While the giant definitely had the advantage of size and being able to attack at a distance, he wasn't very quick on the draw. Not that he was stupid—it was just that he had to stoke up his lungs before he attacked. Plus, he had a habit of closing his eyes when he inhaled, presumably to avoid getting sand or dust in his eyes. Once I figured it out, it was pretty much a boss fight in a video game—except, I didn't have a way to take the big bad down.

Fionn had possessed a magic, barbed, poisoned spear that was impossible to remove once it struck home. All he'd had to do was get close enough to stick it in Áillen's side, and then the giant was fucked. If he pulled it out it'd kill him, because the barbs would rip out his guts. And if he left it in the poison would do its work. As I recalled, it was the latter that did the trick, but I might have been mistaken about that. Despite my heritage, Celtic folklore was not my strongest subject.

Unfortunately for me, my strongest weapon was Dyrnwyn, and I really didn't think a fire-breathing giant would be all that impressed with a flaming sword. Lacking a better plan, I decided to put the sword to the test. Drawing as close to Áillen as I dared, I waited for him to take a deep breath then I ran right at him, drawing Dyrnwyn and slashing at his left ankle as I passed between his legs.

The sword cut him, but no more than a regular blade would. On any other creature, the intensely hot blade would've cut through them like a hot knife through butter. But against Áillen, it was just another piece of steel. Giant skin was both thick and tough, similar to boiled leather armor stacked several layers deep. Thus, I could be hacking at his legs forever and still not get a deep enough cut to do real damage.

So, fire doesn't work—how about lightning?

Sprinting clear of the giant's massive feet—which were currently occupied by trying to flatten me into the world's biggest red velvet pancake—I got some distance to make my attack. Gathering static electricity from the atmosphere, I said the trigger word and tossed a huge-ass lightning bolt at Áillen, landing it just left of center on his chest.

Right over the heart. If that doesn't stop him—

Áillen snorted, blowing smoke out his nostrils for effect. "Oh, druid—yer wee spell tickled me skin like summer rain. Please, continue whilst I fry you like an egg in a skillet."

I suppose the frustration was getting to me, because instead of moving on to the non-existent next phase of my plan, I decided to try my ball lightning spell on him. It had worked wonders on the cu sith, and since I was out of options, I figured I didn't have much to lose.

That is, except for two-thirds of the skin on my body.

Despite the fact that it took a second or two to spool up the spell, I managed to get it off—just as Áillen loosed the mother of all firestorms at me. I raised my arms up to shield my face and eyes as I leapt aside. Yet I moved too late and caught the brunt of the blast over my arms, chest, and legs in the process.

Not good.

I landed on my side several yards away, and the second my body hit the ground, the pain began to register. Instant, searing, debilitating pain exploded across the front half of my body, all except the areas where my nerves had completely burned away. I tried to move, but found that my charred muscles had contracted involuntarily, leaving me functionally immobile.

My eyes felt like they were welded shut. With a cry of agony, I forced them open to survey the damage—and it was severe. My forearms, chest, and thighs were blackened and burned down to the bone. A few dried strips of leathery muscle remained here and there, but for the most part, I'd lost more than half of the skin and muscle on the front side of my body.

Sure, my Fomorian healing factor ensured that the tissue would regenerate, but it'd be several minutes before I'd have anything close to a functioning musculoskeletal system. Clearly, my opponent would not wait for me to recover before finishing me off.

I lifted my gaze from my ruined torso across the sandy, scree-filled beach. There was Áillen, strolling toward me like he had all the time in the world. And he did at the moment, because until my body healed, I wasn't going anywhere. I heard water lapping at the shore close by, and wondered if it would be the last time I'd hear that sound.

Wait a minute... water? Fuck me, but I'm an idiot.

Knowing I'd only get one shot at this, I reached out with my druid senses, connecting with the both the water in the inlet and the air above the lake. Upon making the connection I realized I was too weak, and I wouldn't have the juice to pull off the spell. With a thought, I connected with the Druid Oak, hoping to borrow some of the Grove's power for what I intended to do.

The moment we connected, the Oak sensed my distress. It sent me an image of a bird in flight, a deer fleeing through the brush, and a fox escaping a hunter's snare.

No! I have to beat this guy to get to Fallyn. Just help me cast this spell.

BASED on the feelings the Oak sent through our connection, it was incredibly perturbed that I didn't let it evac me. Despite that, it agreed to go along with my plan. Subtle, powerful druid magic washed through me, clearing away the pain and strengthening my bond with the lake and atmosphere.

When Áillen got close, he stopped and gave a slow shake of his head. "Ye'll not heal yerself in time, druid. No matter how much magic ye can muster."

When I replied, my voice came out in a weak croak. "Worth... a shot."

"Such a shame, ta' hafta do this. Ye lasted longer than most —much longer than Fionn, ta' tell the truth. Bastard tossed that spear o' his at me, just as soon as he had the chance. If he'd missed, well... you wouldna' be here today, eh?"

"Fucker would've... deserved it. His reputation... caused me no end of trouble."

The Tuath Dé giant found that to be highly amusing. He slapped his thigh, chuckling like a middle-aged dad watching a Jim Gaffigan special.

"O', but yer' a funny one. Just fer that, I'll grant ye' a quick death." He lifted his foot, raising it over my head.

"Wait..."

Áillen lowered his leg. "Ye prefer ta' go out another way?"

I nodded. "Fire. Quicker."

He frowned and shrugged. "Yer call."

Your funeral.

As the giant opened his mouth to suck in a roomful of air, I triggered my spell. Alone, it would have taken me several seconds to get the desired effect, but with the Oak's assistance, it happened instantly. A waterspout formed over the inlet, sucking up several thousand gallons of lake water and a fair share of vegetation as well.

I willed the top of the waterspout to point at the giant's mouth, funneling all that water at him while he was stoking up the fire in his belly. As I'd hoped, he sucked in an enormous amount of liquid before he realized what was going on. Sputtering, he opened his eyes in a panic, glancing around frantically to try to determine what had happened.

I released the water spout, too weak and spent to maintain the spell, even with the Oak's assistance. But it appeared to have done the trick. Steam shot out of Áillen's mouth and nose, but not quickly enough to release the pressure building up in his body. His belly expanded rapidly, like a water balloon on a wide-open garden spigot. Within seconds, he exploded with considerable violence, releasing steam and heat in a blast so forceful it sent me tumbling along the rocky shoreline.

Upon recovering, I wiped giant's blood and lake water from my face as I forced myself to sit up. Áillen was now in two pieces: his lower half lay prone where he had stood, and his rib cage, arms, and head were intact and lying face up several yards distant. As for his stomach and other internal organs, presumably they'd been obliterated in the blast. Seeing that he was permanently incapacitated, I rolled over on my belly and slowly, agonizingly, dragged myself to where he lay.

Steam and smoke still rose from Áillen's torso, drawing my eyes to the ruined expanse that had been his innards. Upon closer inspection, I was disappointed to find I could detect no mechanism or anatomy that would explain his unique ability. Whatever strange morphology he'd possessed to allow him to breathe fire must have been atomized when his body exploded.

Despite his current condition, he was still alive. The giant's jaw worked back and forth, and he blew frothy pink sputum from his lips as I crawled to his side.

"Áillen, you have to tell me how to find Dermot."

His chest convulsed as he produced a wheezing sound that I soon recognized as laughter. "Well... done, lad. Didn't think... ye'd be... the one."

"Áillen, where's Dermot?"

"Diarmuid... will find... ye. He's under command... ta' kill ye. Has... no choice."

"Who? Who commanded him?" I asked.

"Who... else? *An t-Athair*." And with that, the giant breathed his last.

'An t-athair'—the father. But which one?

I rolled over on my back, looking up at the night sky while sirens wailed in the distance. Practically speaking, I couldn't just leave the giant's corpse here, but I really didn't know what else to do. So, I reached in my Bag, of which Áillen's fire hadn't singed a single thread, and pulled out a fresh burner phone. Then, I texted Brandon, the fae fixer I'd called earlier.

teL Maeve 2 cum clEn ∧ her meS. Marina on Hudson Bend. BetA Hurry.

Once that task was done, I contacted the Druid Oak through our psychic connection.

Please, get me the hell out of here, I thought before passing out.

WHEN I REGAINED consciousness I was in the Grove, nude and lying in a shallow, spring-fed pool of crystal clear water. While I'd been out, I had shifted back into my human form, presumably after my Hyde-side had healed the massive burns I'd suffered. I was pleased to see that new, pink skin covered the areas where I'd been burned; but honestly, I was mainly concerned about my hair.

After frantically patting my head and looking at my reflection in the water, I was relieved to find that I still sported my usual healthy shock of strawberry blonde hair. With that crisis averted, I spent a few moments recollecting and recompiling the events just prior to regaining consciousness. Dermot had sent another assassin to "test" me, I'd killed Aillén Mac Midgna, and I was no closer to rescuing Fallyn than when I'd started.

With nothing better to do, I headed to my Keebler house. Once there, I magically heated a pint of water and made myself a cup of Luther's special blend, using the pour-over method since there was no electricity. I asked the Grove to grow me some food, which it provided in abundance within a short walk of my house. As I strolled along gathering an assortment of fresh fruit, I chewed my thumb and considered my next steps.

Without a doubt, Dermot was in control—a fact that he'd proven time and again over the last few days. Aillén had said that Dermot's father had commanded him to kill me, and whether he'd meant Donn or Aenghus was a moot point at this juncture. All that really mattered was that his ultimate goal was my death, although it appeared that my suffering and humiliation were also on his agenda.

It was curious to me that Dermot—Diarmuid—was taking such delight in punishing me in every imaginable way. Charming and abducting Fallyn, sending assassins after me, and glamouring my friends so that I would find it difficult to drum up allies to fight him—this all spoke to a deeper wound that went well beyond the gods wanting my head on a platter. I racked my brain, trying to remember what I knew of the beef between Dermot and Fionn, because that was obviously the source of the demigod's issues with yours truly.

I recalled that Fionn and Dermot had fought over Gráinne, the High King's daughter. Fionn was an old fart at that time, and somehow got it in his head that it'd be a good idea to marry a much younger woman. Of course, Gráinne wanted nothing to do with the old lecher, and thus she hatched a plan to escape before the nuptials commenced.

When old man Fionn and his warband came to visit, the princess drugged everyone save the young dudes who she thought might be sympathetic to her cause. Of course, Oisín and Oscar turned her down, not wanting to piss off the old man. And to his credit, Dermot did as well, until Gráinne cast a geas on him that forced him to abscond with the fair maiden.

At least, that's what the stories said. Personally, I think he just wanted to bed her, because the guy never seemed to be able to keep it in his pants. Or maybe Fionn had been such a prick to him, he wanted to get him back. Who knew?

At any rate, Dermot and Gráinne split town, which meant that the Ladies' Man had shit the bed as far as his boss was concerned. A chase followed, with Fionn sending some baddies to go after the couple. Oisín and Oscar betrayed the old man by helping Dermot and Gráinne escape the old man's clutches, Fionn sent a druidress after the kid, Dermot killed her, yadda, yadda, yadda. In the end, everyone got sick of the feud and bloodshed, and finally Aenghus Óg interceded on behalf of his adoptive son. All was forgiven, and Fionn agreed to cede Gráinne's hand and allow Dermot to wed her.

Or so it seemed. As I said, Fionn was a righteous bastard

who could hold a grudge like nobody's business. Years later, he took Dermot on a hunt, knowing it had been prophesied that the kid would be killed by a boar. Of course, Dermot had his guts gored out, and although Fionn had the power to heal him, he chose to let his former rival die. Fionn ate shit for that later—but still, the deed had been done.

And with Dermot being a demigod, it was a toss-up whether he'd resurrect. Gods were what we called primaries, supernatural beings that would come back decades or centuries after you killed them. Many of the more powerful monsters were also primaries, as were the original members of the other supernatural races, such as vampires, werewolves, and trolls.

Every primary could make copies of themselves—offspring, so to speak. Vamps did it through munching veins and a complex process of sharing blood with someone they wanted to turn. Werewolves and other 'thropes could do the same, but their vyrus worked differently so it was a much more dangerous process.

And the gods? Well, they just fucked humans and had demigod children.

The problem was, the farther the apple fell from the tree, the weaker the offspring got. That's how the fae races were made—they were descendants of the gods, mostly. High fae were closer to their forebears, while the lower fae were further down the evolutionary tree or whatever. Sometimes a demigod would be powerful enough to achieve god-like status, sometimes not.

In Dermot's case, he wasn't quite there yet. So, Aenghus took his body away, and would revive him from time to time when he wanted to talk with a corpse or whatever. If that legend was true, then Aenghus had to be involved, else Dermot wouldn't be walking and talking and making my life hell. This all tied in together, but how, I had no idea.

That Dermot was Aenghus' adopted son explained why he

could cast such a powerful glamour. He was said to have been born with the power to charm any woman, and according to legend, it was due to his "love spot." To me, that sounded suspiciously like code for knowing how to hit someone else's *love spot* —but knowing the Tuath Dé, it was entirely due to fae magic. I had no doubt that Aenghus had either graced his adoptive son with the ability, or that he'd taught him the spell craft required to do so.

The legends romanticized it, making Diarmuid out to be a ladies' man. What using his ability amounted to, however, was rape—no two ways about it. Just thinking about it had me seething with fury. Finally, I was forced to face the fact that he might have sexually assaulted Fallyn, despite his promises to the contrary.

Up until that moment, I hadn't wanted to think about it. Thinking about it brought me face to face with my own failure to save Fallyn, and brought to light that it was my fault the fucking scum had taken her in the first place. When I used Fionn's magical insight, it forced me to see the truth of things. So, there was no denying the possibility now.

Bottom line? I would get her back, and quickly—even if it meant sacrificing myself to do it.

22

I stepped out of the Grove and into the junkyard, where Maureen, Hemi, Crowley, Finnegas, and a very bedraggled looking Samson waited for me. The old druid and Hemi were drinking beer and playing cards, using a stack of tires and a rusty car hood for a table. Crowley was examining my wards— trying to steal ideas in case he ever had to lock me out of his place, no doubt. Meanwhile, Maureen tended to Samson, slapping his hands when he tried to force hers away.

As I approached, the Alpha pushed himself to his feet. "Well, you're not dead. Surprise, everyone—the golden boy escapes his own mess unscathed, while everyone else involved suffers."

Finnegas gave Samson a sideways glance, but said nothing. I looked the werewolf in the eye, meeting him stare for stare. "I'm doing everything in my power to get her back, Samson—"

He shot across the clearing like a bullet, slamming my chest with both hands and sending me sprawling on my ass. Knowing better than to provoke him further, I just looked up at him, ready to take an ass-chewing. Anyway, it felt like I deserved it.

"That's the fucking problem," he seethed. "You're always punching above your weight, starting fights with nasty motherfuckers who are way more powerful and ruthless than you. Even on your best day you couldn't take on the least of the Tuath Dé, yet you seem to go out of your way to attract their attention.

"And you have the nerve to act like it's not your fault my daughter got dragged into it? I swear, I wish I'd never taught you to control your *ríastrad*. Maybe if I hadn't, you'd be dead right now, and my little girl wouldn't be in the clutches of some psycho maniac demigod. Fuck!"

He slammed a fist into a nearby panel van, knocking it off the blocks it sat on. I remained seated, keeping my expression neutral while keeping my eyes on his chest. To say I felt guilty as hell about Fallyn's current predicament was an understatement, and if Samson wanted to pitch a fit, I'd let him. Losing it wouldn't get her back, but if it made him feel better, so be it.

He hovered over me, fists clenched and shaking like a drug addict in withdrawal. "Say something, damn it!"

"Dermot—Diarmuid—wants me dead. Or, at least, whoever sent him does. So, I'm going to go trade myself to get her back."

"Oh no yer' not—" Maureen interjected.

Samson held a hand up to silence her, keeping his eyes on mine. "Now wait a minute, Maureen. This is the first bit of common sense to come out of the kid's mouth since I've known him. Saint Ailbhe knows everyone else has been taking the heat for him 'til now. I say we let him take one for the team, for once."

"Saint Elvis?" Hemi whispered in the background. "I knew that bloke was still alive!"

Finnegas cleared his throat. "If I might interject some common sense in this discussion—perhaps Colin doesn't have to. Die, that is."

I looked over at my mentor, wondering what he was about. "Come on, Finn—it's the only way to get her back. No way am I going to beat Dermot, not in a hundred years. We're talking about the guy who single-handedly killed 3,500 warriors in a nine-hour period. Even Fionn was afraid of him.

"Plus, I'm pretty sure he's one of the undead, which means he's going to be hella hard to kill. She didn't ask for any of this, and she sure as hell doesn't deserve to be held captive by that skeezy prick. All things considered, giving myself up seems like the right choice here."

"It was 3,400—and it took him a lot longer than nine hours," Finnegas replied. "And while Fionn respected him, he never feared anyone."

I threw my hands in the air. "Whatever. The guy is as close to godhood as you can get while still being a demigod, and he's been reanimated. I don't stand a chance going up against him, so just let me do the right thing and be done with it."

"That'd be a new one," Samson said as he crossed his arms and leaned against the van. A wry smile crept across his face, but his eyes held nothing but contempt. "Go ahead, kid—knock yourself out. Like you said, my daughter didn't sign up for this. Go, get yourself killed, get my baby girl back, and then we can all go back to living how we did before you came along... in peace."

Maureen walked out to the middle of the clearing, pretty much dead center of the entire group. The only one who didn't have eyes on her was the shadow wizard, who was still examining my wards like pawn broker eyeballing a three-carat diamond. Classic Crowley. He wasn't concerned with our petty squabbles—he simply wanted to ensure that I didn't get back with Belladonna. And if that meant he had to help save Fallyn, so be it.

Meanwhile, Maureen paced back and forth, gearing up for a tirade of epic proportions. "Ya' keep sayin' that the lass didna' sign up fer this, but she did," she said, looking at Samson and me both in turn. "She knew as much as any fool what the risks were ta' datin' the lad. 'Twas her own choice. So stop makin' her sound like some helpless maiden that ya' gotta rescue from a bloody feckin' castle tower. I'd bet my nose that once ya' get her free from that fecker, she'll be the first one ta' rip his balls off herself."

"And free her, he will," Finnegas said, while eyeing his hand of cards with a critical eye. He laid them face down with a scowl before turning to address me directly. "That you can't beat Diarmuid in a free-for-all is true. His powers are beyond you, and his deific heritage provides him with an unfair advantage that will most certainly result in his victory and your defeat."

"Isn't that what I just said?" I replied, with a bit more snark than I'd intended.

"Correct," the old druid countered. "Which is why we need to ensure that it's a *fair* fight."

On cue, my phone rang. It had to be Dermot. I'd changed phones umpteen times already, and no one had that number. I put the phone on speaker and answered the call.

"Yeah?"

"MacCumhaill," Dermot's voice answered. "I see you survived your third trial."

I was about to say something when Finnegas appeared next to me, putting his hand over my mouth as he butted in. "Diarmuid Ua Duibhne, as advisor and druidic counsel to Colin McCool, I hearby invoke his right to a fair duel, by way of seeking redress for harm you've caused to him and members of his fiann, under the law and code of the fianna."

Dermot remained silent for several seconds before speaking. "Finn Eces—I wondered when ya'd make an appearance.

Always slinking around, stickin' yer nose in where it don't belong."

Interesting that his accent is getting thicker. Nervous, much?

Finnegas' eyes twinkled, and the corner of his bearded mouth curled up in a smile as he replied. "Your answer, Diarmuid Ua Duibhne? Should you refuse, you know by the law of the fianna that he wins his dispute by default."

"I took his woman by way of distraint, druid," Diarmuid replied. "'Twas in my right, fer the wrong his ancestor did ta' me, leavin' me betwixt life and death."

Finn's smile broadened. "Ah, but the law of the fianna specifically forbids taking revenge on family members for a wrong done by a member of a fiann. Furthermore, rivalries and disputes between members of the same fiann are always to be handled by a duel fought under fair and honorable rules. Since you've observed neither of these laws, Colin is the one who should be allowed to seek redress."

The demigod laughed. "O' the same fiann? The stripling is hardly one o' the fénnid. The bands haven't existed since times long past. Let it go, old man, and let me do the work I was sent fer."

"On the contrary, Colin MacCumhaill is the sole living descendant of Fionn MacCumhaill, your former rígfénnid. By default, that makes him leader of whatever of the fénnid remain. Making him your rígfénnid, in fact. Diarmuid, you cannot refuse this request for redress by combat."

"I recognize no such authority," Diarmuid snarled. "None! I'll kill the lad as I see fit, however I see fit, an' that's the end o' the matter."

Finnegas frowned. "I'm disappointed in you, Ua Duibhne." Pausing for effect, the old man's smile returned as he continued. "Has the Queen heard enough?"

Another voice came on the line—Maeve's voice. "I have,

Seer. As queen and ruler of this demesne—and your elder, O'Dyna—I recognize Colin McCool's right to seek redress by combat. Diarmuid will accept the challenge and fight a fair and honorable duel, else the Alpha's daughter will be released by him forthwith, and he shall languish in my dungeons until such time as I see fit to release his withered corpse."

"Lady Niamh, let us discuss this matter in private—" Diarmuid objected.

"I'll do no such thing," she replied coolly. "When your father asked that I allow you safe passage through my demesne, he promised you'd take care of whatever business you had here quickly and with as little fuss as possible.

"Instead, you've disrupted the peace, abducted the local Alpha's daughter, placed hundreds of people—some of them, my subjects—under your glamour, and left corpses and bloody messes for my people to clean up all over my lands.

"Oh, and your agent nearly burned down one of my lake houses. So no, I will not speak on this matter again. Seer, let me know when and where the duel will take place, so that I may attend."

With a small burst of magic that emanated from my phone, Maeve was gone. Finnegas cleared his throat, grinning like a Cheshire cat.

"Tomorrow at midnight, Ua Duibhne, at Royal Stadium," the old man purred. "You know of this place?"

"Aye, at the uni," Diarmuid spat. "I'll be there. Say yer goodbyes, MacCumhaill, because tomorrow'll be the last ya' walk on this earth."

Assuming the conversation was over, I hung up on him. "That's all well and good, but how the hell am I going to beat him?"

Samson chuffed. "I thought you were supposed to die, not win."

Finnegas raised an eyebrow at the Alpha. "You think the demigod would release your daughter unharmed, should Colin lose? No, I think not. Diarmuid will want him to go onto the afterlife in shame, knowing he failed despite his best efforts. She'll remain enthralled by the demigod forever, should that happen."

"It'll be war then," Samson growled.

"He'll be long gone by the time you rallied your Pack, and good luck getting in Mag Mell or Tech Duinn," Finnegas replied. "Those peckerheads will have no trouble keeping you out, and I find it doubtful that the other gods would risk Aenghus or Donn's ire by assisting you—no matter how just your cause."

"So it all rests on the kid's shoulders, as usual." Samson punched the van again, sending it skidding into a nearby stack. "Fuck!"

Hemi sat with his hands curled in his lap, lips forming an "o" as he wisely kept his mouth shut. Maureen gave the werewolf a sour look, but likewise remained silent. And Crowley?

He was still examining my wards.

"Crowley, do you mind?" I asked.

He continued his research, hands clasped behind his back. "Not at all. Please, continue your petty squabbles."

I sighed, then looked at Finnegas. "So, do you have a plan for how I'm going to beat this guy?"

The old man clapped me on the shoulder. "Oh, I'm sure you'll think of something." He sat back down at the makeshift card table, turning his hand over for Hemi to see. "Two pair, aces high. Pay up, warrior."

"I'm so fucking doomed," I mumbled.

"Oi, mate, you sure you're up for this?" Hemi said as he sat down beside me on the truck's tailgate.

I'd been hanging out in the junkyard worrying about Fallyn, and just generally thinking about life and my imminent demise. It was early in the morning but still dark out, so things were quiet and peaceful and perfect for being morbid. I'd already had about all the sleep I could stand inside the Druid Grove, so I'd come out here to enjoy the smell of oil and gasoline, and the sounds of the city.

"Hmm... I just came out of the Grove, where Finnegas and Maureen drilled me for hours on how to beat a demigod who's using the Celtic sword fighting style."

"And?"

"I'm not feeling all that optimistic about my chances, but what the hell. No pressure, right?"

He chuckled to make me feel better, then his brow knotted as his voice grew serious. "I could stand in for you. Done it before. Bet Maeve'd okay it."

"Didn't you already make the ultimate sacrifice on my behalf? Besides, you'd be in the same boat as me. Sure, you're demigod material and all, but Dermot's been brought back to life multiple times over the last two-and-a-half millennia. He's had plenty of time to perfect the art of killing people. No, this is my fight, and I'll settle it on my terms."

"I respect that." He looked around the junkyard, then up at the moon. "Peaceful out here. Maki would like it."

"Where's she been, anyway?"

"Here and there, aye? She's taking care of family matters, no big deal."

By "family matters," Hemi probably meant she was either battling with or running from various Maori gods and goddesses. He'd assured me that his mother was okay with his relationship, what with her being the goddess of death and night and all. But apparently, Maki had been ordered to stay in the Underworld by other gods, and by coming here with Hemi, she'd defied that order. So, she spent as much time making sure her family and people were okay as she did hanging out with Hemi in Austin.

"You miss her."

"Loads."

Although I'd really only loved one woman, I nodded just the same. That woman had been Jesse, back when she was fully human and fully sane. Fallyn and I had been getting pretty serious lately, but I'd been taking matters of the heart slowly with her. So, I wouldn't classify what I felt for her to be romantic love by any stretch.

That didn't mean I wasn't freaking out inside, every single second she was with that creep Dermot. Finnegas swore that he'd behave, now that the demigod knew Maeve was onto him. Still, I had to wonder what the Queen's purpose had been in allowing Dermot to come to Austin in the first place.

At first, I'd thought it had to do with revenge. But the way she'd stepped in, forcing the guy to agree to a duel, well—now I had no clue, which was just as well. The day I started understanding the motivations of the fae would be the day I packed it in. Because at that point, I'd know I was batshit crazy.

We didn't say much for a while, so I walked over to Finn's cooler and grabbed one each for me and the big guy. The great thing about having a master druid hanging out in your backyard was having ever-cold beer. Years ago, the old man had cast a nifty little spell on the cooler that refroze the ice in it every time it melted.

Perks of the trade. They were few and far between, but still.

Hemi finished off his beer and fetched two more. "Shift allegiances, bro."

"Huh?"

"Pledge faith to my mum. Then I could have her on standby.

Just in case, aye?"

I accepted my beer from him, popping the cap on the edge of the tailgate. "Sorry, man, no can do. I have a previous commitment."

"So? People do it all the time, cuz."

"I know, but not me."

He tsked. "I don't think your god does do-overs, mate."

"Naw, he doesn't. Well, only on special occasions. But that's kind of what I like about him. Predictability."

"Can't imagine having a god who was never there."

I laughed. "After all the trouble we've had with gods, sometimes don't you just want one who leaves you alone?"

"Lotta Anglicans on Aotearoa. I read that book. Don't think that's how it works."

"Still, I prefer my current situation. It suits me."

Hemi took a swig from his longneck. "Your afterlife, bro. No judgement."

We sat there for several minutes, listening to the cars rush by on Congress and enjoying the night breeze. That was the thing about Hemi—we didn't need to say much of anything to get along. Everything between us was pretty much understood.

Finally, I broke the silence out of boredom. "Did Crowley ever figure out my wards?"

"Naw, bro. Bloke finally gave up and headed back to his place."

My face broke out in a grin.

"What?" the big Maori asked.

"Hmph. That ward spell he was looking at?"

"Yeah."

"Decoy. I buried the real wards under the fence after the place got raided by Cerberus."

Hemi clinked his bottle to mine. "See, mate? Day's looking up already."

23

I whiled much of the day away in my old room inside the ware-house, streaming movies and enjoying the sounds and smells of the junkyard. Then, I got bored and jumpy, so I went out and started pulling parts for customers. Once I'd burned through our order list, I started working on all the cars we were currently flipping, figuring out which ones were a bust and which ones we could fix and sell for profit.

That kept my mind off things until dark, at which time I washed the grease and dust off in my outdoor shower before heading to the Grove. I wanted to be fresh for the fight, and the Druid Grove was the one place where I could really rest and recharge my batteries. After a quick nap and a dip in the stream, I got dressed, grabbed my Bag, and headed back to the junkyard.

Maureen and Finnegas were waiting for me there, sipping coffee and smoking cigarettes like an old couple. Which they were, I realized. Maureen had to be several centuries old, and Finnegas, well—that went without saying. They sat at a cable spool that had been repurposed as a table, on two vintage metal lawn chairs that had more layers of paint than a World War II battleship.

"So, are we ready to watch me die a horrible death?" I said, smiling with false bravado as I approached them.

"Quit'cher whining," Maureen admonished. "Ya' have a solid chance o' beating this tosser, if ya' don't muck it up."

"Maureen's right," the old man agreed. "He might be half-god, but he's been killed before. And, we have a plan."

"Oh, you have a plan. Great. So nice of everyone to let me in on the plan I'm going to have to execute when I fight a demigod in a few hours." A sword lay on the table between them, one I immediately recognized. "Does it have anything to do with Maureen's saber?"

"Aye, ya' smart-alecky brat. That great flaming tree-chopper's fine fer fighting giants, but ta' defeat Diarmuid, ya' need something that's quicker in the hand." She grabbed the saber, unsheathing it. "Meet ma' baby, Torque."

Maureen handed the sword to me, hilt first. I took it, stepping back and slicing it through the air experimentally. After going through a few practice cuts and parries, I nodded.

"It's fast, but with enough heft to cut deeply." I remarked. "And the balance is superb."

Finnegas gestured at the sword with his cigarette. "As the challenged, Diarmuid gets to choose the weapons, but you'll set the terms for victory or defeat. He's bound to choose swords, since that's his favored weapon. He'll want to use Beagalltach, his Little Fury, to dispatch you."

"Wait a minute—doesn't he have a sword that never misses or something?" I asked.

"Aye, lad, but there's nary a chance he'd be allowed ta' use it against ya'. Ta' be a fair match, the weapons each duelist wields canna' give either an unfair advantage."

I looked at the sword in my hand. "And this isn't enchanted?"

She gave me a toothy grin. "Not in any way t'would matter. Now, I know yer' probably eager ta' put this bastard in the dirt, but I suggest ya' demand that the match go best two o' three touches. That way, if he gets the jump on ya', there's still a chance ta' catch up and win."

"What about magic?" I said, addressing Finnegas.

"None will be allowed. It's to be a fair match, which means you'll each have to rely on physical skill alone to win. The only exception being weaponry—a warrior is allowed to use the best equipment he has. But, as Maureen said, that rule precludes using a weapon that would provide either combatant an unfair advantage."

A thought crossed my mind regarding something they'd said, but I kept it to myself. Best they didn't know my plans until it was too late to thwart them. Fallyn deserved much better than half-measures, and I intended to ensure her freedom.

"Anything else I need to know?" I asked.

Finnegas tilted his head as he flicked ash from his cigarette. "Maeve will officiate, since she has the final say in matters dealing with the fae and Tuath Dé in these parts. There will be spectators there to witness the outcome, both for moral support and to ensure there's no monkey business before or after the match. Other than that, I suggest you beat him with as little flash as possible, and quickly. Diarmuid is not to be trifled with, even without his magic." He turned to his assistant and confidant. "Anything to add, Maureen?"

"Kick his arse. An' if ya' nick that blade, yer' payin' ta' have it resharpened. Fae smiths aren't cheap, so I suggest ya' avoid binding the blade in a clash."

"That doesn't give me anything else to worry about, now does it?" I said, sheathing the blade and strapping it to my waist.

She smirked good-naturedly. "Ye'll be fine, boyo. Stick 'im with the pointy end a few times, and it'll be over 'afore ya' know it."

"That's the plan." I looked back and forth between them,

gauging their mood. Maureen was definitely tense, but neither looked as worried as they should've been. Those two certainly had something up their sleeves. "Alright, let's get this over with. I'll just rev up the Oak—"

"No!" they each shouted in unison.

My brow furrowed as I gave them a quizzical look. "What? I thought a little show of force might shake him up a little."

Finnegas frowned. "That's the last thing we want to do. There will be spectators there, from Underhill, Mag Mell, Tech Duinn, and possibly other realms."

"The gods," I muttered.

"Exactly," he replied. "And, your current level of command over the Druid Oak and Grove is not common knowledge among the Tuatha Dé Danann. For now, it's best we keep it that way."

"Whatever," I said with a flippant wave of my hand. "But the hell if I'm driving myself to my own funeral."

When we pulled up to the stadium at a quarter after eleven, there were a ton of vehicles parked in the garage across the street. The place was filled with Harley's, sports cars, limos, and an assortment of other vehicles. Maureen parked the SUV on the street in front of the stadium in a reserved parking spot. Outside the stadium, Pack members were working security, handling parking and keeping out any mundane humans who might've made it past the powerful "look away, go away" spell that had been cast on the grounds.

Finnegas pointed at the Pack members directing traffic and checking people for weapons at the gates. "Maeve forced Diarmuid to release everyone from the glamour but your young lady friend. Understandably, your pack mates are quite upset about the current situation."

"I'm surprised they're so calm," I remarked.

"Due to Samson's influence, no doubt. He knows you're the only chance he has of getting his daughter back." He turned around to speak directly to me from the front seat. "The members of the Celtic pantheon in attendance will portal out at the first sign of trouble. If that happens, the Pack will most certainly turn on the fae out of frustration, forcing the Vampire Coven and Luther to choose sides. Do not fail in this task, Colin. If you do, there will be all-out supernatural war on the streets of Austin."

"Again, no pressure," I said in a quiet voice. *Fuck.*

When we got out of the truck I started heading toward the stands. Finnegas stopped me with a gesture and a shake of his head.

"Nope, this way. We'll be in the locker rooms until the duel begins. I need your head in the game, and that means peace and quiet before the fight."

He led Maureen and I toward the end of the field, into the multi-million-dollar locker rooms the university provided for their prized money-makers. College football was big business in Austin, Texas, and the Board of Regents made sure no expense was spared for the team. It was kind of ridiculous, actually, how much cash got dropped on this place, considering the team's record.

Finnegas had me meditate and do druid breathing exercises and stretches for the next thirty minutes. He also instructed me to pull as much energy from the Grove as I could before we walked out. Diarmuid and I both would be fighting in our natural forms, which meant he'd have a distinct advantage in strength and endurance. Thus, I'd need to be at the top of my natural game when we started the duel.

Finn said anyone who noticed I'd supercharged my muscles before the fight would think it was druid hoodoo, and allow it. I did as I was told, and between the meditation, breathing, stretches, and magic from the Grove, by the time 11:45 PM rolled around, I was calm, collected, and ready to chew lead and shit bullets.

No armor was allowed during the duel, so I dressed comfortably in a stretchy pair of black jeans, a gray t-shirt, and my favorite leather jacket. We walked out of the locker rooms onto the fields with Finnegas in the lead, me in the middle, and Maureen trailing. The old man's eyes were set dead ahead, Maureen scanned for threats, and my eyes were down, because I was supposed to be focused on the coming fight.

As soon as my feet hit the end zone, I heard a roar erupt from our right. My eyes panned up to the home team stands, and to my surprise, the first twenty rows were full on our side. There had to be ten-thousand people and monsters there, and most of them were cheering for me—except for the fae, who were probably here to see me die. Within the crowd were many familiar faces, including the Toothshank Troll clan, the Austin Vampire Coven, the Pack, the Red Cap Syndicate, and even a contingent from the Cold Iron Circle.

A quick glance across the field to our left showed only a small handful of people sitting in the visiting team's stands. However, there were some familiar faces there as well, including Lugh, the Dagda, and Fuamnach, who was scanning the home team stands, likely for some sign of her adoptive son. Additionally, there were others I didn't recognize. A tall, dark-haired woman in traditional Celtic garb, with a severe face and hatchet nose who looked like she lifted weights. A good-looking blonde dude wearing a modern bespoke suit who just had to be Aenghus, and a grumpy fellow in black leather armor with eyes that were nothing but two dark, shadowy pits.

Black-eyes must be Donn. Dermot's two dads showed up. How sweet.

A nasally, high-pitched voice with a Brooklyn accent spoke up from my right. "Hey, druid, I'll give ya' fifty bucks to yell out, 'Are you not entertained?' after you cut 'dis guy's head off."

I looked down at the scrawny, rat-like canid trotting along beside me. "Larry, so nice of you to make it. Where've you been, anyway?"

"Remember when I told ya about my ex?" he said.

"The zombie corgi?"

"Yep, that one. Had a stalker situation to take care of—I'll tell ya about it later."

"Before or after I die?" I remarked, scanning the stands for more familiar faces. I thought I saw Sabine for a moment, but whoever it was, they disappeared behind an ogre.

"Pfft. You're going to kill this dude. I heard what'cha did to his flunkies—everyone has. Trust me, he's shaking in his sandals right now."

No MATTER how confident Larry was in my imminent victory, I wasn't feeling so self-assured regarding the outcome of the duel. Mostly because I knew something everyone else didn't. But also because I was about to fight a demigod.

I'd killed a demigod once before, but that hadn't been in a fair fight. Same went for the god-spawn I'd killed in the Void— I'd had the Grove's help with that. The only thing close to Dermot that I'd pwned on my lonesome was Kulkulkan's avatar, but that was just a giant snake. Plus, I'd hulked out to kill it.

The one place I'd been avoiding as I looked across the stadium was center field, because I knew my opponent would be there. We were almost across the field now, and it was coin-toss

time, so I couldn't help but take a look at my nemesis. My eyes
swept up, and there the prick was.

You mother-fucking, cock-sucking, animal-fondling anus licker.

He didn't look scared at all. Dressed as he was in a patch-
work belted tunic and cloak, wide bronze bracelets, and soft
leather boots, he looked every bit the Celtic warrior the legends
described. By the way he was staring me down, I could tell he
was quite confident he'd achieve a favorable outcome in the
coming fight.

It was bad enough seeing that walking, talking penile erec-
tion standing there with a smirk on his pretty-boy face. But what
really had my blood boiling was that he'd brought Fallyn with
him. She stood next to him in that same sundress she'd worn
days before at the park. It was now soiled and rent in places,
with food and dirt stains here and there marring the once
colorful fabric. Her eyes were vacant, and a thin line of drool ran
down her lip.

Oh, Fallyn.

It was all I could do to keep myself from going stabby right
then and there. I glared at him as we stopped and stood shoul-
der-to-shoulder across the fifty-yard line from him.

"The Druid Apprentice, a Seer, and two mutts," he said with
a smarmy-assed grin and a slight nod to Maureen and Larry.
"The mascot fits. Ya' oughta put that creature on a coat o' arms,
as it certainly suits yer pedigree."

You could hear a pin drop in that stadium as I hawked up a
ball of phlegm and spat it at his feet.

"Dermot O'Dyna, you runny sack of shit, you walking,
talking pile of rat excrement, you are the lowest form of scum
that resides at the bottom of the genetic cesspool that is the race
known as the Tuatha Dé Danann. If I tromped through a
fucking low town pig sty and scraped the sole of my shoe after,
the resulting pile of detritus would have more quality than you.

"You are gonorrhea dripping from an old man's pecker, an anal hemorrhoid of a person who somehow manages to further mar the already damaged image your hateful, worthless kind possesses. The good news is that I am the cure, and I intend to stamp out the venereal disease you call a life here and now, for the entire supernatural community of Austin to see."

His face flushed, and he gritted his teeth in anger before recovering his composure. At that, roughly half the crowd roared while the rest booed and hissed. Over it all, the hatchet-faced goddess on the Tuath Dé side guffawed and slapped her thighs like a pool hall drunk.

"Guess we know who won the first round, aye?" someone with a Kiwi accent yelled from the stands.

When everyone had settled down, Diarmuid chuckled. "Bold words. We'll see how ya' stack up momentarily."

Maureen leaned over to whisper in my ear. "Ya' didna' hafta insult half the stadium with that Tuath Dé remark, lad. Remember that the fae are part o' that cesspool, present company included. Ease up a bit—we may need their support shortly."

Maeve had floated across the field while we were busy hurling insults, resplendent in her full faery queen form and regalia, retinue in tow. As she approached center field, a hush fell over the crowd.

"With that, I believe we'll forego allowing either side one final opportunity to sue for peace," Maeve said, tight lipped. "Let us commence. Diarmuid, you have the right to choose suitable weapons—"

"Wait," I said, raising my hand.

Finnegas winced as Maeve turned to address me. "Yes, Justiciar?"

"I get to decide the terms of defeat, right?"

She gave the slightest bob of her head. "Yes."

I looked my opponent in the eye as I spoke. "Then I want this to be a duel to the death, with no quarter, and Dermot can use any weapon he chooses... but only on one condition."

Maeve turned her formidable gaze on my opponent. "Diarmuid, I'll leave it up to you whether we should allow this breach of protocol."

"Let the lad speak his doom, Niamh," the demigod said with an almost lecherous grin.

The faery queen looked at me. "What are your terms?"

My mouth was dry and my heart was beating out of my chest. I swallowed, trying to work up some saliva before I spoke. "Dermot has to agree to release Fallyn the minute the match is over, whether I achieve victory or suffer death here today."

Maeve didn't have time to address Dermot before he spoke. "Done! I choose spears, an' I'll be wieldin' *Gáe Dearg*, me Red Spear."

Finnegas hung his head, while Maureen hissed her dissatisfaction at my foolishness. The die had been cast, and there was no going back now.

"I accept those terms," I said. "Now, let's get this fucking thing over with."

24

Moments later, I stood on the twenty-five yard-line in my t-shirt, jeans, and boots, wielding a spear I'd pulled from my Craneskin Bag. Sadly, it wasn't the one I'd had created to mimic Lugh's fiery spear, so I wasn't going to be skewering Dermot from across the football field. Still, it was a sturdy weapon with a comfortable haft and sharp, leaf-shaped blade. I thought it would do.

Maureen walked up to me holding her saber in one hand, but whether she meant to whip me with the flat or stab me in the eye remained to be seen. She grabbed the spear from my hands and hurled it across the field at the Tuath Dé stands, where it buried itself tip-first at Aenghus' feet. He scowled, but the half-kelpie barely gave him a second glance.

"Yer' gonna' need somethin' more formidable ta' face down Diarmuid, lad."

She closed her eyes, holding the sword flat across her palms. In an instant, the blade transformed from a basket-hilted saber into a Celtic war spear. The haft was smooth, dark wood with carvings up and down its length—just enough to allow for a positive grip, but not so much as to impede attacks. The blade on either side of the weapon came out in a sharp arc, curving rapidly inward thereafter. This resulted in a long, narrow blade that would part flesh better than the leaf-shaped one I'd held earlier.

Maureen opened her eyes and tossed the weapon to me. "Sorry, all it does is change shape 'n stay sharper than the Queen's tongue. Wish it did more, but it's what we hafta' work with. I'll be wantin' it back, tho'."

Finnegas grabbed me by the arm, turning me toward him. "You stood a strong chance of surviving this encounter before you opened that fool mouth of yours. Now, he'll be wielding his Red Spear. Colin, do not let that spear point touch you! Any wound you suffer from it will never heal, and if it's serious, you'll likely bleed out in minutes."

I winked at Maureen. "Thanks for the pep talk there, Tony Robbins."

Finnegas glowered at me. "False bravado will not win the duel for you, apprentice of mine. It will take every bit of training and guile for you to survive this battle, and if I sent you in blowing sunshine up your ass, I'd not be doing my job."

"Got it. Stick the pointy end in the other guy. Don't get killed," I said, setting my eyes on my opponent across the field. "Now, stop fussing so I can get this over with."

"Smart-ass," the two of them said in one voice.

I yelled at Dermot, who stood on the twenty yard-line some forty yards distant. "You ready, Douchewaffle?"

"When you are, druid."

"Do your worst," I muttered, charging him across the field.

Unlike sword fighting, spear work is an entirely different animal. A lot of people wrongly assume that you use a spear like a quarterstaff, but that's simply not so. The weapon was designed to give a modestly-equipped and moderately-trained footman the advantage against a much better armored and armed swordsman. In that scenario—even considering inequalities in gear and training—the spear is king.

Thus, all that spinning, slashing, and jumping *Game of Thrones* shit was just that—shit. Most spear-fighting styles consisted of jabbing and stabbing at range, with much of that being done by sliding the weapon through the forehand like a pool cue. While you could use the butt end to strike and parry, most of the defense was done with the pointy end. That's because the idea was generally to evade or parry a thrust, and then counter with a stab to the vitals.

Anyone who'd watched that famous fight scene in *Troy* between Achilles and Hektor had an okay idea of how folks used to fight with spear and shield. However, like most movie fights, that scene was highly choreographed, and in real life it was doubtful that two combatants would draw it out so long. As for Dermot and I, we weren't using shields like the actors had in that famous flick. Presumably, there'd be a lot more footwork and a lot less fancy shit.

Or so I thought. As I charged toward him, Dermot stood erect with his spear held vertically in one hand, butt end in the turf. I realized what I was doing was pretty fucking dumb at about the fifty-yard line, when I had twenty yards to go and he was still standing there like a tree. Without the benefit of my Fomorian heritage I was only as fast as, say, an Olympic sprinter. So, I closed that forty-yard gap pretty quick, but it still must've looked fucking stupid for all the time it took.

Instead of committing suicide kamikaze style, when I got within a few yards I screeched to a halt, kicking up a shower of those little rubber balls they use as infill in artificial turf. I started stabbing while I was still moving at him, poking at his face, body, groin, and legs for all I was worth. That's when he started the fancy shit.

My first thrust had been aimed for his eyes, but he could see it coming from a mile away because that's where I'd started the attack. He merely leaned aside to evade it, allowing my spear point to miss his by inches. As I recovered and stabbed at his chest, he pivoted without moving his feet, turning to allow the spear to graze his tunic.

When I stabbed at his groin, he leaned sideways on his own spear while lifting one leg high in the air, much like a circus acrobat. This had the effect of moving his groin six inches to my left, causing me to miss. I tried for a return slash as I withdrew my weapon, aiming for the inside of his thigh, but he leapt straight up in the air—on one fucking leg, no less—using his Red Spear to sort of pole vault several feet away.

The demigod landed with aplomb in a deep stance that favored his rear leg. He stood sideways to me with his spear shaft across his shoulders, the point facing me.

"Yer' quick fer a human, I'll give ya' that," he said with a self-satisfied smile. "But ya' hafta' do better than that to walk outta here alive, druid."

"I HADN'T PLANNED on walking out of here alive, Dripdick," I replied as I circled around him. "Which means I have nothing to lose. So, you'd best quit fucking around and put that pig-sticker in my gut before I do the same to you first."

Dermot shook his head. "Tsk-tsk, but where'd be the fun in that? I prefer ta' make ya' suffer. An' besides, it's what Da requested."

"Did he ask you to abduct the local Alpha's daughter as well, you sick fuck?" I asked with a snarl. "Somehow, I doubt your father would want to risk getting on Maeve's bad side."

Dermot kept his eyes on me, pivoting minutely so he always kept his spear tip pointing at my face. "He didn't specify how I should go about me business, only that I fecked ya' over 'afore I killed ya' dead. Messin' with the wolf lass was merely a bonus."

I continued circling him slowly while I looked for a lapse of concentration that would be my signal to strike. As I did, I examined his spear. It seemed normal enough, just another Late Bronze Age weapon with a wooden haft and a leaf-shaped blade. Despite the inferior material the blade had been made from, it had probably been crafted and enchanted by Goibniu or Lugh. Thus, I had no doubt it was just as deadly as Finnegas had warned.

"Enough fartin' aboot," the demigod said. "Time ta' make ya' pay fer Fionn's mistakes."

Dermot swung his spear around, reversing his grip so that the socket of the spearhead was in his rear hand, and the bronze, butt-capped end was now pointing at me. Then he came at me, closing the distance with quick, precise steps, each one punctuated by a thrust of the spear's butt end. I parried the first two while backpedaling, fighting to maintain range and distance while hoping to position myself for a counterattack should the opportunity arise.

Sadly, that opportunity never came. The demigod never seemed to tire or fade, but instead came at me with an endless barrage of thrusts, feints, and strikes that were almost always aimed at my face and hands. His obvious goal was to diminish me gradually by blinding me or breaking the small bones in my hands so I couldn't hold my own weapon.

Thankfully, I was able to dodge, redirect, or block most of his attacks. However, several strikes did get through, and within a few minutes my lead hand was throbbing and I had a nasty mouse over my left eye. I might not be dead yet, but I was definitely losing this battle. If I didn't go on the offensive soon, he'd get a good one in and finish me off for sure.

Alright, let's play dirty, then.

Waiting for another thrust at my face, I dropped under it and spun my spear, slipping the tail end down into the turf. Once there, I flipped the butt up toward his head, tossing a shower of those little black rubber pebbles into his eyes. They were harmless, but sometimes instinct wins out over common sense, and Dermot reacted just as I'd hoped—he flinched and covered his eyes with his rear hand.

That left an opening when the butt end of his spear dipped. Moving as quickly as my human muscles allowed, I pushed with my rear hand, causing the tip of my spear to dart out and stab him in his shoulder. The crowd gasped, and I tried to follow up with further attacks.

Dermot was having none of it, and he leapt well out of range to avoid being stabbed again. Immediately, the demigod's expression devolved from one of extreme self-satisfied confidence into a rictus of frustrated rage and hate. His eyes narrowed and his jaw worked back and forth as he spoke to me through clenched teeth.

"You will pay for that, mortal."

Dermot spun his weapon around, pointing that gleaming bronze blade at my face. I held my weapon up in guard but he beat it aside, moving in with sharp, staccato steps that caused me to give up ground as I worked my own spear to narrowly avoid his attacks. He stabbed, slashed, and cut at me, high and low, left and right, in a series of short, tight attacks that were almost robotic in their precision.

Within thirty seconds, he'd attacked me as many times. Within forty seconds, I found I was tiring and decided it was only a matter of time before he got through my defenses. And within fifty seconds, I moved just a split-second too late to parry a high thrust to my left eye.

But it was merely a feint. The real, intended target had been the left side of my body. I lifted my spear point up to block, raising my elbow just a hair, and Dermot dropped his own spearhead and drove it home, burying it deep in my left-lower abdomen. When he pulled the spear out, he twisted the haft, and I felt the wound tear wider as the blade withdrew.

DROPPING TO ONE KNEE, I clutched at my side with my left hand. Despite putting pressure on the wound, hot blood flowed freely through my fingers. While I was fairly certain he'd missed my vital organs—the descending colon was there, and I didn't smell my own shit—the blade had bit deeply, plunging through skin and muscle.

"Now ya' know why this weapon's called Red Spear," Dermot gloated as he stepped back, spinning the weapon to sling my blood from the blade. "Once it opens a wound it'll ne'er heal, and the one who receives it'll bleed out 'afore the morn."

My entire left side felt like it was on fire. I was barely able to remain upright as I leaned on the haft of Maureen's Torque. A stream of hot, wet blood ran down my side, dripping off me to form a small but growing puddle by my left knee. Knowing I had to continue the fight, I unbuckled my belt and tore my shirt off, wrapping the belt around my torso and stuffing the shirt under it.

Dermot merely watched as I dressed the wound with my makeshift pressure bandage. "It'll nae' help ya' t'all, druid. Yer' pissin' in the wind wit' all that shite. Nothin'll stop the bleedin' but yer own death."

Ignoring him, I somehow managed to thread the buckle with one hand, then cinched it tight and secured it with the shirt in place. As Dermot had said, blood still flowed freely from the wound, but at least I felt I could stand without my guts spilling out all over the field.

I wiped my bloody left hand on my pants leg and grabbed the shaft of the spear with both hands. "We're not done yet, Dermot. Not by a long shot."

He tilted his head back and laughed. "Do ya' know how many warriors've said those words ta' me 'afore today? Do ya'? Thousands, druid, thousands. Every one bleedin' out from a wound made by me Red Spear or Great Fury."

"I heard it was a Little Fury, but okay," I quipped, wincing in pain as I chuckled at my own joke.

The demigod gave me a dark look. "Joke all ya' want, but ye'll not be jokin' in yer grave."

"Stop jawing, and let's finish this, you slimy sadistic fuck," I said as loudly as I could.

He smiled mirthlessly. Then he leaned in and whispered, so low only I could hear him. "Ya' want ta' finish this? A fight to the death, ya' said. Aye, I'll give it to ya', but nice 'n slow, like I did that lass o'er yonder."

"You fucking pig—"

"Oh, she begged fer it, she did. Under my spell she was, as the love spot's ne'er failed ol' Diarmuid Ua Duibhne. I love ta' hear 'em beg fer it, when their mouth says 'yes' but their eyes say 'nay.' I tell ya', MacCumhaill, it's like the first time, every time."

"Fucking low-life rapist!" I screamed as I lunged and thrust the spear at him.

Of course, that was just what he'd wanted—and I fell for it, hook, line, and sinker. Dermot swept my weapon away easily, returning the favor by slashing and stabbing me in the thigh, arm, and shoulder before dancing away, laughing.

"So easy ta' wind ya' up, druid—it's almost not even sport from where I'm standin'—almost."

Blood dripped down my leg and both arms now, and considering what I'd lost already, I didn't think I had much left to spare. He could've been lying about raping her, but if he wasn't? I needed to beat this guy, and fast, else I was going to die and he'd never pay for what he did to Fallyn.

I tried to step toward him, but my injured leg failed me, causing me to stumble and drop to one knee. Honestly, I didn't know if I'd be able to stand up again. I looked across the field to the sidelines, where Fallyn stood in a glamoured stupor. Poor, proud Fallyn, brought low by some scum who'd magically roofied her and had never even given her the chance to fight back.

If I had to die, at least I knew she'd be free. But how was she going to live, knowing that this sick fuck was out there? She was no shrinking violet—the girl was a warrior, but she didn't fucking deserve to have to live knowing that the guy who'd done this to her walked away Scot-free.

I lowered my head, as if to pray. Instead, I started gnawing on my thumbnail like nobody's business.

C'mon, Fionn's magic, work damn it! How do I beat this guy?

Then it came to me—Hideie's trick.

I'd spent considerable time inside the Grove with Click, trying to learn how the tengu was able to predict my moves. The Welsh magician and pseudo-god had taught me the principles of the thing, seeing the flow of time and speeding it up mentally for a second or two. It was like fast-forwarding a movie, or so Click had said, but I hadn't been able to replicate the trick by the time he'd lost interest and left.

Can I do it now, though?

Being desperate and near death, I had no choice. Besides, I wanted to kill Dermot more than I had ever wanted to kill anyone in my life, and that was saying something. Resolve washed over me like clear, cool water. I slowed my breathing until I was at that still, calm place inside that allowed me to work Gwydion's arts of chronomancy and chronourgy.

Dermot's voice taunted me from somewhere distant. "Prayin' won't help ya' t'all, druid. Give it up, look me in the eye, and go out wit' some dignity."

Opening my eyes, I took in the scene around me in my mind, observing the position of everything in my surrounds in three dimensions. From there, I tapped into the flow of time around us, sensing how it connected me, Dermot, the ground beneath our feet, and even the air we breathed. Then, I shrunk that awareness into a sphere barely large enough to encapsulate us both.

That was where the difficulty lay, Click had said—reaching out too far from where you stood. Time flowed around everything; or rather, everything flowed within time. But the human brain could only deal with so much sensory input. There were simply too many data points to track if you tried to extend your senses beyond your immediate surroundings, and that's what had caused me to fail at the technique earlier.

So, I stayed focused on just the demigod, going so far as to narrow down that little sphere until it contained him and nothing else. Then, I sped it up—one frame, two frames, a dozen, each representing a millisecond of time.

That's when I saw it.

Finally, I knew how to kill Dermot.

25

When I looked up, Dermot locked eyes with me. He'd taken my unfocused stare to mean that I was fading out. Not wanting to miss the opportunity to deal the killing stroke, he moved to finish me. Overconfident and certain that I could neither evade nor counter a simple, straight thrust to the heart, the demigod attacked.

Wrong. Move.

As he stepped forward into a deep, elongated stance, thrusting the spear at me with both hands, I knew what he was going to do before he did it. This momentary window of prescience allowed me to react at the very last second—after he'd fully committed to his attack. As the Red Spear came within inches of my breast, I spun in place, lifting the point of Torque so it entered Dermot's stomach, just under the rib cage and to the left of center.

As it went in, I pushed as hard as I could, driving the razor-sharp spearhead through his heart and out his back. Gáe Dearg grazed my chest as it passed, but I didn't care. I was bleeding out already anyway, and I'd done what I'd come here to do. For a split second, Dermot and I were momentarily frozen in a strange tableau—a still-frame photo perfectly etched in my mind.

Then, everything sped up again all at once.

The demigod dropped his own spear, staggering back as he grasped at Torque's haft with both hands. He clutched at the weapon, trying to pull it out, but as any vampire will tell you, it's damned hard to yank on something that's stuck through your heart. Failing that, he fell to his knees a few feet away, leaning forward with the butt of the spear in the ground.

"I am undone, by a feckin' mortal," he croaked.

I grabbed Red Spear from the ground, using it to push myself to my feet. Stumbling toward Dermot, I turned the stumble into a lunging stab, driving the deadly spear through his left eye and out the back of his skull. The lights went out in the demigod's eyes immediately. As for me, I collapsed on my side, thankfully facing the Celtic gods so I could offer them one final "fuck you."

"Resurrect him now, you son of a bitch," I said, flipping Aenghus off in the distance.

I heard footsteps coming toward me, but they were too late —I was fading out. Vaguely, Finnegas' voice echoed in my ears, as if he were shouting at me from a long, narrow hall.

"Colin, I need you to shift, now!"

Shift? Good idea, old man. Maybe it'll heal me. Or I'll bleed out slower. Sure, why not?

As usual, the change came on fast when I was close to death. Soon, I found myself in my pure, albeit human-sized, Fomorian form. A gasp came from the visitor's side of the stands where the Celtic gods sat.

"I'll be damned, the rumors were true. He really is Fomori," Hatchet-Face said.

Shifting to this form ensured that I wouldn't die as quickly, since my healing factor could replace blood at an astonishing rate. But the wounds weren't closing, and therefore I wasn't going to get any better, either. I'd just be an ugly, helpless dude bleeding out for all eternity.

Or maybe I was still dying, and I just didn't know it yet.

I looked over at Dermot, who remained propped up with Torque through his chest and Red Spear sticking out the back of his head.

Could be worse, I guess.

Finnegas began muttering in Gaelic, casting some sort of illusory spell. Why, I had no idea. Maybe he wanted to give me privacy in my final moments?

"I've cast the obfuscation spell. Do it now, Maeve!" Finnegas yelled.

"The consequences will be severe, Seer. He will hold it against me," she replied.

"Not if you save his life—now, do it!" he said.

I opened my eyes slightly. "Would you two quit shouting? Low blood pressure is giving me a headache."

Maeve started glowing, so I shut my eyes because the light was making my head hurt even worse. "Fuck, turn that down. Trying to sleep here."

"He's daft with blood loss," Maureen remarked.

"He's going to need a blood transfusion soon, so get Luther's medic over here, right away." Finnegas laid a hand on my shoulder. "Hang in there, knucklehead."

Warmth washed over me, making me even more drowsy and incoherent. All I wanted to do was sleep. But whatever Maeve was doing, it was making my headache go away. I started drifting off, and Finnegas shook me awake.

"Colin, you have to stay with us, son. Listen—when I tell you to, I want you to shift back to your human form."

"Huh? I'll die," I mumbled, drifting off again.

"No, you won't," he said. "Just trust me for once."

"Whah? I always truss yew."

"My ass," the old man mumbled. "Maeve, is it done?"

"Yes, Seer. I only hope he doesn't hold me responsible for your decision."

"Colin," Finnegas said, shaking me. "Colin, shift back, now."

"Lemme sleep."

He slapped me across the face, hard. "Shift, damn it!"

"Alright, already."

It was much harder shifting back to human when injured, but somehow, I managed it. When I finished, I lay there for a moment with my eyes closed while Finnegas, Maureen, and a few others around me gave an audible and collective sigh of relief.

I opened my eyes and looked around. Finnegas knelt next to me, with Maureen hovering over his shoulder. Maeve was there, an inscrutable look on her supernaturally-beautiful face. Hemi stood watch, his war club in hand, slapping it in his palm as if daring anyone else to approach.

Wincing, I looked down at my injuries. "Hey, what the fuck? How'd you heal those wounds? I thought when Red Spear killed you, it killed you for good."

Maeve's eyes were taut. "I didn't heal you, Colin. I merely cordoned off the injuries, so they only affect one-half of you. Your Fomorian half."

"Say what?" I said, fighting my way to a sitting position.

Finnegas squeezed my shoulder. "Sssh. We'll discuss this later. Right now, we have company."

FINNEGAS GESTURED toward the visitor's side of the field, where the Dagda, Lugh, Aenghus, and Donn all stood in a half-circle, while Hatchet-Face hung back. Fuamnach was nowhere to be seen, which meant she'd failed to find her son and gone back to Underhill. Or, she was tromping around Austin looking for him while Maeve was preoccupied—take your pick.

Lugh was yelling at us through megaphone hands, but I couldn't hear him.

"Aw fuck—I've gone deaf," I said, while still trying to clear the fog from my mind.

"Yer' not deaf, idjit—the Seer cast an obfuscation," Maureen said, flicking my ear with her index finger.

"Ow! What happened to all those tears you were crying for me earlier?" I asked.

"Hush, you," she replied. "Or else I'll make ya' clean that spear."

Suddenly, it was like the volume got turned up on the world, and Lugh's voice was coming through loud and clear. "I said, 'You can drop the cone o' silence, Seer!'"

"It's done," the old man said with a smug smile. "Dagda, Lugh—a pleasure." He looked at Aenghus and Donn. "You two, not so much."

Donn stared Finnegas down, but there was no hatred in his hollow, raspy voice. "Easy now, Finn Eces. I bear you no ill will. I'm only here to collect my son so that he may finally rest in Tech Duinn."

"My apologies, Donn," the old man said with a respectful bow of his head. "As for Aenghus—"

"Dont'cha get all uppity with me, old man. Trumped up, wannabe god that ya' are. Pfah! Had no use fer you druids back when, got none fer ya' now."

"Now I see where Dermot got his winning personality," I muttered.

Maureen flicked my ear again, this time harder. "Quiet, 'afore ya' find yerself dead."

Aenghus fixed me with his bright blue eyes, a lock of golden, curly hair bouncing perfectly in the middle of his forehead as he spoke. "Ah, the upstart speaks." He looked at each of his fellow gods in turn. "Feckin' shite, but why are ya' puttin' up with this disrespect? Time was we'd have squashed this bug 'n been done with it."

The Dagda stared at the god of love, and poetry, and all that other shit that didn't fit. "Son, there'll be no squashing of anyone, not while we remain in Niamh's realm." He gave me a pointed look. "While we remain in the Queen's demesne, we will respect her rule and law."

Aenghus glared at me, then at each of the other gods in turn. "Fine, but mark my words, this one'll be trouble." He looked at me again. "An' don't think I'll let this"—the god gestured at his now fully dead adopted son—"go without seeking retribution. See ya' 'round, little druid."

A portal formed behind the Celtic god of assholes, as I was coming to think of him, and he stepped through it. Immediately the portal winked out of existence, leaving no trace of the powerful entity who now wanted me dead more than ever.

Lugh spat at where the god of love had stood moments before. "Good riddance, I'd say. That feckin' dandy sows trouble and contention wherever he goes."

"Kind of strange, for a god of love to be so hateful," I remarked.

"You've no idea," Lugh said to me. "Just remember, not all of us are what the legends make us out to be."

I briefly glanced at Maeve. "So I've noticed."

Maeve crossed her arms. "Dagda, I appreciate your support. But if you don't mind, I moved to this realm for a reason—and that was mostly to avoid dealing with my brethren as little as possible."

The Dagda inclined his head. "Understood. We'll be out of your hair momentarily."

"Sooner would be better than later," she replied in a voice that brooked no argument. Manannán mac Lir's daughter didn't mince words, that was for certain. "Donn, please take your time in preparing your son's body for the journey back to your realm. And if you require any assistance—"

"I'll not, but your kindness has been noted," the Celtic death god replied.

"Eh, I'll lend a hand," Hemi said. "Professional courtesy," he offered with a shrug when Maeve gave him a quizzical look. Donn gave him a nod of acknowledgement and nothing more, but I got the impression he appreciated Hemi's gesture.

"Um, one thing," I said, leaning on Maureen as I stood up. "I'll be keeping Dermot's spear. Spoils of war, and all that."

"As is your right," Donn rasped.

Lugh cleared his throat. "Then, if all is settled...?"

"...we'll be on our way," the Dagda finished.

The Celtic god of light winked at me. "Don't be gettin' in too much trouble while we're away, lad."

"No promises," I said, waving my hands back and forth.

"That's just the sort of talk I like to hear from a druid," the Dagda said, just as he and Lugh stepped through a huge portal. Before it closed, he caught my eye. "Don't worry, Colin—I'll tell her you send your greetings."

"I also have business to attend," Maeve said, turning her gaze on me. "I suggest you remain human for the time being, at least until the Seer finds a way to heal you."

"Maeve—"

"Oh, I'll think of a way for you to repay me," she said before stepping through a portal that quickly winked out.

———

AFTER I'D GOTTEN my blood transfusion, and before Donn had

left with Dermot's corpse, I grabbed Red Spear and carefully stored it inside my Bag. I tried to apologize to the god for killing his son, but he waved my apology off, saying I'd done them both a favor.

"Aenghus had kept my boy in thrall all these long years, reviving him only to poison his mind and send him on senseless errands. You've done us no ill here, young druid, so erase those regrets from your mind."

Finnegas and Maureen had dragged me away from the death god, instructing me to leave him in peace. I watched as Donn and Hemi crouched over Dermot's body, but I couldn't see what they were doing. When they stood and stepped back, the demigod's body had been cleaned and his wounds dressed, although he was still quite irrevocably dead. Donn picked his son up with tender care, then stepped through a portal back to Tech Duinn.

"Hey, wait!" I shouted as the portal closed. "Damn it, I never got to ask him if he was the one who sent the Dullahan."

Finnegas puffed on a cigarette, pointing it at me. "What do you think? The so-called 'god of love' didn't look too broken up about his adoptive son being slain, did he? If I had to guess, I'd say that Aenghus enlisted Donn's help in exchange for the return of his natural-born son."

"If that's the case, I can't say I blame him," I replied, meaning it. "You think the Dullahan will come back, now that Donn has his son back?"

The old man flicked ash as he considered my question. "Yes, I believe he will. Not at Donn's behest, of course, but he certainly will return. You've escaped him twice, Colin. The Dullahan is not accustomed to seeing his prey escape."

Escape... hmm, seems like I'm forgetting something.

Suddenly, I remembered why I was there in the first place.

"Shit, where's Fallyn?" I said, frantically searching the stadium for her.

"Don't worry," Finnegas said in a calm voice. "As soon as you killed Diarmuid she collapsed, likely due to exhaustion from fighting the demigod's spell for days on end. Samson had Maeve's healer look her over, then he and the Pack took her someplace safe where she can rest and heal from her ordeal."

"Did anyone... I mean, did she say... did Dermot?" I couldn't bring myself to say it.

The old man's tone was sympathetic as he replied. "No one knows for sure what happened while she was alone with that monster, but Maeve's healer said that she appeared to be unharmed. Meaning, he likely didn't rape her—at least, not physically. Just in case, the healer wiped her recent memory, to save her from the shock of facing those memories when she wakes."

"She's a 'thrope, Finn," I said. "That mind-wipe won't last."

Mind magic that erased memories never held long on werewolves, because it relied on killing brain cells and selectively severing recently-formed neural pathways. With werewolves and other 'thropes, their bodies would eventually heal that trauma. Thus, their memories would return, little by little over time.

"I know, Colin. For that reason, Samson and I both think you should give her plenty of time and space to heal. At least until she reintegrates those memories and is able to deal with what happened to her."

Growling with frustration, I grabbed a fistful of my own hair. "I know it sounds selfish, but I really want to see her. Just for a minute, you know? To make sure she's okay."

Maureen laid a hand on my arm. "Colin, 'tis likely the lass won't want ta' see ya' after what's she's been through. Ya' have ta' respect her space, and let her heal on her own schedule. When the time's right she'll come lookin' fer ya', rest assured."

I exhaled heavily, nodding. "Finnegas, can you at least get a message to her that I want to see her—when she's ready, I mean?"

"Already done," he said. "But right now, we have larger concerns."

"Like what?" I asked.

"The dark-haired, muscular lady who was watching with the rest of the Celtic gods? That was Nemain, one of the three Morrígna. She rarely concerns herself with the dealings of mortals these days, but in times past she was an enemy of Cú Chulainn. After witnessing your *ríastrad*, it's likely that she's gone to warn her sisters you're a threat to the gods. And from what I've heard, Badb already has it in for you."

"Stop beating around the bush, Finnegas. Just spell it out for me."

"In a nutshell?" he said, taking a final puff off his cigarette before discarding it. "What happened here is just a preface for things to come. Maeve doesn't want a war fought between the druids and gods in her demesne, so she's given you three days to pack up and go on a prolonged vacation."

"But, the junkyard... my justiciar work... hell, Fallyn. Shit, Finn—she'll think I've abandoned her."

No way was I leaving her alone right now. I might not have been able to see her, but Fallyn needed to know I was waiting for her during her recovery.

"She'll think nothing of the sort, not after what you did for her today." The old man was already rolling another coffin nail, which he licked, sealed, and lit all in one smooth motion. "And if you're thinking what I think you're thinking, consider that if you stay, you'll merely be placing her in further danger."

Fuck.

"Alright," I said with reluctance in my voice. "When do we leave?"

"Uh, now would be preferable," Larry said from somewhere nearby.

"And why would that be, Larry?" I said in that general direction.

"You know how I can see stuff other people can't?" he asked. "Right now, I see that blond asshole with the curly hair, stalking around invisible-like by the exit to the stadium. He's carrying this crazy, evil-looking sword, and I swear that thing is talking to me."

"What is this sword saying?" Finnegas asked, suddenly very interested in what Larry had to say.

"Gibberish," Larry replied. "But everything it says has to do with blood, killing, and death."

"That would be Moralltach," the old druid said. "Colin, get everyone out of here, now."

"Shit. Alright, gather 'round, people. Except you, Larry— you'll have to find your own ride." No response. "Larry? Larry!"

"Little bugger must've split," Hemi said.

"No surprise there," Maureen observed.

"Well, he's good at looking out for himself, so he'll be fine," I remarked. "Now, everybody hang on while I get us someplace safe."

I reached out mentally, connecting with the Druid Oak.

Time to go.

The only question was, where could we go that the Celtic pantheon couldn't find us?

EPILOGUE

Samson sat by his daughter's side, holding her hand while she rested in a deep, healing sleep. The faery queen's healer had put her under, stating that it might last a few days, or a few weeks. Everything depended on how long Fallyn needed to heal from the trauma she'd been through.

And after that... that's when the real work would begin.

The old Alpha knew that for all his knowledge and experience, he was completely unequipped to help his daughter through the struggle ahead. What she needed was to be surrounded by strong female werewolves who could guide her through the emotional wounds she was about to face. Samson had taught his daughter how to fight, and how to lead a Pack. But he couldn't teach her this.

The door to the cabin blew open, although he was certain he'd locked it. When the Pack had dropped him off here, it was with explicit instructions to set up a cordon a mile out and let nothing through. Yet the being that now stood in the doorway was not anything his Pack members were equipped to deal with. Just as he was admittedly inadequate for guiding his daughter through the difficult path ahead, they were incapable of stopping her from getting past them.

He didn't even bother turning his head, because he'd know his maker anywhere. "Lita."

"Samson." She moved to the beside whisper-quiet, more like a vamp than a 'thrope. She was naked, of course. Lita rarely remained in human form these days. "How is she?"

"Resting," he said, with more strain in his voice than he'd have liked.

"And the druid? He gave his life for hers?"

"Damned near," Samson replied grudgingly. "If not for Maeve's intervention, he'd be worm food right now."

She nodded. "The boy has mettle. He'll make a good mate for her, someday. But not today."

All the while, Samson kept his eyes on his daughter. Lita was ultra-dominant, and the only wolf he could ever be submissive to, a fact that rubbed him wrong even now. It was a gift in a way, given the circumstances, as he preferred to focus on Fallyn for the last few moments he had with her. Besides, it wouldn't do to start a pissing match while his daughter was in her current state.

"Lita, you should know—"

"I heard her cry, my mate. Else I would not be here."

"You being here makes me worry that I'm sending her out of the frying pan and into the fire."

"Nonsense. If you'd told her what she really is, and allowed me to show her what she can really do, that half-breed would never have done what he did to her."

"So it's my fault now? If anyone's to blame, it's the kid."

The she-wolf crossed her arms, still looking at her daughter and not at her mate. "Be that as it may, that young man may very well be her destiny. They were our brethren, once. He's perhaps more compatible with her than even the strongest male wolf."

Samson frowned. "Hmph. I'll say this, though—the kid has balls."

She chuckled, a rumble in the back of her throat. "Good, but we must keep them apart for now. As he grows and matures, so will she. And when the time is right, they will meet again."

"That's what I'm afraid of—well, that, and your crazy family."

"Artemis will look after her, Samson. We will teach her and train her until she comes into her own. At that point, perhaps she'll seek the Fomori out. I for one hope so, because together, they could be unstoppable."

Samson grunted, saying nothing more. The old Alpha leaned over his daughter, the love of his life, kissing her on the forehead. He nuzzled her face, taking in her scent and marking it to his memory.

If only I was more than a very powerful werewolf, he thought. *Then maybe I could protect my little girl.*

His mate walked outside the cabin, into the biting cold and driving snow. Samson picked his only child up in his arms, carrying her like a babe through the door. Once outside, he set her down in the snow, unconcerned about the chill. She was a werewolf, after all, and werewolves didn't catch colds.

"I will take care of her, Samson. Do not worry."

"I know you will," he said.

The Alpha's mate kissed him on the lips, and he returned that kiss, although they did not embrace. Once done, she stepped away. With a final nod to her mate, she instantly transformed into a huge wolf, easily as large as a small SUV. The giant wolf gently picked her daughter up in her mouth, then she trotted off into the night, leaving no trace of her passing.

"I'll see you soon, Pipsqueak," Samson said.

He stood there in the cold for a long time, staring after them.

Then, he silently went back inside the cabin and closed the door.

This concludes Book 9 in *The Colin McCool Paranormal Suspense Series*. But never fear... the story *will* continue in Book 10, *Druid Mystic*.
Sign up for my newsletter at MDMassey.com so you can be among the first to hear when the next Colin McCool novel drops!

CPSIA information can be obtained
at www.ICGtesting.com
Printed in the USA
LVHW021314090520
655281LV00036B/2545